JONATHAN TAYLOR is an author, lecturer and critic. His books include the novel *Entertaining Strangers* (Salt, 2012), and the memoir *Take Me Home: Parkinson's, My Father, Myself* (Granta, 2007). He is editor of the anthology *Overheard: Stories to Read Aloud* (Salt, 2012). Originally from Stoke-on-Trent, he now lives in Leicestershire with his wife, the poet Maria Taylor, and twin daughters, Miranda and Rosalind. His website is www.jonathanptaylor.co.uk.

MELISSA

MELISSA

Jonathan Taylor

CROMER

PUBLISHED BY SALT
12 Norwich Road, Cromer, Norfolk NR27 0AX United Kingdom

Printed in Great Britain by Clays Ltd, St Ives plc

Typeset in Sabon 10/13

ISBN 978 1 78463 035 5 paperback

1 3 5 7 9 8 6 4 2

'Every disease is a musical problem.
Every cure is a musical solution.'
– NOVALIS, *Encyclopaedia*

Dedicated i.m. to Eric Leveridge

Inspired by true events

Contents

1st Mvt:
Musica Mundana

PRELUDE

The Spark Close Phenomenon

THE REAL TRAGEDY, of course, happened before the story begins – seconds before. At 2.35 p.m. on Wednesday 9th June 1999, in Number 4, Spark Close, Hanford, Stoke-on-Trent, Miss Melissa Comb, a seven-year-old girl, died of Acute Lymphoblastic Leukaemia in her own bed, surrounded by family and nurses.

What followed has been floridly described by Stoke-on-Trent's Poet Laureate as a 'musical efflorescence of grief' for the dead girl. This 'musical efflorescence' has been raked over endlessly, by poets, journalists, priests, neurologists, psychologists and parapsychologists. Some have called the 'Spark Close Phenomenon' a musical form of mass hysteria, others a kind of telepathic psychosis, others a millennial judgement on our modern way of life. If none agree in their interpretations or conclusions, a general consensus has emerged about the actual events of that strange afternoon.

Moments after Melissa's family watched her die next door,

sixty-six-year-old Mr. Paul Higgins, ex-Open University lecturer, part-time columnist, part-time right-wing radio broadcaster, of Number 6, Spark Close, was hit by what he later called, in various newspaper interviews, a "ringing, humdinging headache."* He had been dozing, he claimed, with a packet of beef and onion crisps in front of TV insolvency adverts, when he jerked awake, and – as he put it later – the "screen seemed to, like, dissolve in front of my eyes." This was accompanied by an "alarm-ish noise, like some deafening bell ringing in my head. I suddenly felt awful, sicketty-sick. I got off my arse, and – I can't explain it – I felt kinda forced to walk to my front door. I couldn't hardly see anything, and, as I say, there was this huge alarming going off in my head. So I staggered to the door, opened it, and stepped out onto the street. As soon as I was outside, the ringing faded away, and was kinda drowned out by . . . well, by music. Classicalist stuff – y'know, orchestra and violins and all that malarkey. It was dead loud at first. But gradually, it faded away, over the next few minutes or so. It was while it was on the way out I noticed all the doors in the Close were opening – everyone was coming out, holding their heads or ears like what I was."

Mrs. Hayley Hutchinson, and her out-of-work grandson, Frank, of Number 8, Spark Close, were certainly holding their ears: "The siren we heard, it was something out of the war – an air-raid siren raiding my head, if you see what I mean. Came out of nowhere. Goodness me. We thought it was the TV, and Frank here, my grandson (who's a bit of a dab hand with technical stuff), went and whacked it. Then he switched it off at the plug. But the siren carried on with the TV off. I was

* Descriptions of the Phenomenon by residents and other interested parties in this chapter are compiled from various sources, including newspaper articles, transcripts of police interviews and journal articles by Prof. Christopher Sollertinsky and Dr. Terence Williams (see '*Variations: Pavane pour une infante défunte*' below).

almost crying, and Frank, well, he was a bit of a hero. Always knows what to do. This time, he dragged me out of the house into the street – as if it was a different kind of air-raid siren, telling you to go outdoors, not in.

"Suddenly, or perhaps it was gradually, the air-raid siren noise stopped, and instead came this music – like what they play at the Cenotaph, you know. Kind of beautiful, slowish, saddish, yet . . . stirring. Brought a tear or two to my eyes, I don't mind admitting. Like England – but nicer, like in the 1950s, fields and cowpats, you know, and not everyone robbing everyone else. Like when we were in and out of each other's houses down this Close all the time. I couldn't understand why the music was happening, but I was relieved the sirens had stopped. So was Frank. He was standing to attention, next to me, as if on parade. He was in the Territorials, you know, till two years ago."

Frank himself commented: "That music, it made me think back to my time as a soldier, and I felt like presenting arms, or saluting someone or something. Well, I suppose nothing much's happened since then to think back to instead. So I felt eighteen again, like I'd gone back three years into uniform, and the flag was waving and we were supposed to be commemorating something. Without a flag there to salute, I saluted Ms. Kirsten from Number 10 instead. She was wearing a bikini top and shorts – they were Union Jacks, so it was almost as good as the flag. My grandma told me to stop gawping. But Ms. Kirsten didn't see me anyway – or, at least, seemed to be not looking quite at me."

Ms. Kirsten Machin, divorced mother of twin boys, of Number 10, Spark Close, had been out in the back garden. Her statements to the press, doctors and police have been rather confused, if not contradictory. In the immediate aftermath of the Phenomenon, she appeared distracted, and incoherent in her speech when approached by the emergency services. This has led to some fairly wild speculation about the part she played on the day. It has been pointed out that she owns a powerful stereo, and has a taste for playing anti-socially loud music – sometimes, according to one neighbour who will remain nameless, in a bid to "drown out the babies' screams." At least one tabloid commentator has suggested that the whole Spark Close incident might be explained by Ms. Machin's (and I quote) "huge woofers." The simple fact that Ms. Machin's woofers were not accustomed to blaring out orchestral music seems to have escaped this particular commentator. Moreover, the nature of what happened that day on Spark Close, and the testimonies of the many witnesses, all point up the inadequacy of such a facile explanation of events.

Another tabloid explanation of Ms. Machin's behaviour that afternoon is potentially defamatory, and hence cannot be repeated here – sufficed to say, it involves a sun-lounger, a bottle of gin, and twins screaming from an upstairs room. Roughly two minutes after Melissa Comb's death at Number 4, Mrs. Machin seems to have fallen off her sun-lounger: "I got this huge fuck-off pain walloping me on my head – worse than having twins in your brain, if that's possible. Jesus help me, I thought, my brain's going to explode. And then there was the banshee shrieks – out of fucking nowhere. At first, for a tiny second, I thought it was something in the Close, perhaps someone being hacked to death next door. But then I realised it was in my head. In my head, for Christ's sake. I wondered if this was like . . . what's it called? . . . tiny-tuss, tinny-tits, tissy-tinnies . . . anyway, whatever, that whistling-ringing thing you get in your ears. Or perhaps all those years when I was young-ing it up in the clubs were coming back to haunt me. Fucking hell.

"The babies were haunting me as well, I can tell you. I

could hear them screaming outside my head, as well as the screaming inside it. I was only out in the back garden for a few minutes – you know, they'd . . . gone off for their afternoon nap. I'd never leave them otherwise, course not. Always make sure the baby monitor's there, right next to me. Anyway, the babies'd started shrieking at the same time as my head was inside-exploding, like. The two shrieks were getting all mixed up, and I couldn't even stand up straight. I was fucking terrified.

"But, you know, a mother's first thought is always for her kids, isn't it? So I pulled myself to my feet, and legged it into the house. The noise didn't get louder or softer there. It was just like there, in my head, the same wherever I went, whatever doors I opened or closed. I thought I was going Looby-Lou. Except that, if I was going Looby-Lou, so were the babies. I guessed almost without thinking that p'raps they had the noise in their tiny heads too. So I ran up the stairs to them, two at a time. When I'd go to the top and un . . . opened their bedroom door, I found them bawling their eyes out, filling their cots with tears, poor sods. Hysterical, like. I scooped them both up at once, and belted it back down the stairs, and out the front door. I couldn't tell you why I went out the front door. It's not like I was looking for help. Wouldn't expect any help from those knobs-I-don't-call-neighbours. But my feet and the noise in my head carried me out the front door whether I liked it or not.

"That was when the shitty shrieking in my head stopped dead. Then . . . then came this other tune, out of nowhere, kind of creeping up on me, or us, if you count the babies. Dunno how to describe it. Like Mantovani and all that old shit me dad used to like. But not, if you know what I mean. More classy. I tell you what was awesome about it: suddenly the babies were dead quiet too. First time all sodding day. All sodding day . . .

Well, yeah, course, except for that bit when they had a nap, obviously. Might try some of that classical shit on them myself. Worked a treat. Classical Calpol. I sat down on the doorstep with them on my lap, and we all listened inside our heads – if you know what I mean.

"That was when I looked up, and saw all the others – all the knobs-I-don't-call-neighbours – round the street, coming out of their houses too. People like that old bitch from next door, her with the crumpled-up face, and that weird tattoo on her arm. Horrid, faded thing – I mean, the tattoo . . . God, I've got a fucking dragon with its tail down my arse. All she's got are some crappy grey set of numbers on her arm. Rubbish. They obviously didn't know how to do tattoos back in 1066 or whenever.

"I tell you what, they didn't know fuck all back then about music either. It's her who's always complaining to the Council about my stereo. Complain about anything, that one, from my music to the rain to the fucking sunshine – probably her who told the newspaper it was me who was to blame for the whole thing. Miserable bitch."

The so-called "miserable bitch next door" was Miss Rosa Adler, a seventy-five-year-old pensioner, who was the first to alert the emergency services. Whilst her neighbours were gathering in the Close, she initially resisted the urge to step outside, instead dialling 999.

There is an extant tape of the 999 call, recorded at precisely 2.39 p.m., in which Miss Adler is heard whimpering: "Make it stop, make it stop, please please make it stop, do something, it's here, Spark Close, it's in my head and everywhere, *schnell*, makeitstopmakeitstopmakeitstop," over and again. The call-handler attempts to calm her and make sense of the call, but in vain: "Which service do you need, miss? Is there an incident you want to report, miss? Is the incident at Spark Close,

Hanford, Stoke-on-Trent?" In response, Miss Adler is heard sobbing something incomprehensible, followed by the peculiar and unexplained words: "No, it's not Spark Close. It's climbed back inside my head. The *Mädchenorchester*. It's got back in there, and won't stop . . . *Aufstehen!* . . . " Then there's a distant shriek on the recording, as if from somewhere else in the room; and the call-handler is left asking: "Miss? Are you still there? Miss? Can you tell us what is going on?," with no further response from Miss Adler.

Miss Adler later told the police that she abandoned the phone under an irresistible compulsion to go outside, and "feel the sun on her dwindling hair," as she put it. "Ah, it was beautiful outside – the sun, it was shining, and everyone was milling about, even smiling at each other, like the street used to be in times when my hair was fuller and darker. 1977 and all that – how do you say? – jazz. But no, I couldn't smile or . . . 'mill' with them. I couldn't even enjoy my sunny hair, because there was this . . . this terrible *fortissimo* in my head. I have no doubt everyone thought I was being glary and unfriendly at them. But it was not true. My glaring, it was really directed inwards. I was glaring in my head, trying to shush the inside-orchestra. But instead of *diminuendo*ing, it was *crescendo*ing all over. Strings, wind, timpani, trombones, everything. Stop it, I kept telling my head. Stopitpleasestopitmakeitstop, but it wouldn't listen. *I* had to listen to *it*, *it* wouldn't listen to *me*. Like that silly Miss Kirsten who lives next door, with her bang-bang music and bang-bang arguments and bang-bang . . . well, those other activities, shall we say. Babies screaming, men coming and going and shouting, you wouldn't believe. She says I go on about it, but what can you do when you're woken up at three, four in the morning? And I worry about her, I really do. She thinks I don't understand – that I know nothing about what goes on, about sex – that I can't help with the babies, the men and so on. I mean, where does she think my own son came from? And who else knows more than myself about how it's like being what they now call a 'single mother' – and what they used to call many other things? Honestly, what can you do to help someone who doesn't want to be helped?

"Anyway, I am getting away from the subject. At first, I thought it must be her, Miss Kirsten, when the music started. I was washing the dishes, and I thought it was coming through the walls, through the floor, through the windows. But then I realised that the walls, they weren't bouncing as usual. No, it was the walls of my own head that were bouncing. It wasn't like her music. Music sounds all the same to me these days, all horrid, but even I could tell this was different. It was . . . it was old-fashioned – horrid-old-fashioned, as horrid-old as my memories."

Miss Adler is the only witness of the Spark Close Phenomenon for whom the "horrid-old" music was not preceded by some kind of screeching or "alarmish noise." She was also the only witness for whom the music started before she stepped outside the house. She did, though, share with other residents the same peculiar compulsion to leave her house by the front door; and she clearly found the music in her head as disturbing as others found the preceding screeches, sirens or alarms. Whereas others were comforted by the onset of the "old-fashioned" music, which generally superseded these "screeches," or "alarms," she found it hateful.

No convincing explanations have been proposed for the differences between Miss Adler's experience and that of other residents, the majority of reports focussing on the collective experience of the Phenomenon, rather than analysing exceptions.

Another exception was Miss Rosa Adler's neighbour, Dr. Terence Williams, who lived in the only detached house,

Number 14 at the end of the cul-de-sac, and who never 'reached' the musical stage of the Phenomenon. Dr. Williams, a fifty-year-old ex-GP on incapacity benefit, reported hearing a screaming noise at 2.39 p.m. He glanced at his wall clock when it started, and made a mental note of the time, "in case the information would be of use later – you know, for a case study, journal article, *et cetera*. I thought it was one of my seizures, and I always try to remember what happens in the lead-up to them. But looking back on this seizure, or whatever it was, I can't remember much at all after the clock loomed out of the wall at me. After that, everything was blotted out by the noise. It was horrible, hellish, a gnashing of teeth in my head, amplified a thousand times. All I knew, all I could think of was that I had to get out of the front door."

Unfortunately, Dr. Williams suffers from temporal lobe epilepsy, and he collapsed on his own 'Welcome' mat before he could get outside. He was found twenty minutes later by medics, unconscious, cyanotic, hugging his legs, in a pool of saliva, urine and blood. From the evidence available, it would seem he had experienced a full-blown seizure as he was attempting to push a key into the lock on the inside of the front door. One trainee paramedic who found him reported that there was a noticeable dent in the door frame, making it look like he had repeatedly head-butted the door during the seizure, "as if his head was trying to escape any way it could." The paramedic's colleagues on the scene would not verify this claim, declaring that it was not their priority to contribute to media speculation, only to help the injured and distressed.

But in this, the emergency services were at a bit of a loss when they first arrived, given that the majority of the people who experienced the Spark Close Phenomenon were neither injured nor distressed. Prior to their arrival, indeed, most people were visibly enjoying themselves. Ms. Kirsten Machin, for one, was uncharacteristically serene, sunning herself on the doorstep and holding gurgling twins on her lap, who (it would seem) had been lullabyed into half-sleep by the music in everybody's heads; Mr. Frank Hutchinson was standing to attention, saluting, and now and then surreptitiously pulling faces at the twin babies when his grandmother wasn't watching; Mrs. Hayley Hutchinson was standing like a tear in an eye, lost in a Remembrance Sunday reverie. All round the close, people were emerging from their homes into sunshine – at first clutching their ears in agony, and then straightening, loosening, as the inner-music seemed to suffuse their very muscles, bones, marrow. Mr. Rajesh Parmar from Number 9, the Shelley sisters at Number 5, fourteen-year-old Elizabeth ('Lelly') and seventeen-year-old Davy Lawson from Number 3 (both of whom should have been in school, but weren't), the entire Runtill family from Number 2 – all of them burst out of their houses, bent double, hands over their ears, then gradually softened, stood up, listened, brightened. All of them waved and smiled at their neighbours. Even Ralph, the ownerless cat who squatted at Number 1, was seen sitting on an outside windowsill, head to one side, raising a paw in greeting. For a few minutes, the music seemed everywhere, in everything and everybody.

It had spread like a mini-tornado, in a near-complete circle. Within a minute of Melissa Comb's death at Number 4, Paul Higgins at Number 6 was the first to hear the screeching, followed by the unexplained music; a minute or so later, it had spread to Numbers 8 and 10; at roughly 2.38 p.m., Miss Rosa Adler at Number 12 was afflicted by the inner-music, and, at 2.39 p.m., she dialled 999; simultaneously, Dr. Williams from the end of the cul-de-sac heard "hellish gnashing" in his head; then, between about 2.40 p.m. and 2.45 p.m., the musical cyclone circled round to the left-hand (or south) side of the Close, affecting in turn Rajesh Parmar at Number 9, the Shelley sisters at Number 5, and Lelly and Davy Lawson at Number 3; and finally, the cyclone turned the corner again, to hit the Runtills' household, Number 2, on the right-hand side of the close, next door to the dead girl. Estimates vary, but the general consensus is that the Runtills emerged from Number 2, Spark Close at approximately 2.47 p.m. (For a schematic plan of the Close and its residents, see Fig.1).

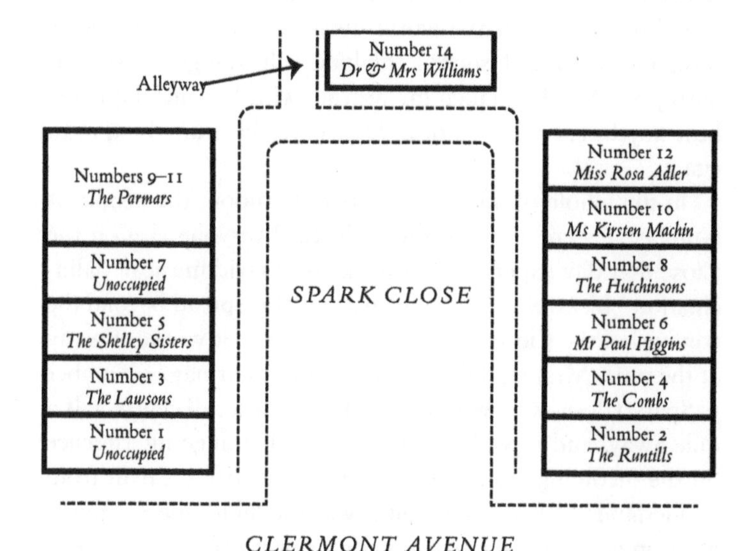

Fig 1. Spark Close residents in June 1999

Meanwhile, no-one at Number 4 heard anything. Number 4 was the silent centre of the musical storm – at this point, the still centre of the story. No-one there so much as looked out of the window, to see what was going on in the Close. All the living who were present in Melissa's bedroom at the time

– including two Macmillan nurses, Mr. Harry Comb, Mrs. Lizzie Comb, and Harry's eldest daughter, seventeen-year-old Serena – have been asked over and again whether they experienced any aural disturbances that afternoon; and they have all repeatedly denied hearing anything. Indeed, Melissa's half-sister Serena has gone so far as to testify to the neurologist investigating the case that those few minutes were, for her, the "silentest moments of my whole life so far. When I remember those moments, it seems as if we were kind of . . . sound-proofed from the world outside. The silent moments went on so long, I started thinking silly things – like perhaps poor Mel had taken my hearing with her, and I'd never hear anything again . . . or at least never hear anything right again."

In the whole of Spark Close that afternoon, the people at Number 4 were alone in their silence. Everyone else on the Close that day experienced some kind of vivid musical 'hallucination.' Bizarrely, this 'hallucination' also spread beyond the confines of the Close, to residents who were at work, or away at the time. Mrs. Sejal Parmar, wife of Mr. Parmar of Number 9, Spark Close, was working in a British Gas call centre half a mile away, and reported that she "heard strange interference on the incoming line. It was during a call from a man from Sunderland. At first, I thought it was the 'hold' music mixing itself up with the callers, you know? But it was so . . . strong, not like the electrical pingy-pongy music they normally use. And I felt it was coming not from the head-piece, but from inside my head – from memories or dreams I couldn't remember. Beautiful, it was, caring music, you know? – something like mothers. I can't explain it in words, and I can't explain why I started to cry, or why I feel like crying now I'm talking about it. I mean, it didn't last long, and then I was talking again to the man from Sunderland, who was very cross. He was much louder than the quiet music, and drowned it out, you know?"

The residents who were not on Spark Close that afternoon, but who experienced "echoes" of the musical hallucination from a distance, all reported that the music sounded "quiet," as if overheard from afar. By and large, their experience of the Phenomenon was less intense than the people who were on the scene. Nonetheless, their testimonies are valuable, if only because they controvert the arguments of those who put forward overly simplistic explanations of the Spark Close Phenomenon. For example, it would clearly not have been possible for Ms. Kirsten Machin's stereo to have been heard in a call centre half a mile away. Any credible hypothesis concerning the Spark Close Phenomenon needs to take account of the "echoes" which reached absent residents of the Close – even those who were miles away at the time.

The most distant of these "echoes" seems to have reached as far as Loughborough in Leicestershire, over fifty miles away. It was there that Mr. Simon Adler-Reeves, grandson of Miss Rosa Adler, childhood resident of Spark Close and long-time friend of the Comb family, was trying and failing to write his Ph.D thesis on 'The Portrayal of Symphonic Music in Second World War Fiction.' At around 2.45 p.m., Simon put down the pen with which he'd not been writing, thinking he could hear white noise coming from the stereo on the other side of the room. He got up from his desk, and stepped over to the stereo. It was switched off at the socket. But he still thought he could hear something: "So I leant over one of the speakers," Simon said, "and put my head against it. It was then that I felt this strange vibration – distant, like listening to an unborn child's heartbeat. I can't tell you if it was really a heartbeat, or music I was hearing; but I can tell you that, for a few minutes afterwards, I felt happy for the first time in months. Even hours later, I was feeling okay, so I decided to pick up the phone and ring my grandma – something I hadn't done for a long time.

"That was when I found out about our neighbours' daughter – about Melissa. I'd known her, off and on, since she was born – and I'd known the Comb family all my life. Because my parents'd been broke, we'd lived on Spark Close with my grandma when I was a kid; and then, when we moved away, I used to visit my grandma all the time and stay with her when my parents were having one of their many splittings-up. And the Combs were the one family on the Close I got to know properly – Melissa, her half-sister Serena, who I played with as a kid, Mel's mum Lizzie, and even their dad, well, a bit. So both my grandma and myself, we were very upset at the news. My grandma, she was distraught and confused when she told me. All she said between sobs was: 'How strange is that, you ringing now? As if you knew.' I said it was pure coincidence. Obviously, I didn't mention the distant noises on the stereo, or the feeling of happiness. It seemed irrelevant. It wasn't till twenty-four hours later, when I arrived back in Stoke-on-Trent, that I realised lots of other people on Spark Close had experienced much more intense versions of what I'd heard and felt."

In all, an estimated forty-five people with connections to Spark Close have been traced who experienced some version of the Phenomenon – who, that is, reported some kind of aural disturbance on the afternoon of the 9th June 1999. There may well be more, who have never come forward.

There were also witnesses who noticed that something out of the ordinary was happening, but who were not directly involved in the Phenomenon itself. Significantly, these passers-by saw what was going on in the Close, but were unaffected by the aural hallucination. One such passer-by was a Mrs. Rebecca Ingram, who was the second person to call the emergency services: "You see, I was on my way back from a meeting with our vicar, and had a new mobile phone with me. I need one, now I'm Neighbourhood Watch co-ordinator for Clermont Avenue. And thank goodness I had one that afternoon. They'd all gone doolally on Spark Close – wandering about, staring into space and . . . hugging each other. At first, I thought it was some jamboree, or an event for Mr. Runtill's 'church,' or some anniversary I'd forgotten about. But I knew no-one had obtained Council clearance to shut the road. So next I thought: gas leak, or that incinerator down the road. Anyhow, the point was I knew something was wrong, and it was high time to call the authorities – the police and ambulance and fire-persons. So I did. It seems someone or other had phoned before me, but you can never be too careful, can you? As Neighbourhood Watch Chairperson, it's my job to be vigilant, and call 999 at every possible opportunity."

Mrs. Ingram's 999 call was received at 2.50 p.m. By this time, a police car and ambulance were already on their way, alerted by Miss Rosa Adler's slightly earlier call. The hysteria of that earlier call concerned the call-handler enough for her to alert both police and medical team: "I thought it might be some schizo-pensioner rampaging on the loose," she said later, "so it was definitely a high priority as far as I was concerned."

But no-one was rampaging in Spark Close – quite the opposite. Once outdoors, the neighbours started to mingle and chat about their shared musical experiences.

This was about 2.55 p.m., by which point the music in most people's heads had swelled towards a final cadence, and was ebbing away. In general, the music's dying away ushered in an almost-euphoric sense of well-being: "I felt great," said Mr. Frank Hutchinson. "The sun was shining, Ms. Kirsten was smiling at me – or at least in my general direction – and by now even my grandma wasn't telling me not to smile back."

"It was the music that made us all happy," said Mr. Paul Higgins. "Those last echoes in my head, I can't describe them, but they felt kinda like throbs of happiness. Like you got when you were young in the seaside in Southport, and you were building sandcastles and digging holes as big as graves, and, y' know, getting on with everyone under the sun." Similarly, Lelly Lawson from Number 3 commented: "God, it was great – weird-great. I hate that kind of yawn-ful classical crap most of the time, the crap she –" (presumably referring to Serena Comb from Number 4) "– tries to play from 'cross the road, plinky-plonky on her piano. But when this classical crap in my head had finished, I almost wanted to say 'come back.' And afterwards, everything felt kind of good, and sort-of-like-I-kind-of . . . liked the people round me. I mean, I've always liked that Machin woman from up the street. She's cool – got great tits, and isn't afraid to show them off in that Geri Halliwell bikini of hers. Doesn't give a shit about what other people think. But it wasn't just her this time. This time, it was sort-of-like I felt everyone was great – just for a bit, you know. So I went over and started chatting with them Runtills. Can't stand them normally, bunch of happy-clappy shites."

Lelly mingled with the Runtills, Mr. Rajesh Parmar chit-chatted with the Shelley sisters, and then started twirling round the wheelchair-bound elder sister in an ecstatic waltz; Mr. Paul Higgins wandered between groups of people, sharing his beef and onion crisps; Mrs. Hayley Hutchinson comforted Miss Rosa Adler, who was still very upset; and Ralph the Cat purred so loudly, he could be heard twenty yards away. Mr. Raymond Runtill, fifty-year-old lay-preacher and nightclub doorman from Number 2, Spark Close, commented that: "It was like Pentecost in the Close, all of us inspired by tongues of fire and chatting with each other – however different we are. After years of just passing one another in the street, the Spirit had descended on us all. I shook everyone's hand, as if Spark Close was my church, and it was time to say 'the Peace of the Lord be always with you.' But I didn't go around saying that, not this time. Don't know why. Instead, I just smiled at everyone, and everyone smiled at me, and we chatted about the music and the sunshine and anything else."

Even Ralph the Cat seemed to want to be a part of the chit-chat and sunshine, so he leapt down from his perch on Number 1's windowsill, and started circulating. Paul Higgins said afterwards: "That mangy cat, the one who slinks round the Close like he owns it, I saw him – y'know, in the corner of my eyes – disappear into the humongous weeds in the garden across the street from us. They got a small front garden, see, at Number 1 – only house with one – or, at least, they would have if anyone lived there. So that cat, he disappears into this garden. I thought it'd got a mouse or dead rat. But no. Few seconds later, it emerges from the mini-jungle, with an old kiddie's football. There it was, pushing the ball towards us with its nose, like. We all took the hint. I crammed what was left of my crisps in my gob – and then me, the cat, that Lelly girl and her brother, that Bible-basher Runtill and his sons, even that bloody wet Indian bloke, all of us joined in, having a kick about. It was like one of my favourite war documentaries – Krauts and British kicking a ball about no-man's-land at Christmas." As in 1914, the football transcended pre-existing prejudices, as Paul Higgins, a local pamphleteer for the BNP, kicked the ball around with Mr. Parmar, as well as the "mangy cat" Ralph, and the "Bible-bashing" Runtills.

At 3.04 p.m., the ball disappeared underneath a police car, which came to a screeching halt in the Close, opposite Number 3. Ralph the Cat is reported to have darted under the stationary vehicle in order to retrieve the ball; but when he emerged, dragging it after him, it was clearly punctured. The game over,

Paul Higgins stepped over to speak to the two police officers, followed by almost everyone else. In his informal report on the incident, PC Daniel Dawson stated that:

> *Upon proceeding to the scene of the 'emergency' at Spark Close, Hanford, and after stepping out of our vehicle, PC Fury and I were immediately approached by a crowd of witnesses, who were talking in an incoherent manner all at once. There was a mood of what can only be termed intense excitement among the witnesses, and, at this point, PC Fury and I could make little sense of what was being said. We quietened everyone down, and requested that the witnesses speak one by one, so we could assess the situation. A Mr. Higgins, of 6, Spark Close, nominated himself as spokesperson for the group, and informed us that some unexplained "mind games" seemed to have affected everyone on the Close. His precise words, which PC Fury noted down, were: "We've all been hearing things, officers, things that aren't there. Our ears have been sent round the twist." Other witnesses then came forwards with more or less similar accounts. Eventually, PC Fury and I consulted together, and decided that the best course of action would be for one of us to remain with the group of witnesses, keeping everyone together and under observation, whilst the other called for back-up, and started knocking on doors to check for further witnesses, or 'victims.' This we proceeded to do, along with ambulance service personnel who now also arrived on the scene.*

It was at this point that Dr. Terence Williams was discovered, lying on his hall floor in a pool of saliva, vomit and urine, by PC Dawson and the team of paramedics. Both Dr. Williams and Miss Rosa Adler, who was in a state of shock, were stretchered into two ambulances, and 'blue-lighted' to Accident and Emergency. Both, however, were discharged the same day, having fully recovered from the incident. Or, that is, seeming to have fully recovered: actually, Miss Adler reported ongoing tinnitus and minor recurrences of what she called the "nowhere-everywhere music" over the next few months. She seems to be the only resident on the Close for whom the musical hallucinations had not entirely ceased by about 4 p.m. on the same day.

For everyone else, the excitement was over by that time, and they heard nothing more. Soon after the ambulances had left with Miss Adler and Dr. Williams, most residents returned to their houses, and what they had been doing (or not doing) prior to the hallucination: "It felt a real downer after the ambulances had gone and everyone started going indoors," remarked Lelly Lawson. "There we all were, in the sun one minute, kinda-sorta liking each other for once, everyone chatting everyone else up, playing football, dancing and shit. Big fucking love-in. Then, the music sodded off, and it was like some hangover after one of my mate's parties – not that I drink, course not – but that afternoon, it felt all kinda balloon-deflated that everything was going back to shitty normal."

Likewise, Mrs. Hayley Hutchinson commented: "Hard to believe that, after the stirring music, after standing together, shoulder to shoulder, after that half hour of Dunkirk on our street, we all went home and carried on as normal – back to front doors and jobs and washing up. Next day, there we all were, just passing-nodding at each other in the Close, not talking again. One has an experience like that, and one thinks: goodness me, that's amazing, that'll change one's life. One's husband comes back from Dunkirk, and continues as milkman-normal. Doesn't even talk about it. My Frank, he comes back a hero from the Territorials in '97, demobbed, and signs on at the Labour Exchange and goes fishing up at Rudyard. Nothing's changed on the surface – except that he wears khaki for fishing. And the same goes for what happened that day on Spark Close. Or at least, the same minus the khaki and fishing. What happened is a nice memory, and all that – people saluting, embracing each other and chatting away. But that's all. Once these things – you know, these Dunkirks, these 'Phenomenons' – have gone, they're gone, and it's back to living or not living, talking or not talking. All the fuss and hubbub dies away, and they seem a million years ago."

For once, Ms. Kirsten Machin's language, in describing the immediate after-effects of the Spark Close Phenomenon, strikingly echoed her neighbour's: "There's this fucking amazing thing that happens, and then suddenly it's a million miles, a million light-years away, and you can't even believe it happened in the first place. One minute everyone's massed together in the Close, all buzzing, like some hot gangbang-orgy – or, at least, an orgy without the sex. The next minute, everyone buggers off, and it suddenly feels a bit chilly again."

At this point, the police started taking statements from each household. This also seems to be the time that someone alerted the local press about the strange goings-on. No-one has admitted doing so, and the local paper was slow on the up-take anyway, suspecting some kind of freak call. They contacted the police for more details, and sat on the story till the next day.

Meanwhile, news was spreading in other ways. For a start, the residents who had been absent from the Close that afternoon, but who had been affected by some kind of aural disturbance, called home, and found out that their experience echoed what had happened collectively on the Close. Indeed, that was initially how the story started to spread – through friends, families, colleagues talking about what had happened. In this way, the story had already 'gone big' before the local newspaper even reported it; and the press in general seemed to be playing catch-up for the next week or so, never quite keeping pace with what was going on. First they treated the Spark Close Phenomenon as a minor incident – maybe a practical joke – and then they consistently underestimated the public's interest in the story, failing to follow up leads, failing to interview key witnesses, failing to provide a coherent account of events. In this, their failures were not dissimilar to those of the police and doctors. 'Confronted with an unprecedented and inexplicable phenomenon,' one broadsheet newspaper columnist wrote much later, in an end-of-year review of 1999,

> *the institutions we rely on were exposed as not only incompetent, but also impotent. It seems they can only handle phenomena that are narrowly classed as 'rational.' What happened that day on Spark Close is a relatively minor incident. Imagine if something of the sort spread across a wider area. Imagine a whole city struck down for a few minutes with 'beautiful music.' Imagine the chaos, the car pile-ups, the inundated hospitals, the shop looting, the aircraft failing to land. Imagine the aftermath: people in shock, the time and money lost to business, the strain on NHS resources. And yet, it seems, we as a nation have no contingency plans in place for such unforeseen disasters – because they are not 'rational.' Such things do not happen, and therefore we do not need to plan for them. Well, judging by 1999 and the Spark Close Phenomenon, it would seem that so-called 'irrational' events or disasters can and do happen – and, if we don't learn this lesson now, perhaps awaiting us in the new millennium are, above all, much harsher lessons in this respect.*

Six months after this article came out – that is, over a year after the Spark Close Phenomenon – Miss Rosa Adler happened across it, while showing her grandson and a local historian the "dossier" (as she called her scrapbook) of cuttings about the Phenomenon which she'd collected. At that time, she was in bed, recovering from a fall, but she still wanted to talk about the Phenomenon, the Combs, her "dossier"; and, despite pain and illness, she sat up when she saw the column. Her response to it, according to the local historian, was angry, impassioned: "It wasn't a disaster," she declared, jabbing a bent finger at it, and finally through it. "For me, it was just horrible and there was nothing but 'makeitstopmakeitstop' that day; but I know that for others it was different. And even for me, you know, it wasn't a 'disaster.' You know, I think all of us, we made a mistake. We got it wrong. All of us on the Close, we had our own thoughts about why it had happened, what the hallucination meant. Well, at least some of us had our own thoughts about it. Some of us didn't seem to think about it at all afterwards, and carried on as if nothing – how do you say? – 'untoward' had taken place. But I couldn't carry on as normal. I could still hear it, the music-noise, *pianissimo*-haunting me in the corner of my head. All that horrid-old-fashionedness was still there, so I couldn't just carry on.

"And those of us who didn't just carry on, we thought it meant something. We thought it meant something about that poor girl – you know, the *Fräulein* . . . Miss Melissa, who died before the screeching and music. Maybe it was a punishment for something, we thought. Maybe we hadn't looked after her enough when she was with the living. Or maybe she was such a beautiful girl, we were being told something from 'up high' about her being at peace. After all, she liked the music, and I used to hear her singing and humming old tunes around the Close – so maybe, we thought, heaven *is* music for her. Not for me: for me it is the other place, full of trombones and fires . . .

"But where was I? Ah, yes, I was talking about the poor *Fr* . . . Miss Melissa, no? She died, we heard the music. We who thought about that music afterwards, we thought there must be a link. But now, you know, I'm not so sure. Now, I wonder if perhaps it wasn't a message about her dying. I think we might have got it all wrong, and because of that everything afterwards went wrong also. The music, it was warning us, not comforting us. I mean, if it was meant to comfort, why did we hear it and not the family themselves, not the sister and mother and father of little Melissa? . . . Or perhaps I'm wrong, and it was doing both, perhaps it was doing everything and nothing, I don't know. I just know . . . I just think that maybe it was also trying to tell us something about the future, not the past. And we . . . we didn't listen, didn't understand.

"Perhaps we should all of us on the Close have guessed what it meant – or, at least, what I now think it meant: that it was a warning, a plea for help, in our heads. That it was like Mrs. Hutchinson says, the 'air-raid siren.' That it was telling us to look after Melissa's family in her . . . in her absence. All of that 'community spirit,' as you say, that came after the music, when people were talking, chatting, even embracing – it went to waste, to nothing, instead of being put to use, instead of all of us joining together to help them, the Family Comb. Perhaps the whole thing, it was her spirit, or a musical spirit on her behalf, begging us to help them through the bad times afterwards – especially that poor sister of hers, especially dearest Serena, who had to live through it all. But we didn't help Serena, we didn't help the still-living family, we didn't listen, did we? People, I think to myself sometimes, care more about the dead than the living. And they don't really listen to either – they don't listen properly, with the open ears, to the living *or* the dead. When you are ancient like me, you realise that no-one ever really listens to anything."

VARIATIONS

Pavane pour une infante défunte

WHAT FOLLOWS IS a selection of cuttings from Miss Rosa Adler's "dossier," as she calls her scrapbook about the Spark Close Phenomenon. From the start, she collected all the newspaper reports, magazine articles, features and even academic papers she could find about the Phenomenon. There are many hundreds, if not thousands, of these; so reproduced here is just a sample, to give a general sense of how the story developed from first reports to later retrospectives. Clearly, there is much that is debatable and controversial, not to mention wildly inaccurate, in many of these accounts; but they all add to an understanding of both the Phenomenon itself, and, just as importantly, its longer-term reception by diverse interested parties.

Excerpts from *The Sentinel* [Stoke-on-Trent's local newspaper], 10th June 1999: 'Street Music.'

The residents of a usually peaceful street in Hanford were amazed yesterday when they all reported hearing unexplained loud music [. . .]

At approximately 5 p.m. [*sic*] yesterday afternoon, all the residents suddenly heard what they later described as "deafening classic music" [*sic*] – music which seemed, as one resident put it, to "come from nowhere." No source for the anti-social music has been traced, and one local GP, who has asked to remain anonymous for professional reasons, claims that the residents might have experienced a "collective musical hallucination."

Whether hallucination or, as another Hanfordian put it, "hoax-ination," local police have described the afternoon's events as "bizarre" and are questioning residents and witnesses. No-one was seriously hurt during the incident, though three [*sic*] residents were hospitalised with shock [*sic*].

From *The Sun*, 14th June 1999: News in Briefs: 'Making Beautiful Music Together.'

A street in Stoke-on-Trent is reported to have been the subject of a daring musical hoax, *The Sun* heard today. On the morning [*sic*] of the 11th [*sic*] of June, everyone on the street complained that they were "hearing music in their heads." Convinced that they were being subjected to some kind of telepathic mind control from a UFO [*sic*], residents contacted the emergency services, who have since reassured local people that the whole affair was some kind of prank [*sic*]. "Why would UFOs come to Stoke?" one paramedic asked our reporter. "Surely they'd go to Washington or London first."

From *The Sentinel*, 14th June 1999: Family Announcements.

COMB, Melissa (1992–1999), of Spark Close, Hanford, beloved daughter of Mr. Harold Comb and Mrs. Elizabeth Comb, half-sister of Miss Serena Comb, passed away peacefully on 9th June after a long illness. Melissa's funeral service will take place at Trentham Parish Church on 17th June at 2.45 p.m. Donations in place of floral tributes to Children's Leukaemia UK please.

From *The Sentinel*, 16th June 1999: Letters.

MADAM,

I write regarding your family announcement of 14th June 1999. I was very saddened to hear of the death of a young girl, Miss Melissa Comb, of Spark Close, on the 9th June 1999. My condolences to the family – I didn't know them or the girl, but I'm sure it's a difficult moment for those close to her. Just remember that time and Christ's love heal all, and their little angel is happy in God's arms.

On a related note, I couldn't help connecting this event with an earlier report in your edition of 10th June 1999, called 'Street Music.' Did the girl die whilst everyone else on Spark Close was hearing beautiful choruses in their heads? Was this a sign that her soul was ascending to heavenly bliss? Was this the angels singing her to her rest?

Name and address supplied,
St. Basil and All Saints, Talke Pits.

From *Millennium: A Magazine of the Mystical World*, 18th June 1999: Notices and Announcements.

On the evening of the Summer Solstice, The Musical Society of Mystic Hummingbirds will be holding a candlelit vigil in Spark Close, Hanford, Stoke-on-Trent, to celebrate the life and beautiful death of Miss Melissa Comb, whose musical soul still hovers over the area. The vigil starts at 7 p.m. and is free, but suggested donations of £40 a head to the Society are welcome. Light refreshments will be provided by the Society, but please come prepared with your own candles, blankets and necessary provisions. We have supplied a copy of an artist's impression of 'Melodious Melissa' below, which you can enlarge, photocopy, cut out and bring along if you so wish. If you are a registered member of the Society, you will also be entitled to a free glass of Cava and slice of pizza, on production of your membership card.

Feature from *The Weekend Sentinel*, 26th June 1999: 'Hummingbird Chorus.'

A candlelit vigil has been held at Spark Close, Hanford, by a little-known sect called 'The Musical Society of Mystic Hummingbirds.' The vigil took place on the evening of the 21st June, to commemorate the Summer Solstice, as well as the life of Miss Melissa Comb, who died on Spark Close earlier this month. The organisers claimed that the vigil aimed to "recreate the strange musical phenomenon which occurred at the time of Miss Melissa Comb's death earlier this month" [. . .]

Leader of the candlelit vigil and Chairman of the Hummingbird Society, Sir Peter Rosamunde, commented that: "The evening was a great success. Melodious Melissa's soul-music is still audible if you listen with open ears. During our Solstice vigil, we opened ourselves up to receive it. We were merely the vessels, channelling the cosmic vibrations into our all-night chants."

Some of the residents of Spark Close, however, were reportedly less happy about the Society's "channelling" and "chants." Ms. Kirsten Machin of Spark Close told *The Sentinel* that: "I had to turn up my music to top volume to drown out the weirdos outside. That was the only way I could get my babies to go to sleep. They were very disturbed."

One of the most disturbed Spark Close residents, Mr. Raymond Runtill, a lay-preacher and nightclub usher, is alleged to have burst out of his house at 2 a.m. in the morning, and heckled those taking part in the Society's vigil. He is reported to have accused the Society of a form of "devil worship," and a scuffle is said to have ensued. No-one, however, was hurt, and the police say that the only complaints made to them at the time were from residents unable to sleep.

PC Henry Fury has since issued this statement on behalf of the local constabulary: "All we ask is that, next time, any group planning a meeting in the vicinity of Spark Close contacts us beforehand to make the necessary arrangements. Furthermore, we ask anyone visiting Spark Close to respect the privacy of the residents, and particularly that of the Comb family, during this difficult time. While we understand that Spark Close is now a place of special interest for certain spiritualist groups, we would ask for sensitivity on the part of visitors to the area" [. . .]

Though the police denied that they had received any complaints specifically from the Comb family, PC Fury did express concern about a number of incidents of alleged harassment involving the family. There are reports that people have been knocking on the Combs' front door day and night, asking to see Melissa's bedroom, or what they call her "shrine." The family have also reportedly been pestered by phone calls, journalists and even tourists, who were under the mistaken impression that the Combs' house has been open to the public since the Spark Close Phenomenon [. . .]

From *The Potteries Advertiser*, 28th June 1999: 'Combing for Evidence.'

Police are said to be taking "very seriously" claims that the Comb family of Spark Close, Hanford, is being subjected to severe harassment [. . .]

The family recently received a threatening letter from an unknown source, accusing their older daughter, Miss Serena Comb, of responsibility for Melissa Comb's death – a claim strenuously denied by the family. A police spokesperson confirmed that there is no evidence that Miss Melissa Comb died of anything but natural causes, and they are not looking for anyone else in connection with her death. The police are now "doing all they can to alleviate the situation and prevent the harassment from continuing."

"We will do everything in our power," said PC Henry Fury, "to find and prosecute with the full force of law the person responsible for this unpleasant letter."

From *The Potteries Advertiser*, 29th June 1999: Apology.

The Advertiser would like to apologise for the contents of the article 'Combing for Evidence' (28th June 1999). *The Advertiser* fully acknowledges that it should not have named the recipient of the anonymous letter in question, and apologises fully and unreservedly to the family concerned for any distress caused by this error.

From *The Guardian*, 3rd July 1999: 'Biteback' Column, by Ursula Birch: extract from 'Pavane on the Death of an Infanta.'

[. . .] and as for all this endless drivel about the so-called 'Spark Close Phenomenon,' with its hallucinations, millennial visions, miracles, mass delusions – anyone would have thought a blonde princess had died. Oh, sorry, my mistake: a blonde princess *did* die, or should we say a provincial infant infanta, of the name Miss Millicent [*sic*] Comb, who has been posthumously elevated to princess-dom by the sentimental right-wing press:

Blonde princess dies = wailing, gnashing of teeth and lots of group hugs + hearse-loads of weepy music by Elton John, or John Taverner – or, in Millicent Comb's case, just made up in our own heads . . .

. . . this is becoming an equation we can recite more easily than times-tables. From Monroe to Kelly to Spencer to Comb, the millennial epidemic we have to worry about is not 'flu, computer bugs, nor even (for that matter) music in the head – it's an epidemic of blonde princesses dying.

Meanwhile, for us non-blonde, non-blue-blooded, still-living proles, this fatal epidemic is accompanied by another, compulsory, long-and-drawn-out epidemic of collective grief for said blonde princesses. Society, the media, and now (it seems) even the music in our own heads compel us to gather round the necropolis of blondes and mourn continuously – because that is our subservient role, as middle-aged brunettes or redheads. These days, it seems compulsory collective grief is a condition of living [. . .]

From *The Guardian*, 10th July 1999: Letters.

My dear Sir,

I wish to complain in the strongest terms about Ms. Ursula Birch's article last Saturday, entitled 'Pavane on the Death of an Infanta.' It was unfeeling and unworthy of the national institution that is *The Guardian*, which I have read and otherwise enjoyed for many years. What is more, I have to say that the column was erroneous in all respects. For a start, Miss Melissa Comb, the charming young girl who died on Spark Close, was not blonde, but leaned towards auburn on the hair spectrum.

Yours with all due regards,

Miss Rosa Adler, Spark Close, Stoke-on-Trent.

From *The Sun*, 20th July 1999: 'Y' What Y' What?' Column, by Kevin Rite: extract from 'Who's A-Freud of the Big Mad Professor?'

[. . .] and our old friend, Professor Christopher Sollertinsky (right) of St. B***'s University Hospital, London, eminent psychologist [*sic*], brain surgeon [*sic*], agony uncle [*sic*] on Neurology FM, spokesperson for the FIN ('Fat is Neurology') campaign, and advocate for sexual music therapy [*sic*], has been seen snooping around Spark Close in Stoke-on-Trent, the scene of unexplained musical hallucinations in June [. . .] Prof. Sollertinsky is said to be investigating the so-called 'Spark Close Phenomenon,' alongside a local quack [Dr. Terence Williams], with the intention of writing a book [*sic*] on the subject – a book which will no doubt tie up the events on the Close with his own bizarre theories. This second Sigmund Freud is said to believe in everything from telepathy, telekinesis, poltergeists and "a direct link between IQ and body weight" [*sic*]. He is also notoriously obsessed with sex: "Everything boils down to our primal desires," he has been heard to say [*sic*], "and it is our job as doctors to uncover those desires" [*sic*].

Well, Prof. Christopher Sollerts-*kinky*, *The Sun* has beaten you to it: here, you can see a photo of lovely twenty-five-year-old [*sic*] Ms. Kirsten Machin, 36-DD, of Spark Close, her desires uncovered just for us . . . [*finger pointing at half-page spread of Kirsten Machin in a school girl's outfit, the blouse lowered to show her bare breasts*.]

From *The Sun*, 29th July 1999: Apology.

The Sun would like to acknowledge and correct some factual errors in Kevin Rite's 'Y'what? Y'what?' Column of Tuesday 20th July: 'Who's A-Freud of the Big Bad Professor?' *The Sun* would like to point out that Prof. Christopher Sollertinsky works as a Consultant Neurologist, not psychologist, at St. B***'s University Hospital, and the quotations in the article were misattributed to him (the actual source has yet to be identified). *The Sun* would like to apologise for these errors and for any inconvenience caused.

Extract from 'A Neuroscientific Investigation into the Spark

Street [*sic*] Phenomenon,' by Prof. Christopher Sollertinsky with Dr. Terence Williams, in *Journal of Neuro-Musicology*, vol. 5:2, Autumn 2000, pp.5–64.

> [. . .] so, taking all this into account, a definitive explanation of the bizarre occurrences on Spark Street [*sic*] in June 1999 seems as elusive as ever. In its place, all we have are hundreds of competing explanations, from the mystical to the dismissive.
>
> Rather than summarily dismissing the Phenomenon, however, we would like to suggest the following hypotheses along neuroscientific lines, based on our field investigations, interviews and tests. We offer these hypotheses with the proviso that they are just that – hypotheses – which demand further research for their verification or falsification; and we are aware that they may be controversial among our more single-mindedly rationalistic colleagues. But, for what they are worth, here are the tentative and initial hypotheses to which we were led by our investigations:
>
> 1. That the Spark Street Phenomenon was not a hoax, but was experienced as 'real' by residents of the street.
> 2. That it was related, in some way, to the death of Miss Melissa Comb, and might be seen as a spontaneous and collective outpouring of repressed grief for the young girl.
> 3. That its aetiology lies in some form of shared neuro-pathology.
> 4. That this neuro-pathology remains obscure, but it seems significant that at least two residents of the street have been diagnosed with degrees of tempo-

ral lobe epilepsy. Perhaps Spark Street – for some hidden environmental reason – represents a kind of epileptic 'hotspot.' Hence, we believe the Phenomenon may represent an outbreak of what we have chosen to call 'mass neurogenic illness' – that is, a peculiarly neural version of 'mass psychogenic illness,' more popularly known as 'mass hysteria.' (As a point of comparison, we might refer to the rather similar case of the Dancing Plague of 1518, when up to 400 people danced themselves into a frenzy and ultimately – over a period of weeks – to death by exhaustion. Significantly for our study, many of the dancer-sufferers in this case screamed they could hear music in their heads).

5. That the initial unpleasant 'screech' or 'siren-like' noise experienced by residents was a species of collective tinnitus. Tinnitus is, of course, common as a precursor to full-scale musical hallucinosis: the brain, assailed by a chaotic, or 'screech-like' noise from the ears, makes sense of that noise by reshaping it in terms of more familiar musical imagery. That is to say, the tinnitus is received and processed as noise by the basal ganglia, but is then reshaped into recognisable musical patterns by the 'higher' parts of the brain, and the thalamocortical systems. Hence, on Spark Street, it is possible that the musical hallucination was itself merely an extension of the original 'screeching' noise, reshaped into a recognisable form. We will be presenting our hypotheses about the nature of the 'recognisable form' assumed by the hallucination in a separate, forthcoming paper.
6. That the fundamental mystery of the Phenomenon remains quite how and why a spontaneous and col-

lective outpouring of grief for Miss Melissa Comb occurred, prior to any of the residents outside her house consciously knowing of her death. In this regard, we would like to suggest that the Spark Street Phenomenon is one of the most compelling cases yet to point towards some form of communal telepathy. Though we risk the ridicule of our colleagues for admitting as much, we believe that the Spark Street Phenomenon may prove to be the starting-point for a new branch of socio-neurology; specifically, it may point the way towards a socio-neuroscientific form of C. G. Jung's collective unconscious, whereby certain 'lower' sections of the brain – such as the so-called 'mirror neurons' in the premotor, primary somatosensory and posterior parietal cortex – may be connected with a proto-linguistic, and, above all, musical mode of telepathic communication [. . .]

Extract from 'A Musicological Investigation into the Spark Street [*sic*] Phenomenon,' by Prof. Christopher Sollertinsky with Dr. Terence Williams, and the assistance of Miss Serena Comb, in *Journal of Musical Neurology*, vol. 7:3, Autumn 2000, pp.153–98.

[. . .] I, Prof. Christopher Sollertinsky, suggested in a previous paper [see above] that the musical hallucination experienced by residents on Spark Street [*sic*] assumed a 'recognisable form,' following the initial tinnitus-like 'screech.' No-one, though, seems to have managed to pin down precisely what this 'recognisable form' was; and it is a curious fact that none of the residents who experienced the hallucination have been able to name, nor even decently whistle, the music they heard on 9th June

1999. No doubt this is partly because almost no-one who experienced the musical hallucination actually professed to liking the genre of music involved under normal circumstances. This was the case both for those residents who regularly listened to music and for those who didn't. The music they heard on the 9th of June was not to their taste, or at least not to their usual taste, even though (in the majority of cases) the hallucination was extremely pleasurable.

To be more specific, judging by the various witness statements, the hallucinatory music was clearly of a classical and orchestral nature, yet no-one who experienced the hallucination admitted to listening to classical music on a regular basis. Conversely, the two residents on the street, Mr. Harry Comb and his first daughter Miss Serena Comb, who both listened to and, indeed, played classical music, were among those who did not experience the musical hallucination: that is, members of the Comb family and their medical entourage at Number 4. The Spark Street Phenomenon, like some kind of audio negative, reversed the musical *status quo* on the street: those who were not fans of classical music were suddenly possessed by it, whilst those who had some prior knowledge of it were reduced to silence.

In this paradoxical context, my colleague and I came to the conclusion that the Combs – Harry and Serena – might somehow hold the key to the puzzle: given their predilection for music of a classical nature, that is, they might be able to help the residents (and, indeed, ourselves) discover what exactly the music was which people had heard on the 9th June. Harry Comb, however, refused to help in this regard, so I turned to his first daughter, Serena. She agreed, and I spent a pleasant afternoon in the company of this exceptionally astute, if understandably sullen, young lady. There was an intelligent intensity to her sullenness, her unspoken grief, which I found intriguing, almost disturbing – and it crossed my mind that she herself might be the epicentre of the Phenomenon, as much as her dead half-sister. Perhaps, I wondered in an idle moment of superstition, what we were dealing with here was a kind of auditory poltergeist, centred on this strangely-fascinating teenage girl.

Despite what my detractors claim, though, I am ordinarily neither superstitious nor suspicious of the female sex; first and foremost, I am a scientist, but I – unlike those detractors – am open about my own emotions, prejudices, irrational beliefs. It is vital, I believe, to be open about these predispositions, to bring them to consciousness, in order to understand and transcend them, for the sake of scientific enquiry. And that is precisely what I did in this case. After initially pondering on Miss Serena Comb and her own part in the Phenomenon, I decided to move swiftly onto the main business of the afternoon. I subsequently interviewed various residents of the street whilst Serena played the piano, in an attempt to discover the precise nature of the hallucinatory music.

After a few hours, we were near to giving up the search for this musical needle in a haystack – until, that is, we came to an interview with Mrs. Hayley Hutchinson and her grandson, Mr. Frank Hutchinson, from Number 8, Spark Street. The former had memorably described the hallucinatory music as "like what they play at the Cenotaph . . . Kind of beautiful, slowish, saddish, yet . . . stirring." So Serena set about trying out simple piano arrangements of some of the pieces played on Remembrance Sunday. Eventually, she hit upon 'Nimrod,' the famous variation from Edward Elgar's *Enigma Variations*. At first, the Hutchinsons seemed convinced this was the right piece; but then back-tracked and declared that it was "almost right, but not quite."

We subsequently played the Hutchinsons an LP (owned by Harry Comb) of the entire *Enigma Variations*. Given that the piece is all about friendship and community, it seemed peculiarly apt as music for the Spark Street Phenomenon – which similarly ushered in a momentary sense of camaraderie among residents. Nevertheless, none of the variations seemed "quite right" to the Hutchinsons.

Finally, Serena Comb tentatively put forward a suggestion which we found rather compelling: that perhaps Spark Street's hallucinatory music was – and we quote – "the 'Enigma' in the *Enigma*. There's supposed to be some kind of hidden meaning or mystery or, well, 'Enigma' in the Elgar piece – some kind of 'invisible' tune which isn't said by the orchestra out loud, but which kind of hangs over the whole piece."

Many people, of course, have tried to solve the 'Enigma' in the *Enigma Variations* since it was first performed in 1899 – an 'Enigma' first set out by Elgar himself in a lost letter quoted in the original programme notes:

> *It is true that I have sketched for their amusement and mine, the idiosyncrasies of fourteen of my friends . . . The Enigma I will not explain – its 'dark saying' must be left unguessed . . . Through and over the whole set another and larger theme*

> *'goes,' but is not played . . . So the principal theme never appears, even as in some late dramas – e.g. Maeterlinck's* L'Intruse *and* Les Sept Princesses – *the chief character is never on the stage.*

Like the 'Enigma' in the *Enigma Variations*, the chief character to the drama on Spark Street – Melissa – was never on stage, had left the stage never to return, immediately before the Phenomenon; and, indeed, the more one reads about the 'absent character' that is the 'Enigma' theme, the more uncanny seem the connections between the *Enigma Variations* and Spark Street. For example, among the many candidates put forward by critics for the 'Enigma' tune – candidates which include Bach's orchestral music, Beethoven's Fifth, Schubert's and Schumann's piano music, *Eine Kleine Nachtmusik*, 'Auld Lang Syne,' 'Abide With Me,' and many others – one eminent musicologist has suggested a piece of Elgar's own, a cantata called *The Black Knight*. According to this musicologist, the intervals played by the first violins in the opening two bars of the *Enigma Variations* – whereby two pairs of falling thirds are divided by a rising fourth – are pre-echoed in *The Black Knight*, at the precise moment the chorus sings the line: 'He beholds his children die' [. . .]

Extract from *The Sentinel*, 4th November 1999: 'Tourist Boom is "Spark Close Effect."'

[. . .] And it seems it is not merely eminent neurologists who are intrigued by the so-called 'Spark Close Phenomenon' [. . .] In a leaked memo, a source from the City Council's Tourism Services has linked the surge in tourism to the unexplained events on Spark Close in June [. . .] According to the figures, which *The Sentinel* reported yesterday, there was an average increase of 6.7% in the number of people visiting Stoke's major attractions during peak Summer months, July to September, as compared with the same figures from 1998. Attractions surveyed included Wedgwood, Gladstone Pottery Museum, Hanley Museum and Alton Towers. According to the leaked memo, many of the visitors also visited Spark Close in Hanford, following extensive coverage of the 'Spark Close Phenomenon' in the national media. One inside source, who did not wish to be identified, commented that: "People are coming to Stoke now because they saw Spark Close in the papers and want to see for themselves what all the fuss is about" [. . .]

The City Council declined to comment on the specifics of the leaked memo, but said that they "were committed to their policy of developing tourism in the city at all levels."

Extract from *The Guardian*, 4th December 1999: Travel Supplement: 'Holy-Daze and Mad-gical Mystery Tours: The Twenty Strangest Packages of the Millennium.'

[. . .] and at number 13, it's *Spirit-USA-Way*'s three-day break in the Potteries. Not that we've got anything against touring the Potteries – they make good Oatcakes, there's Wedgwood, and the shopping centre's okay, though maybe you wouldn't come all the way from San Francisco to visit Topshop in Hanley. But these aren't the attractions for *Spirit-USA-Way* tourists. Oh no. They're paying good money – an average of $12,500 each – to be bussed round (and we quote from the brochure) 'all the major sites associated with the Spark Close Phenomenon, and that dear departed cherub, Miss Melissa Comb (1993[*sic*]–1999). You will stay in the luxury North Staffordshire Hotel, located near the centre of the city, with fellow Spark Close *aficionadi*. There will be presentations, concerts and slide shows. The tour will then take in Melissa's local school and hospital, where she received treatment for the illness which was eventually to transfigure her into music. You will see the playground in Hanford that she visited, and the swings which are haunted by her angelic spirit, now moving backwards and forwards in the musical breeze. The tour will culminate in an evening visit to the musical epicentre itself, none other than Spark Close, Hanford, Stoke-on-Trent, where well-known psychic Madame Irene Phillips-Zabetsky will lead a séance and spiritualist service of thanksgiving.'

Extract from *The Sun*, 18th February 2000, 'Sparks Fly in the Close: Machin Love with the Neighbours: World Exclusive.'

Inset (under photograph of a reclining Kirsten Machin, in stockings, suspenders and a negligée pulled down to reveal her breasts): Readers will, of course, remember 28-year-old [*sic*] glamorous escort Kirsten Machin as the top Potteries totty of Spark Close, Stoke-on-Trent, who posed for one of our most popular Page 3 pictures last year. Today, in an exclusive and shockingly frank interview, she reveals all again, recounting how beautiful music led to hot love on the Close [. . .]

Excerpt from interview: "[. . .] Harry Comb rang me up one day, out of the blue, and asked if he could come round. I thought he was just another punter, so I did myself up to welcome him in the usual gear – black fishnet stockings, red suspenders and so on. But when he got here, he sobbed all over my best bra. He wanted comforting, because he'd lost his daughter and was lonely. So I did just that: I comforted him. In fact, I comforted him all night, all over the house, in all possible positions. It was electric, and we arranged to meet again the next evening and the next one after that.

"It's not often a woman in my line of business feels anything during sex, but with him it was different. It was the most mind-blowing sex I'd ever had. People have only heard of him as the grief-stricken father of the 'angel' Melissa Comb who died – that's how he's been portrayed on TV and in magazines. He never says anything about what happened on Spark Close. Just keeps himself to himself. In my wide experience, though, it's always the quiet ones who are smouldering with passion underneath. And my Harry, he could smoulder for hours at a time.

"I don't know what his wife thought he was doing away from home in the evenings. But I didn't care. I just wanted him and he wanted me. Nothing and no-one else existed when we made love."

This all happened, Ms. Machin says, a few months ago, and Harry has since returned to his loving wife and home: "But that doesn't stop us having the occasional 'reunion.' Sex with Harry is like a drug. I just can't give it up" [. . .]

From *The Sun*, 25th February 2000: Apology.

The Sun would like to apologise to Ms. Kirsten Machin

of Spark Close, Stoke-on-Trent, for appearing to imply that she worked as an 'escort' or was in any way connected with prostitution in the article of 18th February 2000, 'Sparks Fly in the Close.' The implication is in no way based on fact, and was printed in error. *The Sun* would also like to acknowledge certain factual inaccuracies in the printed interview which formed part of the article. If you would like to receive an accurate transcript of the interview with Ms. Kirsten Machin, please write to our solicitors, with whom the matter currently rests, at the address shown below [. . .]

Extract from *The Sentinel*, 12th June 2000: 'Not Comb-ing Home.'

Police have reported that Mr. Harry Comb, father of Melissa Comb, who died on Spark Close, Hanford, almost exactly a year ago, has disappeared, and are seeking information as to his whereabouts. The family, including his wife, Elizabeth Comb, and daughter from his first marriage, Serena Comb, are said to be distraught, and have pleaded for him to return. Melissa Comb's death in June 1999 triggered what has since become known as the 'Spark Close Phenomenon' [. . .]

2nd Mvt:
Musica Humana

THEME

Eine Kleine Nachtmusik

LONG BEFORE THE Spark Close Phenomenon, long before the beginning of that story, there was a moment when a consultant first said to Mrs. Lizzie Comb: "Don't worry yourself over-much. It's a curable disease, and the large majority of children survive. It's one of those miracle areas, in which medical science has made incredible progress over the last few years. And girls have an even better outlook than boys. So, you know, your daughter should be fine."

Lizzie's daughter Melissa didn't look fine. She'd been tired for weeks, maybe months. On her fifth birthday, she'd slept in till 10.30 forgetful of presents. A week later, her father had found her crawling around the living room like a baby, because she said her legs felt "funny-heavy."

"I actually really feel like Schubert felt . . . no, feels," she'd explained, referring not to the composer, but to one of her pet spiders; they were all named after the composers whose work she'd heard her sister play on the piano.

"What do you mean?" her father had asked.

"I mean I feel all legs," she'd answered; and, from the floor, she'd started singing some nonsensical song: "All legs, all legs, all-legs-all-legs-all-legs," to the tune of the opening movement of *Eine Kleine Nachtmusik*, an arrangement of which she'd heard her sister play.

Melissa made up these nonsense songs all the time, often for her pet spiders, whom she kept in her *Star Child Home Planetarium*™. She'd furnished the inside with dolls' house beds, a sofa, TV and a kitchen, all of which were covered with thick spiders' webs. Just as her sister, Serena, played music to her in their living room, so she would sing music to the spiders in their miniature home – in fact, given that the spiders' names were Bartôk, Schubert (which she pronounced 'Sherbert'), Brahms (which she pronounced 'Bras'), Schoenberg (which she pronounced 'Show-berg') and so on, she would often echo back to the spider-composers the music their human counterparts had first written. And they would, in turn, echo music back to her: at night, she told her mother she could hear them singing whilst spinning their webs in the Planetarium. Lizzie told her to stop being silly – that it was not the spiders, but the Planetarium itself which was designed to chime Brahmsian lullabies, whilst spinning slowly on its axis.

At night, as the Planetarium spun round, and its residents spun webs, the busy spiders would cause the circling stars on Melissa's ceiling to flicker, go out, reappear; new constellations would form, and spider black holes would swallow others whole.

One morning, Lizzie cleaned out the Planetarium whilst Melissa was downstairs. When Melissa found out, she cried and stamped her foot and shouted: "Mother, you're silly and horrid and silly."

"Don't call me that," said Lizzie.

"What?"

"Any of it – silly or horrid, or Mother, for that matter. Call me Mummy instead. And as your mummy I say you can't keep spiders. They're dirty and scare your mummy."

"That's cos you're a silly . . . 'ee-rak-niff-obe,' Mother," screamed Melissa.

"'Arachnophobe?' Gosh, darling, where did you learn that word from?"

"From Dadda," pouted Melissa, and Lizzie couldn't help suspecting that he'd taught Melissa the word deliberately, knowing that, at some point, it would be used to needle her. Melissa shouted it a few more times for effect, each time stumbling over it in a different way: "Iraq-noth-obe! Or-rakk-newfobe! You're an . . . a-rack . . . one of them because you actually really do not understand my spideys."

"I do understand them and I don't want them in my house."

"It's not *your* house, Mother." Lizzie's eyes widened slightly, wondering what her daughter was about to say. She was relieved when Melissa added: "It's actually really my Planetarium-ium-my-house. It's not yours. And I really actually want my spideys in it." She stamped her foot again, and stuck out her lower lip.

"But they start in there, darling," said Lizzie, "and then they spread their webs all over the 'big' house. All over *our* house." Lizzie looked up at the ceiling, as though for spiders' webs. "It's hard enough keeping this house clean and tidy, what with your dad's crackers and your sister's black mascara. It feels like . . . as soon as I stop cleaning for a moment, the house starts falling to pieces, and dust and spiders' webs start appearing everywhere, and then ants, and then mould and damp and holes, and then – I don't know . . . Gosh, if I weren't here, dusting and hoovering and mopping all the time . . ." She looked back down at Melissa, and patted her on the head: "Well, you wouldn't understand, darling, but we need to keep the dirt at bay. We need to be vigilant."

"But Mother, you actually really don't understand too: my spideys' webs aren't dirty. They're part of the house. They hold it together, you know, like sticky glue."

"What a funny thing to say, darling," said Lizzie.

"It's not a funny thing, Mother. It is not. And I am going out to find my spidey friends again. I think they are actually probably in the Close or the alley – hiding from you because you're horrid and silly." Before Lizzie could inform her that most of them were in the Hoover, Melissa had thumped downstairs and into the living room, where her half-sister Serena and one-time neighbour Simon Adler-Reeves were lazing around with books. Melissa grabbed Simon's book, threw it away, took his hand, and pulled him out of the front door – and they both went a-hunting for "spideys."

During that spider-hunt, dizzied by a circling cockchafer, Melissa had tripped and bruised her knee. When Simon came to visit a week later, the bruise was still there. That was the first time anyone remembered noticing the bruises, blooming on her legs, her arms, across her chest.

Gradually, over the next few weeks, other people started noticing them too, and Lizzie started noticing their noticing: at the school gates, friends' parents peered down at Melissa's arms, and then up at her mother, and then down again; at the end of a Saturday tap class, a teacher took Lizzie aside and asked her if everything was all right at home.

No, everything was not all right. Melissa had started pushing away her favourite beef spread and ketchup sandwiches, staring blankly at butterscotch Angel Delight. Her mother found her in the upstairs toilet one Sunday afternoon, pretending her pet spider Bartôk was being sick.

Melissa got cold after cold, bruise after bruise.

Melissa no longer moaned when it was time for bed, or

made up songs to Beethoven's Fifth: "I don't want tooooooo . . . Go to my bed . . ."

Instead, Melissa fell asleep on the sofa when her sister played piano arrangements of Beethoven's Fifth to her.

Melissa fell asleep during school lessons.

Melissa fell asleep on her sandwiches.

"I'm sooooo tired," Melissa said, her head hovering above the sandwich box during school dinner-time, "so really tired of egg and cress."

Melissa's teacher, Mrs. McNicholl, found her, face bruised with egg and cress, surrounded by laughing and pointing children. She cleaned Melissa up, and rang her mother at home: "Your daughter is tired constantly, Mrs. Comb. Is she getting enough sleep at home?"

"She sleeps all the time," answered Lizzie, yawning at the thought of it.

"Do you think that's . . . healthy?" asked Mrs. McNicholl.

Lizzie Comb yawned again: "It's good for her, I suppose. I wish I slept more."

Mrs. McNicholl sighed: "Look, all I'm saying is that she might need checking up. I'm sure it's not . . . narcolepsy, like my brother had, or anything serious like that. But perhaps, you know, just in case, you should get her seen by someone."

Lizzie put the phone down, and went to collect her daughter from school, grumbling all the way: "Bloody interfering old cow. Bloody prissy missy so-and-so. As if I haven't got enough to do today." She yawned and changed down gears, turning right into the school drive.

And there, in front of her, was her daughter, waiting with Mrs. McNicholl on a bench. Maybe it was the way Melissa didn't sit forwards on the bench, waiting expectantly for her mother, but was instead leaning against the wall behind, panting slightly; or maybe it was the way the afternoon light fell on her, the sun having just appeared over the roof of the junior block, seeming to shoot white light through her like an X-Ray; whatever the reason, that was the moment when Lizzie Comb first realised something was wrong. Everything afterwards merely served to confirm that realisation, that diagnosis by sunlight.

"God, Melissa," Lizzie said, trying to sound calm, joky, even airy, but ending up just sounding brutal, in front of Mrs. McNicholl: "you look crappy. What kind of boy is going to be interested in you if you look like that when you're older? You'll end up as boyfriendless as your sister, and you'll have to spend all your time on that bloody piano."

Mrs. McNicholl hissed through her nose: "I'll leave Melissa in your . . . capable hands, Mrs. Comb." She stood up, turned and stomped off.

"Stomping hell," said Lizzie, pulling her daughter off the bench, and patting down her collar and hair, "what a prissy missy you've got there, Melissa, dear. Her and her flat heels and mauve blouses. Never seems to take anything I say the right way. Silly moo."

"You're the silly moo-moo, Mother. She's nice and I do actually extremely like her," said Melissa. "She looked after me today when my tummy went wrong and my eyes fell asleep."

"Oh well, I suppose that's good of her anyway. Let's get you home and then to the doctor's, if we bloody well must. No shop-shopping for Mummy today."

Lizzie rang up Melissa's GP, but he was booked up that day. So she had to ring up first thing next morning, to find he was booked up again. On the third day, with Melissa asleep on the sofa, she finally stamped her feet and got an emergency appointment. The GP checked Melissa over, looked at her bruises, felt her neck lymph nodes – which were swollen. He asked them both to wait outside, whilst he phoned someone somewhere; and then packed Melissa and Lizzie off to the North Staffs University Hospital.

Once there, Melissa was attached to a drip for fluids, and had some blood taken for a test. The test confirmed that she was anaemic, and had too many immature white blood cells. "Explains why she's always so stupidly pale," said her mother. "She's so white, sometimes I get this urge to slap some tan on her – and I have to chase the silly girl all round the house trying to catch her."

"You don't understand," said a nurse, shaking her head. "This isn't – well, isn't just about skin colour. You don't understand what the doctor is trying to say." She pronounced every syllable of the next sentence in time with her shaking head: "He is trying to say that there is a possibility your daughter might have Leukaemia. Leu-kae-mi-a. Only a possibility, mind you. There are other tests to be done first."

The other laboratory tests took place next day in Birmingham Children's Hospital, and included a bone marrow aspirate. Melissa was taped down on a table, given a local anaesthetic, a needle was inserted and twisted into her hip bone, and then the marrow drawn up into a syringe.

Afterwards, a consultant, flanked by two nurses and registrars, came to see Melissa and her mother. The consultant smiled at Melissa in the bed, and took Lizzie aside, into an empty cubicle. He stared down at his clipboard and muttered: "The pathologist has had a chance to examine the sample. I'm afraid to say, Mrs. Comb, that she has confirmed our initial diagnosis. Your daughter has Acute Lymphoblastic Leukaemia, or ALL as we prefer to call it."

"ALL?" Lizzie wanted to ask, "My daughter has 'ALL' – you mean everything?" Instead, she said nothing, just leant against the empty bed behind her.

"You shouldn't worry yourself unduly," said the consultant, still not looking up.

Lizzie coughed: "Shouldn't worry? Shouldn't bloody worry?"

"Please, Mrs. Comb," said the nurse .

"I quite understand your emotion, Mrs. Comb," said the consultant. "It's only natural in the circumstances. But I do mean what I say when I say don't worry. Worry can only be counterproductive, and you need to be strong for your daughter. Just remember, if your daughter had to get one form of Leukaemia, this is the better one. With B-Cell ALL, her prognosis is good. This is a curable disease, and the majority of children will survive – especially girls."

"What about the minority?"

"We will do our utmost to ensure that Melissa isn't in the minority."

"But Mel's always in the minority," said Lizzie, "in everything she does. You don't know her. She's a very odd-one-out kind of child."

The consultant shook his head, "We must hold onto the fact that treatment is successful in 85% of cases of ALL, or thereabouts. Statistics are on her side, especially these days: medicine has made great strides over the last few decades. Before, the prognosis would not have been good. But now, your daughter has the whole of medical science behind her."

Lizzie was tempted to ask how the whole of medical science could squeeze into her daughter's hospital pillow; but she restrained herself. "So what do we do now? What happens now?"

"Now, your daughter needs a bit of rest. We'll transfer her into a room of her own, in the Thomas the Tank Ward, to decrease the risk of infection. Then, as soon as we can, we will commence the programme of medication. We will discuss all this tomorrow, Mrs. Comb, when we have more time, and you have had a chance to collect your thoughts."

The consultant's time was up till tomorrow, so he moved onto the next bay, before Mrs. Comb could think of the questions she needed to ask.

She stepped back over to her daughter's bed, and sat down in a plastic chair next to her. Melissa was asleep, and Lizzie watched her still face, and thought about nothing, nothing at all.

Finally, after thirty or so minutes of nothingness, a nurse stepped over and offered Lizzie a lukewarm cup of sugary tea ("I was going to give it to you earlier, but I got called away on something else"), and a leaflet. The nurse bustled away, leaving Lizzie staring down at a page swimming with acronyms, medical terms, drug names, tests, statistics, diagrams and charts which made as much sense to her as the black dots and Italian phrases on her stepdaughter's piano music. Leukaemia music, she thought: Leukaemia music, which would march them forwards, never sideways or backwards, never stopping, just forwards, forwards and downwards from now on. She closed her eyes, let the leaflet fall from her lap, and tried to stop her left index finger incessantly tapping a rhythm – one-two-three-four, march-two-three-four – on the arm of her chair.

A couple of hours later, her husband, Harry, found her like that, and went to the desk to ask if a doctor could come and explain what was going on. Eventually, a registrar turned up, and took them both into the day room. It was only then that Lizzie's questions bubbled up to the surface: "So what is this illness? What is the treatment? What is going to happen?"

Without understanding a great deal of it, she was told by the registrar that ALL is a form of liquid cancer, in which the bone marrow accumulates too many immature lymphocyte-precursor cells, or 'blast cells.' The haematopoiesis – the process of blood formation in the bone marrow – malfunctions, and too many blast cells are produced. The blast cells can't mature into full-grown white blood cells, which fight infections, so Leukaemia sufferers become prone to infections; and the profusion of blast cells also inhibits the production of normal blood cells, reducing the number of red cells, white cells and platelets. This results in anaemia and bruising – as they had seen in Melissa's case.

The next stage, they were told, would be a series of tests: blood tests, temperature monitoring, chromosome analysis, chest X-Rays, Lumbar Punctures, injections, further bone marrow aspirates, ECG, MRI and CAT scans, tests on liver and kidney function, and so on and so forth – to establish how widespread the cancer was, and how susceptible to treatment Melissa would be. A Hickman Line would be fitted under general anaesthetic – that is, a narrow plastic tube would be channelled under the skin of Melissa's chest into a large vein just above her collar bone. Outside her chest, the line would be attached to a three-pronged port, through which infusions of drugs could be administered, blood transfusions given, blood tests taken. The Hickman Line would be taped to Melissa's chest, and remain in place permanently whilst the chemotherapy continued – Melissa would no doubt become quite fond of it in time, as a kind of pet, or extension of her own body. Nurses would, of course, show Melissa's parents how to clean it out.

Lizzie felt sick.

The registrar didn't notice, and continued with his explanation.

Melissa's treatment would probably be 'shared care treatment' between the Principal Treatment Centre, Birmingham, Paediatric Oncology in North Staffordshire, and possibly Great Ormond Street in London as well, depending on what was necessary. The treatment proper would commence as soon as possible following the initial tests, which would determine the exact nature of that treatment. Most likely, there would be a month of intensive chemotherapy, or remission induction, on a cocktail of cytotoxic drugs, aiming to disrupt the production of blast cells. These drugs would be administered orally, in thigh injections, or through the Hickman Line, in blocks of five or six days; and they would probably include Vincristine and Prednisolone plus an anthracycline (Daunorubicin, Adriamycin, Buridazone or Idarubicin).

"Are you following me, Mrs. Comb?" asked the doctor.

"Yes, yes, of course," she said, studying a nail which was about to break.

"Then I will carry on," said the doctor. And he carried on to tell her that the remission induction phase would aim to destroy all the Leukaemic cells in the bone marrow and bloodstream. In addition, he told her that that there was a slight possibility that Melissa's Leukaemia had already crossed the barrier into the Central Nervous System and penetrated the cerebro-spinal fluid. That would be determined by initial tests, but it was unlikely. Melissa would be unlucky if that were found to be the case.

"Unlucky?" asked Mrs. Comb, wondering what the definition of lucky or unlucky was in this man's vocabulary.

He didn't understand her tone. "Yes, Mrs. Comb, unlucky: only a few in a hundred child cases at this diagnostic stage would be found to have Leukaemia cells in the CNS." If Melissa was affected in this way, then she would have to have CNS-directed therapy, because normal chemotherapy would have limited effect in the cerebro-spinal fluid. This would include a drug called Methotrexate being injected directly into the fluid around the spine, by intrathecal injection, probably under general anaesthetic. She would also immediately be put on a drug called Allopurinol, which would stop her developing kidney damage as a side effect of the treatment.

"Of course, all the treatment from here on in has certain . . . unwelcome effects, which we will do our best to control. The chemo may – or may not – cause such things as hair loss, weight loss, diarrhoea, sickness, lethargy, infections, colds, influenzas, viruses, and so on."

"And so on?" asked Lizzie.

"Don't worry. We have other drugs, like steroids and antiemetics, to deal with some of the side effects of the chemotherapy drugs," the doctor said – and Lizzie wondered if there were drugs to deal with the side effects of the drugs dealing with the side effects of the drugs. Shutting her eyes for a moment, she saw a strange vision of a black hole of drugs circling drugs circling drugs circling . . .

"Mrs. Comb? Are you following me?"

Lizzie opened her eyes, and nodded – not at the doctor, but at her lap, unable to meet his gaze. She felt like a naughty school girl who hadn't been paying attention in a science lesson.

"As well as drugs," the lesson continued, "there will be other aspects of care. For a start, Melissa may well need regular blood transfusions and platelet transfusions when her blood count gets low. Washing regularly will be important because of potential neutropenia. Fluids are also crucial, especially at the remission induction stage."

During this stage, the registrar said, it might prove necessary to give Melissa some early cranial irradiation therapy – the initial tests would show whether that was needed or not. They liked to avoid it if possible; but they would take all necessary steps to induce remission during this first phase of treatment.

Once remission had been induced by chemo and other means, the second treatment phase would be consolidation or delayed intensification therapy. The apparent disappearance of Leukaemia cells from the bone marrow did not necessarily indicate the end of the disease. It might be lurking somewhere, biding its time. To prevent a relapse, therefore, Melissa would be given two more blocks of powerful chemotherapy over the following year. She would live at home during this second phase, and would receive regular visits from social workers, psychologists, educational advisors, health visitors, occupational therapists, district nurses; and Macmillan or Marie Curie nurses might come round to take blood. She would also need regular GP, clinic and hospital check-ups, blood tests, weight tests, heart echoes, liver function tests, platelet and haemoglobin tests, maintenance treatments, and, no doubt now and then, re-admission to the ward for short periods. Due to the immunosuppressive nature of chemotherapy, she would be prone to infections, and might need antibiotics, maybe isolation, maybe other forms of treatment. It was impossible, at this stage, to predict what treatment Melissa's particular case would necessitate during consolidation therapy. Once again, they would do everything necessary to induce Melissa into the third and final phase of treatment.

The final phase would be maintenance therapy. This would take up to two years, during which time Melissa would be given low-dose chemotherapy; drugs administered might include daily tablets of Mercaptopurine and weekly doses of Methotrexate. On a monthly basis, she would be given Vincristine injections into a vein, steroid tablets, and, if necessary, further intrathecal injections and antibiotics. During this period, Melissa would be an outpatient, and things would hopefully, gradually, slowly, return to 'normal.' In full remission, Melissa would be back at school, and their everyday lives would be returned to them, as before, intact and whole again.

That's what the registrar told Lizzie and Harry would probably happen.

What he didn't, couldn't tell them was what actually did happen.

What he couldn't, didn't tell them was that, at first, Melissa seemed to respond well to the remission induction therapy. After a few weeks, the chemo seemed to have eliminated all the Leukaemia cells from her blood and marrow. She was very sick, and the nurses told Lizzie that this was a good sign: "It's like the cancer being ejected from the body," said one, somewhat unscientifically, while Lizzie held the emesis basin underneath her daughter's chin, trying to keep her own sleeves out of the way. "You see, she'll be right as rain soon enough, terrorising those pet spiders she's always on about. No need to worry yourself, Mrs. Comb."

Nor, it seemed, was it a matter of worry that they found Leukaemic cells in Melissa's cerebro-spinal fluid. Admittedly, this was "unlucky" on Melissa's part, but the intrathecal injections and, later, cranial irradiation seemed to "do the trick," as one consultant put it. Dazed and half-asleep after the irradiation therapy, Melissa murmured incoherently to her mother that the theatre had been "really actually full of spideys . . . full of spideys weaving musical webs . . . full of spideys' music webs . . . full of webs of musical spideys . . . full of webs weaved between me and the . . . huge . . . linna achoo-ator" (by which she meant 'linear accelerator').

Through the musical webs, past the linear accelerators, Melissa went straight into the second phase, delayed intensification therapy – hair-less, a bit tottery on her feet, but surely getting there. "She will get her hair back, won't she?" asked Lizzie, to half a dozen passing doctors, always on their way to somewhere else, somewhere more urgent. "She had that lovely auburn hair. I was so jealous – much better than my lank stuff. I don't want the other children laughing at her. I'd hate that. Auburn, it's such a lovely colour. Much better than all of our colours put together. She will get her hair back, won't she? Won't she?"

"All you worry about is her hair," complained Harry.

Lizzie looked at him with narrowed, incredulous eyes. "Of course, darling. Of course that's all I worry about. All I spend every sleepless hour of every single bloody night worrying about is her hair. All I never stop crying about, all I never stop shaking with horrible terror about, all I ever want inside to scream and scream and scream about is her hair. That's all, nothing else. Nothing bloody else. After all, the doctors, nurses and everybody are always telling me not to worry about anything else."

But soon, there were other worries. Three months later, Melissa started to develop rashes, started to have headaches, started to feel tired. "It's probably merely an infection of some kind. Her white blood count is low. Nothing to worry about. The risk of relapse is small, no more than 20% or so," said her GP; but, just in case, he referred her back to the North Staffs, and then to the Children's Hospital for tests.

They found more Leukaemic cells, both in the Central Nervous System and, more worryingly, in the bone marrow itself. 30% of Melissa's white blood cells were blast cells again. She was put back on remission induction, moved back to the start square. Concerned now that the Leukaemia cells might be resistant to the drugs, they devised a new relapse protocol, shuffled the drugs around, increased the dosage. But the Leukaemia had developed Multi-Drug Resistance, as if it were clever, as if it had seen the doctors coming. Weeks bled by. A second remission seemed a vanishing horizon.

Finally, they grabbed at the horizon, and Melissa was pronounced in remission for a second time. But the doctors didn't seem quite so pleased, quite so sure this time round. Melissa was now tiny, pale, bone-thin, as if she herself – the person-who-was-Melissa – were gradually disappearing under the sheer weight of therapies, tests, drugs, illnesses, acronyms. She barely smiled at the news of remission, which she didn't really understand, and which didn't mean much to her. Churned through pancytopenia and nadir sepsis, remission seemed merely a new cycle of illnesses.

And then, three months later, there were more illnesses, more rashes, more headaches, more tiredness. Her gums started bleeding and wouldn't stop when she brushed her teeth. She was taken in for more tests, and they found more Leukaemia.

The doctors started to mumble about BMT – Bone Marrow Transplantation. Allogeneic transplantation, or an allograft – that is, a transplant of stem cells from a donor – seemed the safer option, given that it would be more likely to eliminate the Leukaemia. There was a good 50% to 60% chance of total success, they said. The risk was rejection of the new body by the transplanted stem cells. They had to find someone whose white blood cells matched. They looked on the National Blood Transfusion Register, and the bone marrow donor register, and also closer to home.

Closer to home, the phlebotomist found someone, someone who passed the Histocompatibility Antigen Test, someone whose white blood cells, whose proteins, whose Human Leukocyte Antigens matched Melissa's – someone who loved her half-sister: Miss Serena Comb.

Delighted, the doctors got ready to harvest the stem cells from Serena. In preparation, a week before the harvest, they took a couple of pints of blood from her, in case a blood transfusion proved necessary during the operation. The following week, she came to the hospital for two days. She was put under general anaesthetic, and a surgeon harvested bone marrow from the bones at the back and front of the pelvis. The surgeon inserted a needle and sucked out the bone marrow through a syringe; then she did it again in another place; and then another, until three-quarters of a litre of bone marrow had been extracted.

Serena stayed overnight in hospital. Dosed up on painkillers, she was discharged the next day, feeling horribly sore, bruised, stiff for a week afterwards; and there were odd times, even months, years later, when the memory of that bone ache returned like new-born pain.

Meanwhile, to prepare for the transplant, Melissa had been receiving high dose chemotherapy and total body irradiation twice daily over three days – a conditioning regime designed to kill off all the existing bone marrow, and force her into remission. She was too weak to complain much about this regimen – except once, when she murmured: "I am really actually extremely bored of this, you know," to the radiographer over the intercom. "Please can we stop now?"

But the treatment didn't stop, and nor did the painful boredom.

After the conditioning regime, Melissa was given the transplant drugs, and the bone marrow infusion from the donor was pumped through her Hickman Line. The bone marrow found its way to its new home, and, over the next few weeks, started to foster new mature blood cells, which were released into the bloodstream.

At this time, for weeks and weeks, Melissa and her mother were bricked up in an isolated corner room of the ward, away from infections, away from the world. Lizzie had to leave all her make-up and jewellery at home. No-one was allowed to bring flowers or food. People wore masks when muttering to or about them. The only visitors they were allowed from outside the hospital were Harry and Serena – for an hour a day – until a desolate time when the two of them caught a cold, and had to stay away for a week.

Melissa did the same puzzle over and over again. Lizzie read the same page of her page-turner over and over again. Doctors came and went. Nurses orbited them. Whole days echoed one another, till Lizzie wasn't sure whether it was today, tomorrow, yesterday.

Everyday, there were new illnesses, old illnesses, repeated illnesses, new, old and repeated threats, new, old and repeated treatments. Melissa was given growth factors through her Hickman Line, encouraging the bone marrow to make new cells quicker. She was given transfusions of blood and platelets. She was given mouthwashes to avoid infections, and lollipops to ease the soreness in her mouth. For a few days, because of the soreness, she couldn't eat anything, so she was fed nutrition through her line. She was prone to infections, high temperatures and viruses, because of her low white blood count. Her red blood count fell too, and she became floppy-tired and needed more transfusions. She had daily blood tests. She was given morphine, anti-nausea drugs, antibiotics.

And then, one day, out of the blue, the morphine, anti-nausea drugs, antibiotics stopped; and a registrar said, "You can go home today." Lizzie looked up, and asked her to repeat herself. For the first time in weeks, though, there was no repetition: the registrar had already turned and left. When a nurse bustled in a few minutes later, Lizzie was still staring at the door. The nurse frowned at her, and asked: "Are you all right, Mrs. Comb? You look like you saw a ghost."

"I think I kind of did. Did she just say what I think she said?"

"Who? What?"

"That we're going home today?"

"That's right, you can pack your stuff. Melissa's blood count's up. The temperature's gone. It looks like the transplant has been successful."

"Successful?"

Given how her daughter looked, Lizzie wasn't sure what

"successful" meant; but she did as she was told, and packed up their bags. Later that day, the two of them tottered out of the isolation room, out of the ward, out of the hospital jaws into daylight, an ambulance – and then home.

"Are my spideys actually okay?" was the first thing Melissa croaked to Serena, when she opened the front door of home.

"Yes, they're waiting in your Planetarium, looking forward to seeing you at last."

That night, Lizzie slept – or, rather, lay awake – on Melissa's floor, watching the constellations from the Planetarium revolving, appearing, disappearing, blotted out by the magnified silhouettes of gigantic spiders. For what seemed like hours, Lizzie tried over and over to sob, "I love you," to the darkness, as if it were a magic spell, as if it might ward away the spider-silhouettes – but over and over, her voice stuck in her throat, and the words wouldn't come out.

When she finally did doze off, after hours of mute sleeplessness, her nightmares seemed comforting by comparison.

Still, there was now some comfort in waking hours: Melissa seemed a little brighter; she had an appetite sometimes for beef spread and ketchup sandwiches; she liked sitting in the living room listening to her sister playing Elgar, Schubert and Brahms on the piano. Ten days later, she had an out-patients appointment, with X-Rays, blood tests and a general medical examination, in which she was pronounced well – relatively well.

Then . . . then she started getting pains in her tummy, pains which turned into diarrhoea; she developed conjunctivitis, and rashes reappeared on her skin, this time on her feet and hands. Her eyes went yellow, then her face, then her whole body. She was referred back to hospital, with suspected acute Graft Versus Host Disease, GVHD. A biopsy, along with liver function tests, confirmed the diagnosis. Despite the immune suppressant drugs she'd been given to prevent this very eventuality; despite the closeness of the match between the donor tissue and her own; despite everything that had been done, everything they had been through, the T-lymphocyte white blood cells in the transplanted marrow recognised their new home as foreign, and started attacking Melissa's body from within. The match of donor tissue and her own wasn't quite close enough, and full-blown GVHD took hold.

Rated as "moderate to severe, two to three on the GVHD scale of four," the disease meant that Melissa was hospitalised again, where she was treated with new drugs, high-dose corticosteroids, Methotrexate and Cyclosporin A. "You see," explained one passing consultant, "the only way we can prevent – or, in your daughter's case, treat – GVHD is by using drugs to try and suppress the immune reaction between transplant and recipient. Do you understand, Mrs. Comb?" Lizzie was so used to nodding her head, that she continued doing it automatically, even when the answer was no.

The consultant continued, regardless of her answer: "The thing is, Mrs. Comb, that blood cells and platelets can be irradiated to avoid GVHD. But we can't do this with bone marrow transplants beforehand, because that would kill off the stem cells we need. So there's always a risk that the transplant cells will start attacking their new home, even when the donor seems like a good match. Only identical twins are perfect matches for transplants. Still, GVHD's normally only a 25%-ish chance in this kind of transplant – and, in this case, given the patient's age, and the closeness of the donor, even less than that, I'd have thought. But you can't predict these things, and Melissa's just a bit unlucky, I'm afraid. You might be surprised to know, Mrs. Comb, that I still remember what you once said to me, a long time ago: that Melissa is always in the minority, always an odd-one-out kind of girl. It's just a shame it's the 25% GVHD minority."

The consultant turned away, and then, on second thoughts, turned back: "Look, it's sometimes the case that GVHD can even work in our favour. It can actually turn on the Leukaemia cells too, in what we call Graft Versus Leukaemia Effect, or GVL. You never know, this might prove to be a good thing, so don't worry yourself, Mrs. Comb, unduly." He seemed strangely jovial, good-humoured, when he said: "This isn't the . . . end of the story, you know, Mrs. Comb. We are doing everything we can to ensure that it's a long way from that."

No, Graft Versus Host Disease wasn't the end of the story; but later, the family remembered it as the beginning of the end – when, that is, they consciously recalled the events at all, which wasn't very often.

Finally, one day, Melissa said to her mother, "Can I actually hear Seri playing the piano?"

And her mother looked around, and said, "No, I don't think you can."

"I don't mean, *Mother*, that I'm actually hearing things in my head again like before. I mean: please can I hear Seri actually *really* play the piano?"

"Not unless they bring a piano onto the Thomas the Tank Ward, darling."

"I don't mean that too, Mother. I mean: I want to hear Seri on the piano at home. And I want to check up that she's not actually, you know, poisoning my spideys – or that you've let them all out again, Mother."

"I haven't, but you can't. You can't go home. You've got to stay in the hospital till you're well."

Melissa said, "Don't be silly, Mother."

And Lizzie said, "Don't call me that."

And Melissa said, "What?"

And her mother said, "'Silly' or 'Mother.' Call me 'Mummy' like normal little girls."

And Melissa said, "But you *are* being silly, Mother. They're not actually going to make me better. I've heard them all whispery-whispering about it. And it all hurts too much. I want to go home and hear Seri play Sherbert on the piano."

"You can't, darling. And the whispers you heard, they're in your head. You're hearing things because of the drugs again. The whispers aren't true."

And Melissa said, "Silly-silly Mother."

When Lizzie mentioned what Melissa had said to the consultant, she was surprised to find he agreed: "Yes, Mrs. Comb. Perhaps she's right. Why not. Let her go home for . . . well, let's say a little while."

So they took her home, for a few weeks . . .

And about those last few weeks, there is nothing much to say, nothing much to remember: the family, Lizzie, Harry, Serena, Melissa just orbited her sickness and it sucked everything, even their memories, out of them – so that afterwards they recalled almost nothing but the orbiting, orbiting, orbiting, being flung round in elliptical orbits so powerful that, even when the centre had collapsed and disappeared, they would carry on orbiting blackness, automatically, unthinkingly, in empty echoes of that terrible era, when their lives spun between work routines, care routines, pill routines, washing routines, vomitting, headaches, spots, bleeding, transfusions, waiting, boredom, relapse, analgesics, infection, waiting, haemorrhage, transfusions, boredom, pain, bleeding, infection, possible liver failure, boredom, infection, kidney failure, boredom, infection, in and out of hospital, in and out of ambulances, between doctors, between infections, between transfusions, between half-finished puzzles, between spider races, between piano sonatas, between breaths, until finally . . .

VAR I

Mack the Knife

FOR TEN DAYS after Melissa's death, the family only heard about the Spark Close Phenomenon in passing. They were too taken up with the paraphernalia of death, and what Lizzie busily called "logistics," to think about anything else: who would sign and pay for the death certificate? Who would talk to the vicar? Who wanted to go and see the body one last time in the funeral parlour? Who would go in whose car to the funeral service? Who would pick up this person from that address, whilst this person would also be waiting? Who would give a reading at the funeral service? What hymns should be sung at the service? Should the family accept flowers, or substitute donations instead? To which Leukaemia charity? Who would do the catering for the wake, and what time should it be – how long after the service? Who would do this or that, where and how?

In the living room of the Comb household, these questions were rehearsed again and again: "So, what's the arrangement for . . .?," "Remind me, who's picking up cousin thingy from Stoke station?," "Did you manage to check if Marks and Sparks do sandwiches with the crusts off?" – all in the same tones of voice, Harry Comb's monotone a living tick-list, Lizzie's high notes teetering on the edge of a precipice, Serena's grumbling monosyllables never quite answering the questions asked – and no-one ever seeming to speak directly to anyone else, conversations more like atonal counterpoint than human interaction.

One conversation which Harry had with himself over and over concerned who would play music at the service. Everyone was agreed, he said, that there had to be music – Melissa had asked for it. The organist would be there in the church; but that wasn't the point. There should be a pianist, playing something Mel herself had enjoyed listening to. Who would, should be the pianist? Who? Who?, he kept insisting, over and again.

"Who?" was a rhetorical question, and no-one dared answer it. No-one said: look, it was Serena who played the piano for Melissa whilst she was alive, so it should be Serena who played for her dead. No-one answered Harry in this way, perhaps because no-one wanted to upset Harry; or perhaps because everyone had more important things to think about; or perhaps because everyone knew the answer Harry was looking for, and simply couldn't give it to him.

In the absence of that sought-for answer, Harry eventually answered himself: he decided he would play. He hadn't played to any kind of audience, or even himself, for years; and the piano in the Combs' living room had been locked up since Melissa's death. But he obviously felt this special occasion demanded something of him as a father – a special kind of strength. It might also help others, he seemed to think; or, at least, it might help them comprehend what a lost talent he was. Someone who could play heart-rending music, even under such harrowing circumstances: now there was a father. There was a pianist.

So, on Thursday 17th June 1999 at 3.13 p.m., after Trentham Parish Church had filled with mourners, well-wishers, and hangers-on who'd heard about the Spark Close Phenomenon and wondered if something else miraculous might happen at the funeral; after 'Abide with me,' 'All Things Bright and Beautiful,' prayers and sermon; after the vicar had intoned the order of service at the mosaic floor below his microphone, seemingly unable to look coffin or congregation in the face; after 'Blessed are they that mourn, for they will be comforted,' and 'You are tender towards your children and your mercy is over all your works. Heal the memories of hurt and failure'; after all this and more, Harry the pianist took his place at the tatty old grand in front of everyone, adjusted the seat, flexed his fingers, and placed them on the keyboard. He nodded at the vicar, as though the latter were conducting an accompanying orchestra, and the vicar read from a prompt sheet: "And now, in place of a eulogy, Mr. Harold Comb, father of the deceased, will play a piece of music Melissa loved: 'Kind im Einschlummern' from Robert Schumann's *Kinderszenen*."

There was a hush, and everyone looked at Harry. Everyone seemed to hold their breath, expecting something to happen, expecting something extraordinary of Harry and the music.

Harry hadn't practised the piece, hadn't even unlocked the piano in the front room on Spark Close. He knew he didn't need to. He remembered the piece well, and it was relatively easy to play. Harry found most pieces easy to play. Maybe that was one of his problems: he'd never had to struggle for his talent, so had never made much of an effort.

He'd have to make an effort now, though: he'd have to make an effort to play well under these terrible conditions, whether or not 'Kind im Einschlummern' was an 'easy' piece.

His fingers were on the keys, poised over the first E-minor chord.

And in the E-minor silence which followed, he found himself recalling other silences; and out of those other silences surfaced incoherent mutterings and tap-tappings; and out of those incoherent mutterings and tap-tappings came his own voice, clear as if it were happening now – and he was talking about music, and his own musical history.

In the silence, he remembered . . .

In the silence, Harry remembered the silences in the front room of the house on Spark Close – the silences when Lizzie, Serena and Melissa had left the room on various errands to the kitchen, their bedrooms, or, later on, the clinic, hospital, intensive care – and he was left alone. To fill these silences, his fingers would start fluttering involuntarily on the arm of his chair, tap-tap-tapping on the upholstery, as if playing an invisible keyboard; and underneath the tap-tap-tapping, he'd start mumbling and muttering and humming – like Glenn Gould and other piano-heroes, accompanying his armchair pianism with groans of overflowing emotion.

And then, if someone dropped by to see how Melissa was, how the family was – say, Rosa Adler from Number 12, or that pesky grandson of hers, Simon Adler-Reeves, home from university, visiting his grandmother and old childhood neighbours, sniffing round Serena, now she was 'legal' – Harry's groans would gradually deepen, solidify, coalesce into words, and he'd start talking to whoever would listen – as if he were answering something that had been asked, or continuing a conversation that had been going on all the time: "You see," he would say, "I used to play. I used to play Bach, Brahms, Beethoven, the *Moonlight*, the *Waldstein*, the *Hammerklavier* – well, most of it – and the *Pathétique*." And then he'd mumble under his breath "*Pathétique . . . Pathétique . . . Pathétique*," until the visitor asked him something else, preferably about his playing.

"What else did you play?" Rosa or Simon would ask out of politeness – though one couldn't stand music, and the other wasn't really interested, was just biding time, waiting for Serena to return.

"Oh, lots of things," Harry'd say, pleased to have been asked, relaxing slightly, picking up an Arrowroot biscuit from the stool next to his chair, nibbling a corner of it. "Lots of things. Things like . . . things like the *Kinderszenen*, Chopin's *Études*, the Liszt Sonata . . . But no, actually not that. Not quite. I couldn't *quite* get it." He'd suddenly slam his biscuit down into crumbs: "But I could have. If they'd let me. If the school had bothered to notice they had someone special on their hands. If my dad hadn't been so bloody mean as to sell the piano just because he'd got laid off. If . . . if the stupid talentless bint who was meant to be giving me lessons hadn't been so precious about me looking down her top, when she leant over and corrected me."

He'd talk about his teacher like this, whether his audience was Rosa or Simon or someone else – because his intended audience was really no-one but himself. He'd smile to himself, or half his face would, as that old sense of irony, which he seemed to have lost during Melissa's illness, returned, just for a moment, on one side of his face: "But bloody hell, perhaps it was worth not making it as a so-called pianist after all. Perhaps it was worth it, just for those fleeting glimpses of . . . of her Beethovenian orbs. Bugger Liszt. I used to make deliberate mistakes, just so I could look down that top. No wonder I never got there, no wonder I never got up – what d'you call it? – Mount Parnassus, when two of the bloody foothills were so distracting."

"What do you mean, 'there'?" Simon – if it were he who

was being talked at – would ask. "You must've got fairly there, you know, up the mountain, if you could almost play the Liszt Sonata. You must've been fairly brilliant."

Harry would smile strangely, as if he were listening to the Liszt Sonata in his head. "Fairly brilliant," he'd mutter, "but not fairly brilliant enough. When I was eleven, I was fairly brilliant – my school teachers told me that when I played Schubert in assemblies. When I was twelve I was fairly brilliant – my piano teacher told me that, when I played her my own blues arrangement of 'Silent Night.' When I was thirteen I was fairly brilliant, and everyone kept saying that one day 'I would happen.' Those were their exact words, you know: 'One day, son, you'll happen, with fingers like that.' I was going to go beyond fairly brilliant. My mother said so, my piano teacher said so, even the judge of the Penkridge Music Festival said so. They can't all have been wrong. They all admitted I was fairly brilliant at eleven, twelve, thirteen.

"But at fourteen, I was just fourteen. I was meant to be brilliant by then. It was meant to have happened, that I'd edged beyond fairly brilliant. But somewhere between thirteen and fourteen I ground to a halt – and it was like, well, now he's growing up, now he's obviously no longer a kid, being fairly brilliant isn't good enough for anyone." Mimicking the voices he could still hear in his head, Harry would get carried away: "Look at him, he's no longer a near-prodigy, he's too old, only another adolescent with a decent talent, which needs a lot of work if he's going to get anywhere, which he probably isn't, because he's not really that outstanding, and there are lots of other, easier things he can do, and the Northern College of Music is too far away and no doubt too expensive for the likes of us, so let's take away his piano at home anyway, and stop his lessons, and give his assembly-concerts to talentless imbeciles instead, to make doubly, triply sure he'll never get anywhere, and . . . and . . . fucking and . . ." His listener would wonder if the sentence would ever end – if Harry would be stuck in 'ands' forever – but finally, he'd take a deep breath, and the sentence would wind down, peter out: "and . . . and it's all their fault . . . and it's all everyone's fucking fault . . . and . . ."

He'd take a bite out of his Arrowroot, and sigh. "Most of all it was my ridiculous Uncle Alex's fault, for warning me it would happen – for being a kind of living warning, if you see what I mean, which you probably don't, because you never knew him, and nor did anyone else round here.

"He was a silly old bugger was Uncle Alex. He was my father's brother, Serena's and Melissa's great uncle. He died when I was twelve, I think, 1970-ish – it was another twelve years before Serena was even thought of. He was a huge bloke in ill-fitting Sunday suits, who used to fill our front room with his tenor. And everywhere else, for that matter – down Hem Heath colliery, along the street, buying the groceries, he lived in his own personal opera. At our house, he made me accompany him on the old piano in stuff he loved, like Gershwin and Ellington and Weill – 'Mack the Knife' was his 'show-stopper,' he used to say, though I just thought he needed a sodding gobstopper. No-one else seemed to notice he was off-key – perhaps because he was so shouty-loud, they were all too deafened to hear it. 'Better than the Italians,' he used to bellow at me, 'they *bel canto*, I *can belto*.' Wasn't even his own joke, the tosser. Anyway, he belto-ed so loud, his legs fell off."

"Eh?"

"That's kind of what I thought as a kid. His body shook so much when he shout-sang that I thought all his bits were going to shoot off in different directions. And in the end they did – or, at least, his legs did. No-one told me but I guess that, because of the diabetes, they had to saw his legs off. Last time I met him, he was in a second-hand wheelchair, still trying to sing 'Mack the Knife.' Shame they hadn't amputated his voice. 'Don't end up like me and me legs,' he smoke-wheezed-bellowed in my ear, when I was told by my mum – you know, Serena's grandma – to bend down and give him a kiss goodnight. 'Remember me as a lesson, son, and use your legs, don't lose them' – he was full of these crappy commonplaces and rhymes – 'Use your legs and go places, see new faces. You'll be playing with the Hallé and Barbirolli, mark my words. I can see you now, my boy, sitting where I should have been standing, but can't now, on the stage of the Free Trade Hall, banging away at Tchaikovsky or Rachmaninov or stuff like that. Remember the space where my legs used to be whenever you doubt that's going to happen to you.'

"Soon enough, the daft bugger was gone, and even the echoes of his deafening tenor died out of the front room. He'd asked to be cremated, so he was burnt at Burslem Crematorium. I thought that was the end of it – that, once and for all, the million-decibel voice of Uncle Alex had gone, thank Christ. But then we took his ashes down into Hem Heath mine – down and down the Number 2 shaft lift, 1,000 yards under the earth, with me holding the urn all the way. At the bottom, we got out, and scattered his ashes in one of the galleries by the old Winghay seam.

"Coming back up, I couldn't get those bloody ashes out of my head. I couldn't seem to shake off the thought of them all lying there in the dark – like they were conspiring with one another. I knew in a way I was being stupid, but, well, I was an imaginative kid, and at night, I had this half-awake nightmare, that somehow all the tiny pieces would be magicked together – or, rather, musicked together, one cinder starting to squeak 'Mack the Knife,' followed by a second, which joined the first, followed by a third, followed by a million others . . . until there stood a complete ashy Uncle Alex, all of his dead cells belting out the tune in unison, a huge chorus of cinders . . . and me, 1000 yards above, in my bedroom, convinced I could hear that off-key, undead tenor far below, and that it'd never go away . . ."

For a wavering moment, Harry's middle-aged face would itself seem to recall this childish haunting, all white eyes and pursed lips. Then half of his face would relax into a knowing grin, and Rosa or Simon would feel at liberty to release the smile she or he had been bottling up, in case he was totally serious. One could never be sure with Harry. Even now, his half smile would flicker only for a moment or so, and would be replaced by what Melissa used to call "Daddy's clever-clever face" – an arched eyebrow, narrowed eyes, a forefinger rubbing his lower lip. "Daddy is thinking again with his clever-clever face on," Melissa would laugh, "which means he is going to say a clever-clever thing that no-one actually knows what it really actually means." Then Harry would get cross at her, tell her to shut up, and wait for whoever was in the room to insist he reveal what the "clever-clever" thing was. To his disappointment, no-one would do so: Lizzie would bustle about, pretending his expectant silence wasn't happening; Serena would turn the volume on the TV up with the remote; and irregular visitors like Simon would prefer a peaceful life, choosing Harry's disgruntled silences over his manic monologues. Only Melissa, before she got too ill, would stop laughing, and drag it out of him: "Come on, Daddy. Tell us what the clever-clever thing is then. I actually really want to hear it, you know. I'll understand it probably when I'm dead old like you." Harry would hesitate, until he was won over with: "Honest, Daddy, I do want to hear how clever-clever you are."

Harry Comb certainly liked to think of himself as clever-clever, though Simon Adler-Reeves – puffed up with his own academic 'successes' – sometimes wondered if Harry's intellectualism consisted mainly of scraps of half-knowledge and facts he'd picked up from school, TV, books he'd flicked through at work, and books he hadn't flicked through, but of which he had read the blurb.

During his recollections of Uncle Alex, Harry would put on his clever-clever face for a moment, and then come out with one of these strange scraps of pseudo-knowledge: "You know, I found out that Marconi, the guy who invented the wireless and stuff, came to think that no sound waves ever totally die out – that, if you have equipment powerful enough, you'd be able to pick up Christ's Sermon on the Mount, maybe even the Big Bang. Anyway, the point is . . . well, I don't know what the bloody point is. All I know is that I'm with Marconi. If I listen hard enough, I can still hear Uncle Alex's belting tenor echoing down the mine, or in my head, or both."

With that, Harry would start to hum the tune of 'Mack the Knife' under his breath. Within the hum, muttered lyrics would gradually coalesce. At first, these would be words, and then phrases, familiar from the Louis Armstrong or Bobby Darin 'Macks' – words and phrases like 'shark,' 'pearly white,' 'scarlet billows,' 'oozing life,' 'done something rash.' But as the words and phrases started taking over from the hum, they'd seem to piece themselves together into a much-less-familiar pattern, an oft-forgotten final stanza:

Some in light and some in darkness
That's the kind of world we mean.
Those you see are in the light part.
Those in darkness don't get seen.

And after that, the hum would again subsume the lyrics – an ever-repeating hum stuck on the tune of that last line: 'Those in darkness don't get seen.'

In an effort to break the cyclical hum, Rosa or Simon would start to ask Harry a question – any question, about biscuits, the TV, Uncle Alex, anything at all to interrupt the endless drone. As soon as they'd open their mouths, though, the drone would stop, and Harry would say – as if in answer to whatever question they were about to ask – "Yes, it was his fault, Uncle Alex's, the bastard. I could've been a Glenn Gould or John Ogdon or Dinu Lipatti or whoever, but instead I was haunted by Uncle Mario Lanza and his out-of-tune mediocrity. Uncle Alex said he wanted to be a warning to me, but instead he was just a fucking curse – one frustrated mediocrity begetting another."

Harry would think for a moment, and his "clever-clever face would come back. He'd smile a knowing smile, and sa "You know, musicians beget musicians – I mean, look at Ba and his multitudinous offspring. So I suppose *frustrated* mu cians beget frustrated musicians."

"But Serena isn't frustrated," Rosa or Simon would s wondering if Harry had forgotten about his first daughter, a her musicianship. "She enjoys playing – seems quite ha with how she does. Not everyone can be a John Ogdon."

Harry would grunt and shrug his shoulders: "Happy amateurism – can you imagine anything worse? A happy m ocrity. God. My frustrated-fairly-brilliant musicianship b mere contented mediocrity in the next generation. Pe that's what happens too: musicians beget weaker musi who beget weaker musicians. Look at the Bachs again: t comparable J. S. one generation, the good C. P. E. and J. next, the eminently-forgettable W. F. E., whoever he w next. Geniuses beget musical mediocrities who beget am who beget sub-amateurs who beget critics. An ever-dec circle."

At this point, Rosa would nod sympathetically, pat

knee, and decide it was time to go and make him a cup of tea in his own house; or if it were Simon listening, he'd feel agitated into some kind of reaction by Harry's stream of self-indulgent pessimism: "That's not true," Simon would say. "I mean, what about J. S. Bach himself? How did he happen? Someone had to beget him in the first place, for him to go on and beget the lesser Bachs."

"No they didn't," Harry would say.

"Of course they did . . ."

"No. J. S. Bach just happened. Spontaneously. No-one begets a Bach. A Bach is like a psychopath, like a Macheath – he comes out of nowhere, and is fundamentally inexplicable. No-one can explain the origins of either Bachs or psychopaths."

Simon would look at Harry's face whilst he said this, but there'd be no sign he wasn't being serious. "Look," Simon would say, after a pause, "that doesn't make any sense, and it's also historically incorrect." But Harry would just yawn, as if it had been Simon, not him, talking for the last half hour.

Harry often – it seemed to his listeners – oscillated between sulky silences and verbose tirades, manias and sudden stases. Now, he'd suddenly decide the tirade was over, everything had been said that needed to be said, and he'd dismiss the whole conversation with a wave of his hand. Turning back to the TV, he'd mutter something under his breath – something which may or may not have been a response to Simon's last comment – something which may or may not have been the one word: "Critics."

Back on Thursday 17th June 1999 at 3.13 p.m., back in Melissa's funeral service at Trentham Parish Church, back at the piano stool, in front of the congregation, Harry again may or may not have been muttering something else under his breath

– something which may or may not have been directed at his fingers, poised ready on the first E-minor chord – something which no-one could hear, but which may or may not have been a command or curse: "Move, for fuck's sake, move."

His fingers didn't move.

He willed his fingers to depress the keys: "Please don't let me down now. Please. Move, for fuck's sake." But they just hovered on that E-minor chord, unmoving.

Nothing happened. The church was silent.

Some of the onlookers who'd come to church because they'd heard of the Spark Close Phenomenon, and wondered if another miracle might happen at the funeral, thought: "Now is the time."

But no. Now wasn't the time. Now, the church was silent, music-less. Now, nothing happened.

Harry's fingers didn't move.

No-one so much as coughed . . .

. . . until one little boy – a school friend of Melissa's – whispered audibly to his mother: "He's not very good, is he?," like the little boy in the fable of the *Emperor's New Clothes*. And that was that: the silence was gone, replaced by congregational coughing, whispering, shuffling.

Finally, the vicar got up, stood at the front again, and recited directly to Harry at the piano: "'I was dumb with silence, I held my peace, even from good; and my sorrow was stirred . . .'"

Harry, though, was not stirred by the impromptu Psalm. He just stayed where he was, his fingers still poised over E minor, where they remained for the next hymn, the prayers and the commendation. Only during the recessional did long-suffering family friends, Rosa Adler and Simon Adler-Reeves, step over to him, to take his hands away from the unsounded E-minor chord, and lead him out of the church. If they hadn't, perhaps he'd still be there, his hands stuck forever in that pre-'Kind im Einschlummern' silence, his fingers never quite sounding E minor, the chord always just about to happen.

VAR II

Harry

FOR THE TWO years before and the three months after Melissa's death, Harry Comb had got up at 7.05 a.m., showered, dressed in trousers, cardigan, shirt and tie, breakfasted on black toast with jam or marmalade, left the house at 7.55 a.m., walked down Spark Close, right onto Clermont Avenue, and right again onto Church Lane, to wait in rain, snow, fog, or sunshine at the bus stop. From there, at roughly 8 a.m. every morning, he'd catch the Number 21 Bus to Talke Pits, via Hanley, run by PMT (standing for Potteries Motor Transport and nothing else). Getting on the bus, he'd pay his fare, and sit three or four rows from the front, never speaking to any of the commuters with whom he shared the same thirty-minute journey for two and a quarter years. He'd never read, never listen to a personal stereo, never even look out of the window, having seen it all so many times before – just stare fixedly ahead at the back of strangers' heads, the driver's gear-stick, blurred tarmac.

Nearing his stop in Shelton, he'd press the bell, get up

roughly twenty-five seconds before the bus pulled over, hang on till the bus had stopped, and then step off it onto the pavement. Glancing at his watch, he'd see that it was usually about 8.30 a.m., give or take five minutes. It was a six-and-a-half-minute walk from the bus stop to his workplace, a corrugated iron hanger on an industrial estate, where he'd make a coffee and grunt "Good mornings" at people he'd half-known for years. Finally, at 8.50 a.m. every morning, he'd be sat on his chair in the smaller of the two offices, his back to a colleague called Mary Slight, otherwise known as 'Smelly Mary,' because she always smelt so strongly of Potpourri. On hot days – Harry once told his wife – Smelly Mary seemed to "sweat dead flowers."

Ensconced in the office, inhaling flowery fragrances, Harry would enter purchase invoices onto the company computer for eight-hour stretches, with a twenty-eight-minute break for lunch. His rate of invoice entry was approximately seventy invoices per hour – an excellent overall average which took into consideration time for queries, special cases, new accounts, phone calls, sorting the post, tidying his stationery, and occasional forays into the sales ledger.

Sometimes, when he was back in the living room at home, mechanically tap-tap-tapping the arm of his chair, his fingers themselves seemed uncertain whether they were playing an unheard melody on the piano, or merely tap-tap-tapping his work keyboard, entering invoice after invoice:

> *Enter account number.*
> *If new account with no pre-existing number, enter name of company, address, company number & contact phone number.*
> *Enter invoice number.*
> *Enter purchase reference number.*

> *Enter price, quantity, description code &, where relevant, ISBN of items purchased.*
> *Enter NET invoice amount.*
> *Enter total invoice amount inclusive of VAT, where relevant.*
> *Once invoice is completed, make sure total invoice amount is equal to the sum of the individual purchases on the invoice. If it isn't, delete & enter the invoice again.*
> *Once a complete batch of purchase invoices is entered, make sure the total for that batch of invoices matches the total held on the central purchase matrix. If it doesn't, start the batch again.*
> *If it does match, start the process again with a new batch.*
> *& then again.*
> *& again.*
> *& again.*

Up till two-and-a-quarter years ago, he hadn't had to put up with all these infinite '& agains.' Instead, he'd been the manager of a cubby-hole of a bookshop, located down the road, opposite Staffordshire University – a bookshop owned by the same company for which he now entered data. He'd spent his years there selling law, chemistry, art books he knew next to nothing about to students who wouldn't read them, and who would try to sell them back to him at the end of term. And he'd been rather successful at the selling and buying, he thought, having worked his way up from sales assistant to deputy to manager – which were, incidentally, the only three positions in the shop.

But then the success had been cut short: Melissa had become ill, an alternative position in accounts had come up, and he'd decided it was probably best to swap – temporarily – a job with unfixed hours, managerial responsibilities, stock takes and cash tills, for a nine-to-five job in a forgotten corner of the company. Admittedly, it meant taking a pay cut but, in the circumstances, it seemed like the logical thing to do: set hours, no distracting take-home work and no dependent staff – all of this would free him up, mentally and physically, to deal with his daughter's encroaching illness.

In the initial meeting about the change in roles, the Managing Director – a Mr. Gary Southend – hadn't tried to talk Harry out of doing the logical thing, much to the latter's disappointment. Nor had the MD offered to match Harry's old salary (which wasn't very much anyway) in the new role, or provide any special dispensation for having an ill daughter. There had been no "Oh, don't take a pay cut, Harry – we'll keep your salary as it is," or "You can't change jobs, Harry, you're invaluable where you are – just take some time off to spend with your daughter," or even "How is your daughter getting on in hospital, Harry?" Instead, it had just been: "Yes, that's fine, get Smelly Mary to fill in the paperwork, won't you? We'll have to go through the formality of an interview, but consider it done and dusted, dusted and done." Then, Gary had stood up and shaken Harry's hand, as if he were offering him a promotion, not a £7-an-hour job in data entry.

"How on Earth will you pay the mortgage on £7?" asked Smelly Mary on Harry's first day in accounts. "I mean, your house in posh Trentham . . ."

"Hanford," he corrected.

". . . even so, I mean, Hanford isn't Bentilee. How do you afford it? Do you rent?"

"No, we own it."

"How do you afford it?" she repeated, heading into a monologue: "I mean, I have to rent on my salary, and my salary's a bit more than yours, if you don't mind my saying, as head of this sub-office, and as kind of PA to Gary – although not really a PA, but might as well be, the way he gets me to buy his BLT sandwiches and keep his diary. And then, gosh, there are so many bills these days, I'm always broke at the end of the month, and it's always at that precise moment, isn't it?, that a dress you really want appears in your size in Dorothy Perkins, and you just can't get it, and have to wait till pay day – by which time some bitch is swanning around somewhere in it, and you're not. Do you find that? I suppose you don't, being a bloke and all, although, having said that, I did know someone once – a boyfriend he was – used to ring me up saying he was wearing a wedding dress, white stockings and all. Soon put a stop to that one, I can tell you. Not into that kind of stuff myself, are you? No, you wouldn't tell me if you were, and you don't look the type, though you never know – the quiet ones are often the worst. And you're being awfully quiet about the house question. Perhaps you think I'm being nosy? I don't want to be nosy, people say I am, but I'm not, I'm genuinely interested. Do you rent the house or not?"

"No, as I said, we own it."

"Oh yes, I remember now, and I don't know how you afford it then, unless you have a rich wife or inheritance or something, which, of course, is always possible, and I wouldn't want to be nosy, but what kind of house prices are they round there? House prices have gone up and up, haven't they? – although perhaps they haven't in your street, because I'm sure I heard something from someone about Spark Close in Trentham, or Hanford, something about a woman on your Close who, well, was doing a bit of – how do you put it? – all-over-massaging and phone-sexing on the side, someone called Kirsty or Kristen or Caitlin or something, who this other person said was even in some dodgy . . . readers' wives magazine – which I don't read so I don't know if it's true – with, well, her boobs out, and everything else for that matter, which no doubt drummed up lots more trade for her, including, I found out, from the someone I knew who knew her, and had visited her, shall we say, without me knowing. Seeing as this other person was another soon-to-be-ex-boyfriend at the time, when a small tweety bird told me about it, I was livid, I can tell you – but not with Kurtain or Kir-ching or whatever her name is, but with him – got rid of him sharpish, I can tell you, although he did deny he'd had anything to do with the massage woman on your Close. Is there someone called something like that on your street who was a reader's wife, and does she do that sort of thing? And if there is and she does, does it, like, reduce the house prices, bring down the tone, if you know what I mean? Is that how you can afford having a house there, because having that kind of massagey stuff next door takes the house prices down?"

Harry could have answered – if he'd wanted to – that he and his wife Lizzie couldn't and didn't afford the house, couldn't and didn't afford most of the furniture, couldn't and didn't afford Lizzie's collagen replacement therapy. He could have answered that his previous £12 an hour wage, and current £7 an hour wage, plus Lizzie's dwindling inheritance and pittance from her part-time post as a so-called 'teaching assistant' couldn't and didn't amount to a house in Hanford. He could have answered that, deep down, he'd always half-believed that something better might turn up without his doing much; that perhaps someone from his pianistic past would reappear and insist he sign a lucrative contract with EMI; that tapping the keyboard in data entry was only a prelude to tapping a different kind of keyboard for a living; that there were huge audiences out there *sans* pianist, waiting for him; and that it was neither here nor there that he never practised any more, or even touched the piano: he knew it would all come back to him when the time was right.

The time was not yet right, and he could also have answered Smelly Mary by admitting that he, Lizzie, Melissa and Serena survived mainly on the maintenance money sent from Ottawa by Serena's "successful" mother, his ex-wife.

He could have answered in any or all of these ways, but he didn't. At that point, his head a carousel of questions and possible answers, Harry made a mistake with his new colleague, and he shrugged his shoulders, turning back to his monitor, and turning the (one-sided) conversation to stone – in fact, unwittingly turning it to stone for the next two and a quarter years. Taking his shrugged shoulders as a sign of disinterest, or rudeness, writing him off as taciturn and aloof, Smelly Mary tutted and also turned away to tap at her computer keyboard. Thereafter, conversation was never fully brought back to life, beyond "Good morning," "How was your weekend?," "How is your daughter getting on?," "Do you know anything about this account?," and so on. Even when these desultory mini-conversations gained a bit of colour, and seemed to breathe for more than a couple of exchanges, they wouldn't last, and soon sunk back into inanimate silence. For the remainder of the hours upon hours of work, the pair sat in near-silence, their backs three feet away from each other, the only communication between them her cloying fragrance, and their tap-tap-tapping keyboard duet. In the near-silence, Harry tried to convince himself that such a duet was at least preferable to another monologue from Smelly Mary.

The wordless duet carried on until three months after Melissa's death. Then, on Monday 13th September 1999, Gary Southend, the company's MD, squeezed into the back office, and perched himself on the corner of Harry's desk, head and shoulders above Harry. Smelly Mary coughed, but kept her back to both of them, leaning forward, concentrating on her monitor. Gary picked up a hole punch on Harry's desk, looked at it, and then played with it during the whole of the ensuing conversation, squeezing it up and down in his hands.

"How are you feeling, Harry, any better?" he asked, trying to frown his customary smile away.

"I'm okay," said Harry, staring down at his fingers, which had frozen above the keyboard.

"Good, that's good," Gary nodded slowly, and looked again at the hole punch. "Nice hole punch you've got here, Harry."

"Thank you," said Harry.

"Yes, nice hole punch," repeated Gary. "Good colour too."

"Thank you," said Harry. "It's very useful. It . . . punches holes."

There was a long pause. "Useful, yes," said Gary. "Useful," he said the word a few times with different intonations, squeezing the hole punch in his hand, a few inches away from Harry's head. "Useful, useful, useful," he said, sounding like a pianist trying to get started, but stuck on a particularly difficult phrase, trying out different dynamics, emphases, speeds. Eventually, he hit on a slow but steady *moderato*: "Useful is kind of what I wanted to talk to you about, Harry. That's why I'm paying you a visit."

"Oh," said Harry flatly.

"No, Harry, please don't be worried," reassured Gary – although Harry had expressed no such emotion in his voice or actions. Rather, Harry sat perfectly still, whilst Gary carried on: "Don't be worried, Harry. Gosh, of all things, I don't want you to be worried." Something about the way Gary drew out the word "worried" reminded Harry of Melissa's consultants in hospital, but he dismissed the connection as soon as his mind involuntarily made it. "Don't be worried," continued Gary. "You've had enough to worry about, Harry, without my adding to your anxieties. No, I'm not here to worry you. I just want to have a talk with you . . . a chat, if you like, just you and me."

At the words "just you and me," Harry automatically glanced behind him at Smelly Mary – and then returned to staring at his fingers.

Gary noticed the glance, and said: "Oh, don't worry about Mary. She won't interrupt our chat, will you, Mary?" Mary shook her head without turning away from the screen, without moving the rest of her body at all. "Mary's fine. She won't bother us. And anyway, we have no secrets here, do we, Harry? That's the strength of Alma Mater Bookshops. We have nothing to hide. With us, it's all about communication and consultation, which is why I wanted this nice chat we're having today."

"Yes," agreed Harry.

"And this chat isn't to make you worry. Remember that. You mustn't worry about the chat, any more than you should worry about Mary being here with us."

"Okay," said Harry, "I won't worry."

"That's right," said Gary, "worry, I always think, is counter-productive. There are so many managers out there who think worry gets more out of staff; there are so many managers who thrive on inducing nothing short of paranoia in their staff. But I think you know I'm not one of them, don't you, Harry? I think you know me well enough to know I don't want you to worry about things here, when you've got so much to worry about in the big wide world outside our cosy little company. Obviously, you know all this by now – I mean, when you were worried about your daughter's . . . illness a couple of years ago, I made sure you were taken care of, and transferred here. So you could concentrate on your family. And we all know, don't we, that's what's really important in life, don't we? We all know what's really important is a healthy work-life balance, with the emphasis firmly on life. Certainly not on all this here." He waved the hole punch around, as far as was possible in the small space, to indicate the office and, by extension, the company as a whole. "There's no point worrying about all this, letting it sap your energy, when, for example, a member of your family is so . . . unwell. That's what I thought back then, and I stand by my decision to accept your request and move you here. Other managers, of course, might not have been so understanding, but I was brought up to know what's more important – family or work. As I like to say to people, we work to live, not live to work. You'll have seen that on the calendar above my desk, so you know I live by that motto."

"Yes," said Harry, for something to say, "I have seen it."

"That's because you're observant, Harry. You're one of the observant ones. I know that." Gary nodded to himself. "And being one of the observant ones, you'll know that I've quietly – without a fuss, without making too much of it – been looking out for you, these past few months." Gary put his free, hole-punch-less hand on Harry's shoulder. "As I've said to you before, Harry, and I'll say it again, I was very sorry to hear about your daughter's . . . passing away. I was only saying to you, Mary, yesterday, wasn't I, how sorry I was?"

"Yes, you were," said Mary, unmoving

"Yes, I was. Very sorry. It must've been a hard, worrying time for you. Of course, you needed the whole week off for compassionate leave when it happened, plus an extra day's leave the next week for the funeral. That was important. But since then, I've been happy to see you've come back . . . well, if not rejuvenated, then certainly with the same . . . hard-working attitude I've come to expect from you. Expect, but not taken for granted, certainly not. I never take my staff for granted, as you know."

"No – I mean, yes," said Harry.

"Indeed," continued Gary, "only bad managers take their staff for granted, and I'm sure you don't think I'm one of them, after everything we've been through together, Harry. It's been a . . . worrying time for you, I know. A time for grieving, yes, but also for taking stock, no doubt, and thinking about the future. But hopefully not worrying about the future. Worrying is, of course, the enemy of work, as I always say. So I don't want you to worry, or become in any way paranoid: your future is secure if . . . you want it to be. I'll make sure of that, because I've known you through thick and thin, haven't I, Harry?"

"Yes."

"I mean, when I think of what you and your family have been through whilst you've worked here . . . First the divorce – gosh, I remember that difficult time, Harry. You'd only just got the managerial position in the bookshop when all that stuff, shall we say, 'kicked off.' But we rode that storm home. And then, just when we thought things had settled down, your poor daughter goes and gets ill. That must've been so hard for you all, that battle. Two whole years of it. And then she . . . passes away after so much fighting. She was a brave girl, your daughter. I never met her, but I can see that much. She certainly didn't worry: she faced what she had to face, right to the end. And that is what I've come to expect of you, Harry, too. Dogged determination, right to the end. Right to the end. It suits you in this position, as, I'm sure, it'd suit you in any position you cared to take on, in this firm – or, if you chose, another firm – at any point in the future. It's what I'd put on your reference: 'dogged determination right to the end.' The end. The end." Gary kept repeating "the end" under his breath for a few seconds, as if it were a sweet he was rolling around in his mouth.

Then, deciding to wrap up the conversation, he said briskly: "I'm glad we've had this frank chat, Harry. I'm glad we've discussed things over, man to man. I always enjoy our chats, Harry, even though they don't happen as often as I'd like. Gosh, I know that when something terrible happens like with your . . . daughter, well, people sometimes clam up because they don't know what to say. They feel embarrassed, and even cross the street when they see the person who has, shall we say, 'loved and lost.' But I think you know that's not my way, Harry. My door is always open for you. I hope we can have another chat like this again soon. It stops unnecessary . . . worrying, doesn't it?"

Harry nodded. There was a long pause, as Gary looked at the hole punch again. "Good hole punch this, Harry. Very useful piece of office equipment. In a small but neatly formed company like ours, you know, everything, down to this humble item of stationery, has to be useful. We can't afford hole punches – or anything else for that matter – which isn't useful. We're not that kind of company. Everything, from hole punches to desks to –" he looked around the office, to find something else for his list – "computer monitors to larger things like *human* resources, everything has to prove its usefulness on a day-to-day basis. I mean, we wouldn't keep this hole punch, would we, Harry, if it had broken?"

Harry shook his head.

"No, of course we wouldn't. It would no longer be useful. And that's what matters. Continued usefulness. A good manager notices these things. A good manager notices the usefulness – or otherwise – of even the smallest of things. Do you see what I mean, Harry?" Harry nodded again, moving his head up and down, as Gary moved his hand up and down, as if weighing the hole punch he was holding. He suddenly stopped, seeming to come to a decision. "Yes, I like this hole punch. It certainly seems . . . useful. Would you mind if I borrowed it for an hour or so, Harry?"

Harry shook his head, and Gary popped the hole punch into his pocket. "Good," he said. "Good. I'm glad we're all clear now. All done. Gooooood," he elongated the last "good," and when he reached "d," hopped off the desk, and strode out of the room, closing the door behind him . . .

. . . leaving Harry wondering what was "good," what was "done," what was "clear" – leaving Harry wondering if, during the conversation, he'd been sacked, demoted, promoted, told he wasn't going back to the manager's job, told he was going back to the manager's job, or told to look for another job in another firm entirely. Harry couldn't work it out; and his wondering was interrupted by Smelly Mary saying out loud: "God, what a cunt."

"Pardon?" asked Harry, turning his swivel chair to face her.

Her fingers remained on her keyboard, but she nodded at the closed door, and repeated: "Him – God, what a cunt."

Harry frowned. His mind already befuddled by the previous conversation, for a moment he thought that Smelly Mary meant that God was a cunt. But then it dawned on him what she really meant, and he nodded in agreement.

They both nodded in unison at the door.

And that was that, and they returned to their keyboards, invoices, monitors. But something had changed: reflected on both monitors were shy, corner-of-the-mouth smiles. Through those unison nods, after two and a quarter years of near-silence, the two employees had decided that they rather liked each other after all.

So it was a bit of a shame that that afternoon was the last time Harry ever saw Smelly Mary.

VAR III

Pathétique

IT WAS HARRY'S fault he never saw Smelly Mary again. As he himself more or less admitted, Harry was the sort of person who wanted to freeze relationships in time. After two and a quarter years, he'd finally hit it off with Smelly Mary, finally shared a smile with her – so he wanted to make sure that their smile froze there. He hated that he could spend a good day with someone, and then the next day it was something different again, and then the next and the next.

Months later, after his final disappearing act, Harry's wife Lizzie explained this aspect of his character to a sympathetic police officer, over a cup of tea and Custard Cream: "Harry, you see, always wanted us to be on our first secret date, or our first best secret date, or something like that. He was always dwelling on times when things were at their best, always saying 'I wish time would stop now' when things were good. He was like that with all of us – Serena, me, even Melissa, who wasn't old enough to remember lots of what he remembered.

"What I remember is one day, when he was subjecting us all – even Mel, who was a baby then – to one of his LPs in the front room. It must've been years ago, when he still listened to them. The LP was something crappy by Beethoven, which took ages to finish – you know, all that endless to-ing and fro-ing you get, thud-thud, pom-pom, thud-thud, pom-pom. God, I could never get on with that stuff. I'm more of an Andrew- than-Julian-Lloyd-Webber-type person, if you know what I mean. Harry used to call me a Philistine, but it never bothered me much. Anyway, finally, the LP stopped, all loud and triumphant and pom-py-pom, and he turned to me as if the music had somehow been him, all beaming and triumphant himself: 'You see,' he said, like we were continuing some silly conversation in his head, 'that's what I'm talking about. In music like that, you reach the joy at the end, and that's exactly what it is – the end. The problem with real life is that the joy isn't the end. You have a moment of joy, like our wedding, and then you wake up next day.' 'Thank you very much,' I said to him. 'I don't mean that,' he said – although he did, really. 'What I mean is that you get to the end of music like that, and it really *is* the end. But in real life, you'd have to have another movement after it. And then another movement after that, and so on. In music, even if the piece ends in tragedy – you know, like in Tchaikovsky's *Pathétique*, or Mahler's Sixth Symphony – well, at least that's the end of it. Nothing could come after that A-minor *pizzicato* at the end of Mahler's Sixth, or the growling double basses and cellos at the end of Tchaikovksy's Sixth . . .'" Lizzie paused after she'd repeated this, and leaned her head to one side: "Did I remember all that rubbish he was spouting right?"

The sympathetic police officer shrugged her shoulders and said, "No idea."

"It doesn't mean anything to me either, all that *pizzicato* and *Pathétique* stuff – the only reason I remember it is that Harry used to get cross if he thought I wasn't listening, and ask me questions about what he'd said afterwards. Later on, with Melissa ill and all, I'd tell him where to stick his questions. But the first few years of marriage, I'd get lots of headaches trying my best, like a good wife, to concentrate on what he was saying, not to get distracted by a hang nail or split end, not to pee him off. That way, I could answer his 'were-you-listening-to-me?' tests properly: 'What was I just talking about?' '*Pathétique* cellos and A minors and *pizzicatos*.' 'How does Tchaikovksy's Sixth Symphony end?' 'With growls and double-Mahlers.' 'And what did I say comes afterwards?' 'How can anything come after the end?' 'Precisely,' he said, folding his arms, 'that's precisely my point. Nothing comes after the double-M . . . the double basses and cellos at the end of Tchaikovksy's Sixth. That's it. Finale, finish, conclusion, the end, *kaput*. But in real life even tragedy like that is not the end. You have to carry on afterwards, plodding away on your double basses and crap. Sometimes, all I want is for things to finish, the end, full stop.'

"I got cross then, and told him to shut up, stop being morbid in front of the kids. I told him I didn't know what he was going on about, and I didn't want to hear any more about crappy double basses. I told him we'd listen to some of my Whitney Houston instead, to cheer us up. That got him out of his chair, I can tell you, the lazy so-and-so. He sprang up and told me he'd play me the two pieces he'd mentioned – by Tchaikovksy and Mahler – to 'illustrate his point,' as he put it. I said they both sounded long and boring and loud, and I didn't have time or ears to put up with them. I had to make tea and sort out Melissa's nails and do a dozen other jobs which were more important than listening to growling double basses. 'But you can do those things afterwards,' he said to me. 'And that's exactly what I'm getting at: in real life, one moment you've got Tchaikovsky-ish tragedy going on in the double basses, or Beethovenian C Major on trombones, the next you're filing your daughter's nails, making tea. Why can't things finish like they do in music, instead of growling on forever?'"

Six and a half years after he asked this rhetorical question, Harry answered it at Alma Mater Bookshops by trying to arrest forever – by, that is, trying to freeze in time his job, and his shared smile with Smelly Mary. Put simply, the morning after the chat with Gary Southend, and the mutual smile with Smelly Mary, Harry didn't go into work.

He got up, as normal, at 7.05 a.m., showered, ironed his shirt and tie and put them on. He wandered into the front room with his piece of toast, on which he'd spread marmalade to disguise the black stripes, and sat down in his customary armchair.

At some point during that black and orange breakfast, he mentally resigned his job. There must have been one particularly ashy crunch, or maybe one particularly sweet strand of marmalade, which made up his mind, once and for all – as far as it was a conscious decision. Perhaps if the toast hadn't been burnt, or he'd replaced the cheap toaster a few months before, or the marmalade hadn't been Sainsbury's best, but their usual buy, perhaps he would have left the house at 7.55 a.m., caught the Number 21 at the bus stop on Church Lane at 8 a.m., gone to work, entered invoices, talked or not talked to Smelly Mary, and come home for tea.

Instead, only that perhaps-ghost caught the bus for him, took up his empty seat, three or four rows from the front, turned up at work, and entered ghostly invoices all day. That day, Tuesday 14th September 1999, Harry Comb divided in two, and was living two parallel lives at the same time: the perhaps-him, who should have gone to work and did, and the real him, who should have gone to work but didn't.

At 8.05 a.m., Serena was the first to come across the Harry-who-didn't. Getting ready for college, she wandered into the living room to watch some TV, drying her hair roughly with a towel. When she emerged from beneath the towel, she noticed the back of her father's head in front of her, and she almost jumped. For her, it was the real him – the one who didn't but should have gone to work, the one who was now sitting, staring at a blank television screen with a plate of half-eaten toast on his lap – who was the ghost.

"Dad?" Serena asked, as though she were speaking to the dead.

Harry didn't answer.

"Dad?" she asked again.

He didn't answer.

"Dad, are you okay? Are you, like . . . alive?" she asked.

He nodded: "Yes."

"Oh," she said, not knowing how to pursue the conversation further. So she left the room, finished drying her hair, straightened it, sorted her rucksack out, and drifted out of the house to catch her bus for Sixth-Form College – all without saying another word.

A bit later, at 8.35 a.m., Lizzie drifted out of the bedroom in her dressing gown, yawning, wishing she'd not bothered to get up on what wasn't a work day. Wandering into the living room to switch on the television, she too was confronted by the back of a head. Like Serena, she stopped, as her mind tried to work out what the back of a head would be doing in Harry's armchair.

"Harry, is that you?" she asked.

He didn't answer – perhaps couldn't answer what would have seemed to most people a simple question.

"Harry?" She took a step forwards, and then hesitated. Of course it was him – she thought she recognised the back of that head – though absolute stillness makes anyone difficult to recognise.

"Harry, is it you? Are you okay?" she asked the stillness.

"Yes," the stillness answered.

"Then why are you here?" she asked, now moving forwards, parallel to the armchair and his profile.

The stillness didn't answer.

"Harry," she said, looking down at him, "are you unwell?"

"Nope," he said, casually shaking his head.

"Then what the hell are you doing?" she asked, starting to lose patience.

"Sitting here," he said.

"I can see that," she said. "I can see you're bloody well sitting there, Harry. Harry!" She tentatively touched his shoulder, and pushed it a bit, as one might push a body to see if it's alive. He wriggled under the touch, and moved away slightly. She withdrew her hand.

"Harry," she said.

"Yes?" he said.

"Harry, why are you here and not at work?"

"I'm not going to work."

"Why?"

"I'm not going to work," he said, as if the repeated statement answered her question.

"What are you going to do then?" she asked.

"I'm going to sit here," he said, "and wait."

"Wait for what?"

"Wait for . . . I don't know . . . a musical hallucination to pop into my head." He spoke without a smile. "Everyone else on this shitty street has had one. Why not us? Why not me? I want one. All I hear is bang-bang-crash-crash-discord-discord. That's all I get from the world, from work and home and TV and computers and families. That's all my ears give me these days. Well, I don't want any more bang-crash-discords. I want a beautiful musical hallucination." He sounded like a spoilt boy, demanding a toy that everyone else had. "I demand a musical hallucination, and I'm not moving till I've had one."

"Harry, you're being silly."

"I'm not," he pouted. "I'm not being silly. I'm sitting here, waiting for a musical hallucination. I want one now. I want Wagner in my head. No, perhaps not Wagner – that way lunacy lies. And National Socialism. I don't want to invade Poland, not yet. I wouldn't want to be mad or a Nazi, now, would I? Would I?" He was almost shouting, certainly not laughing.

"No. I wouldn't," he said, calming down and answering his own question. "Not Wagner – perhaps Haydn or Mozart. They'll do for starters. I'll order Haydn and Mozart, with a side salad of early Beethoven, and a spicy Schubertian relish. Yum yum." He turned to Lizzie and smiled a forced smile. "Yum yum, Berlioz to go, please."

There was a long pause.

"You're being s . . ."

"No no no. I'm not. I'm not being silly. Why is it silly to want what everyone else on this shitty Close has had? For fuck's sake – I'm the musical one, not Serena, not you – God help us, not you and your Whitney-fucking-Houston – and not anyone else on this street. Me. It's me who's the one with talent, who knows a musical something from a musical nothing. It's me who can play the piano, who can whistle Bach in counterpoint. Me. I'm surrounded by musical imbeciles, who listen to Whitney Houston, or techno-rave-bang-bang-rubbish, or happy-clappy-tambourine-God-is-the-dog's-bollocks-crap. And yet who is it who gets the hallucinations? What kind of fucking joke is that? What kind of fucking joke is *all* of it?"

Faced with this onslaught, Lizzie pulled herself up to her coldest height – a formidable five-foot-eleven – and glared down at him. "I don't care," she said, "I don't care about any of that. All I care about, *darling*, is who is going to pay for our twice-weekly trip to Tesco's, if you're not working and Serena is in college? We can hardly pay for it from my part-time pittance, can we?"

"I'll tell you who's going to pay," said Harry, "the very person who's been paying Tesco's on our behalf for years, the very person who pays for the hive we call home . . ."

"Hive?"

"Yes, hive. Where bees live, stupid. A nearly-empty hive, with we three bees buzzing round in it, sometimes bumping into each another by accident, but mostly just buzzing, buzzing, buzzing . . ."

"Harry, what the hell are you going on about? Are you ill? Honestly, Harry, I haven't got time for this."

"No, you haven't, of course you haven't, because you've got an appointment no doubt with your outrageously gay hairdresser, or your outrageously heterosexual personal trainer, or your pedicurist-nail-filer-general-by-appointment-to-Her-Majesty-the-Queen, or someone else paid for by my *ex-wife*. Because it's her and only her who pays for everything, from Tesco's to this dump of a hive to Serena's gothy mascara, to the cement you use to fill in the cracks in your face. It's her, not my £7 an hour after hour after hour after hour . . ." He stopped himself by shutting his eyes, and then opening them again: "No, it's not my £7 an hour which pays for us, and nor is it your so-called 'teaching assistant' job – otherwise known as colouring and sticking all day, no wonder there are only two of you in the whole LEA, what a waste of their money – and nor is it any of the here-today-gone-tomorrow-half-an-hour jobs Serena does when she can be bothered. It's none of us here – none of us pay for it. So why should we bother? Why should I bother? I might as well stay at home, waiting for the musical heavens to open in my head. Waiting for the Hallelujah-cination Chorus to descend on me from on high."

Involuntarily, Lizzie found herself looking up at the ceiling for a moment – and then corrected herself.

"Are you listening to me?" Harry asked. "Do you understand?"

"No I don't," said Lizzie, stamping her slippers. "I told you: you're talking nonsense, Harry."

"I'm not. Stop saying that. Look, *darling*, we get the money from my ex anyway, whatever I do. We take her money, we spend it. If we need more, she sends more. If we need less, she still sends more. If we asked her to buy the crappy house outright, she'd probably do it. Because she's so-so-so *kind*, such a *loving* mother to her daughter, Serena. She'd do anything for her. Anything at all. Apart from maybe come over and see her."

Harry turned to Lizzie and smiled again – or at least turned his mouth up at the corners: "And you know what? I'd do anything for you too, *darling*. Anything you wanted. So if you said to me now: go to work. Don't sit in this chair, talking 'nonsense,' waiting for nothing to happen. Go to work. I command you. All I want from you in the world is for you to work, earn £7 an hour, spend your earnings on council tax and half a gas bill a month and not much else. All I want from you is you to work, work, work, enter invoice, invoice, tap, tap, tap on the keyboard forever and ever – if you said to me now: I want you to go into work and do all this, and not sit here and think or not think about any of the shit that's happened to us, just plod on and on, never stopping, never thinking, never remembering, just going to work and coming home and eating tea and watching TV and going to bed and not having sex ever ever again – if you said to me now: that's all I want, well, my darling, of course, your wish is my command."

Lizzie looked down at Harry looking up at her. Gradually, her jaw set, her eyes narrowed – and then she swivelled round on one heel and left the room.

"Goodbye, *darling*," said Harry, watching her go.

Harry didn't go to work that day, or the next, or the next. He'd still get out of bed at 7.05 a.m., still shower, dress in trousers, cardigan, shirt and tie – he'd still be tidy, or at least tidyish, in his appearance – and he'd still breakfast on black toast with jam or marmalade. But now, instead of leaving the house at 7.55 a.m., he'd sit down in his armchair, and watch TV – sometimes on, sometimes off. Sometimes, he'd wander into the kitchen and bring back a snack, usually of cheese and crackers, to his armchair. Sometimes, mid-morning or mid-afternoon, he'd wander to the local shop on the A34 for a newspaper or a new packet of crackers. Back in his armchair, he'd slowly, methodically butter the crackers, slowly, methodically cut himself a slice of cheddar, slowly, methodically take small bite after small bite. Away from work, all he had to do now was slowly, methodically fill stretches of empty time with cracker-eating, TV watching, people watching, waiting, nothingness.

After three days of nothingness, at roughly 2.15 p.m. on Friday 17th September, Harry seems to have got out of his armchair, walked out of the living room, walked down the hallway, stepped out of the house, turned right, instead of the usual left, walked past Numbers 6 and 8 (Mr. Paul Higgins's and Mrs. Hutchinson's houses), and stopped outside the front door of Number 10. No-one knows for sure how long he stood there, staring at the door – though Mr. Paul Higgins said that he saw Harry walk past his window at about 2.16 p.m., and Ms. Kirsten Machin said she didn't hear a knock at her door till 2.25 p.m. Maybe he'd knocked before, without an answer, because Ms. Machin said that sometimes she didn't hear the front door, "what with the fucking stereo-howling from my twins."

Ms. Machin's supposed version of events on that afternoon has, of course, already been widely circulated in a now-notorious interview she gave for *The Sun*, which was published on 18th February 2000.* Following its publication, the interview was the subject of controversy, scandal and, indeed, legal action. As is well known, Ms. Machin herself was unhappy with the 'editing' her version of the story received in the national press. What follows is the full version of her story – what she said *really* happened between herself and Harry Comb – in a recorded interview with her solicitor:

> *So it all went like this. First off, about 2.25 I think it was, I heard the banging at the door. When I got to it and opened it, I saw him there. I knew who 'him' was, course. I'd seen his face around – and not a bad face it isn't – and I knew, like, he was father of that poor girl Melissa what died. Before she went and got sick, I used to see her all the time in the Close, singing, skipping, searching for wood-lice and spiders, and shit like kids do – stuff what I know her mother, precious bitch, hated, because she went and ruined her prissy-princessy-all-pink-and-girlie outfits. Poor little mite, having a mother like that bitch. And poor little mite, getting all ill, like. Anyhow, I knew this was her father, and I knew his name was 'Harry' from the papers. I think I'd have known it was him – y'know, that he was the father of the dead girl – even if I hadn't known, if you get me. It was all over his fucking face. Don't blame him, either. It'd send anyone Looby-Lou, wouldn't it, watching your kid fall to pieces in front of your eyes.*

* See 'Variations: Pavane pour une infante défunte' above.

He was standing there, all saggy shoulders and blank face, and he didn't say anything, so I just goes: "Hello," like. He still didn't say anything, though his mouth was going like a frigging fish, opening and shutting, so I goes: "Hello" again, and asked him if he'd like to come into my "humble abode." He nodded, and I took his elbow, and guided him in, like he was some kind of fucking disabled.

He shuffled into the living room, and I plumped him down in the armchair. I asked him if he wanted a cup of tea, or gin. He didn't answer, but instead stared up at the ceiling with dead wide eyes and whispered: "What's that?" He sounded kinda spooked, if you know what I mean, like it was some kind of fucking ghost or zombie yelping upstairs. Twin fucking zombies, more like. I told him it was just the twins in their cots, having an afternoon snooze. Afternoon snooze, my arse.

Anyway, whatever they were doing up there, Harry seemed kinda relieved, and his eyes came back to the living room. I asked him again if he wanted something to drink – gin or tea – and he nodded. I kinda assumed the nod meant gin, so I went and got him some, and poured myself one for good measure. Then I sat down on the armchair next to him. "Cheers," I goes, "here's to you," and we clinked glasses.

Harry didn't say nothing, and I was just looking at him, like you do. Sizing him up. Why had he just knocked on my front door out of the blue? Never really talked to the bugger before, let alone had a drink with him. It didn't take a genius to work it out. I mean, I don't do that kind of stuff any more – well, only on the side for a . . . as a favour to old mates. I tell you fucking what – the phone sex is much more lucrative than that old-style escorting stuff. And, well, I can do the phone shit round the kids – they don't know what I'm going on about, what it all means.

The point is, that I reckon he'd heard somewhere 'on the grapevine' about my . . . past. I don't advertise no more, so he must've heard from someone who heard from someone. Or p'raps he'd seen my boobs-picture in The Sun *– y'know the first one I done, that summer, which I didn't mind as much as the shite they printed a few months later. So p'raps he'd seen that, got all turned on, like, and come round to mine to see what might happen. I s'pose it's kind of convenient for him – next door but one. Not much different to going to the fucking paper shop.*

Still, I thought it might've been a bit awkward, if I saw that bitch Mrs. Harry out the window next day or so. I definitely, like, feel awkward now it's all come out – y'know, the lies in the papers. She fucking hates me now. Not that she ever gave me the time of day before. Not many of them do round here. There was only that one day of all weirdy days – you know, The Musical Day – when the stuck-up-knobs-I-don't-call-neighbours were almost real neighbours, became kinda nice. Niceness round here never happened before or again, tell you that for nothing.

Not that I really blame Mrs. Harry-Lizzie-Bitch-Comb for being not-nice. Kind of understandable, given the bollocks they printed in the papers about me and Harry. And I'm grateful to you, like, for listening to my side of the story, even if I am paying through the nose for the privilege.

Course, that's what those journalist bastards pretended to do: listen. They said they'd listen to my side of the story and give me a measly bit of cash for the interview. Bastards didn't even pay me proper in the end, let alone write up the story I told them. All that crap about all-night 'romps.' None of it was fucking true. But now everyone round here thinks I'm some nasty slag, vulturising or something on a dead girl's family.

But I'm not the slag people think. Whatever happened between me and Harry Comb was not started by me, honest. He banged on my door, came in, sat in my living room, and knocked back my gin. And he didn't half knock it back, I can tell you.

I took his empty glass, and offered him another. Thought he needed it, so I went and got the bottle of gin and the bottle of tonic, and plonked them in front of him on the coffee table. "Help yourself," I said, and he did. He was, like, leaning forwards in the chair, kind of panting like a dog after that second one. But he didn't say much. I think that's one thing I liked about him. I didn't say much either – such as, like, asking why was he fucking here in the first place?

So we just sat there, not asking stupid questions, and I poured another for us both, and he took his and downed it again. I kinda sipped mine, and looked at him. Poor sod – probably wasn't bad looking once upon a time, and he was still, well, clean and shit. But he looked kind of hunched and all white eyes and starey-like.

Yeah, poor sod just sat there, staring at the coffee table, downing my gin. In the end, I did ask him a question, cos I couldn't think of anything else to say. So I asked him if he was okay, and touched his elbow – and, fuck, he didn't half jump. Like he was sleep walking or something. "Look, are you okay?" I asked again. "D'you want me to take you home?" He shook his head, and turned to look at me – or to look at my chest, anyway. Don't worry, I'm used to it. After all, it's a pretty good one, if I do say so myself. No shitty silicone in there, I can tell you.

He mumbled something to my chest, and when I asked him to repeat it, he couldn't seem to find the end of his sentences: "I want . . ." he said, "I want . . . I want . . ." Well, I kinda knew what he was trying to get to at the end of his sentences. I tell you, what with that drooling mouth and unfocussed stare, I reckon he looked like he hadn't had much of the end of sentences for a long while, if you know what I mean.

Now, as I say, all of that kind of shit was in the past for me. Most guys who came onto me in pubs and clubs, who'd heard from someone who'd heard from someone else about me, I kneed in the bollocks and poured their lagers over their fat heads. I tell you, I don't take that shite from no-one. I'm not one of those nicey-nice, aren't-they-kind-underneath, non-existent-bollocks kind of prossies you see on movies. Oh no. In fact, get this straight, I'm not a prossie at all, never liked the name – it's like an excuse so people can treat hard-working business women like shit. Well, they can all fuck off, as far as I'm concerned.

And I would've told Harry Comb to fuck off too, if he'd come in, all up-his-own-arse, crowing about how he'd heard about me and wanted some of that, here's some cash, let's get down to it on the living-room floor, you dirty slag. But he didn't come in like that. He came into the house, I plumped him down, and he just sat there, not saying anything. I reckon if I'd let him alone to drink my gin, he wouldn't have said anything ever. He'd have just got smashed, and then staggered home before Mrs. Bitch-of-a-Wife came back from her school-teacher-ing, or whatever shit she does. He wouldn't have made no complaints, would never have asked me to get my kit off.

Because he didn't ask, I decided to do it anyway. The twins were safely shut up in their cots, I was a bit wankered already on the gin, and, well, I kinda felt turned on that he didn't say anything. I felt horny cos for once I was, like, in a situation where we didn't have to do it, could've just stayed sitting. Kinda sexy. And on top of the sexiness, I felt sorry for the poor sod. I thought, freebie or not, he deserves a bit of fun, and if he's not had a bit for a while, it won't last long anyway. Probably not even get to the main event.

So I put my hand on his knee, leant forwards, kissed him on the cheek – all romantic-like – and whispered that he should give me a couple of minutes to get dolled up. I ran upstairs, put dummies back in the twins' mouths, went into my bedroom, and took my dress off and everything else. Did all the normal shit, but faster. For once, well, for once I felt kind of nervy and shaky, not sure why, and couldn't seem to get the suspenders to clip right. God, I've had enough practice with those fuckers. So I just got some hold-ups instead, smeared some red lippy on, dug out the old scuffed stilettos, and then paraded downstairs like that – starkers, apart from the shoes and stockings. Good fucking job no-one was looking in through the front window, let alone that old biddy-bitch next door. Would've finished her old heart off.

For a second, I thought it was going to do the same to Harry Comb, when he saw me coming down the stairs. Fucking hell, he looked like he was seeing the zombies he'd heard before. Thought for a moment I must look shit or something, and checked my nose for dangling bogies. But no – he just hadn't seen anything like that, I guess, in the longest of long fucking times. Poor fucker. His balls must've been bursting.

So I get downstairs, all seductive and wiggly-like, and then sit on the opposite end of the sofa to him. I know how to fucking play them after all these years. I still got it. Harry, though, he didn't take the cue, so I patted the empty space next to me on the sofa. Almost bent double, he got up and came and sat next to me. He was having a good stare, I can tell you. "Go on," I said, "you can touch if you like."

Ever-so-slowly, like I was going to shatter or something, he reached forward with his finger to touch the top of my right boob. Christ H. God, it was so fucking slow it must've made me tense, cos when his finger finally got there, I almost jumped, like I was being wasp-stung – as if, I don't know how to put it, y'know, he hadn't touched anyone for so long that there was all this . . . horror or something bottled up inside him. God, now I'm talking fucking weird spiritual shit like those people who camp outside in the Close. Still, it was weird. After years of . . . practice, you don't expect to flinch at anything – but this time I did, just a bit, and it made him take his finger away as well.

He stared at the carpet for a while – I'd obviously put him right off, and he wasn't going to do anything else on his own. So I took his finger again, and popped it in my mouth, and moved it back and forth – like you do. Well, you probably don't, but you know what I mean. Finger-fucking always gets them going, and I didn't feel that wasp-sting shit this time.

I took his finger out – I kinda realised by this time that I was going to have to do all the frigging work – and kissed him smack on the lips. Don't always do that, but thought he deserved it. He grabbed one of my boobs while we were snogging, and copped a good grope.

Then, with my eyes closed, and my tongue in his mouth, I suddenly tasted salt. My first thought, y' know, was "God, that's not, like, possible yet." I was dead confused. So I opened my eyes to see what the fuck was going on, and realised he was crying everywhere, all over our two faces. Fucking hell, them tears were flowing out of his eyes not like separate, but all together, making everything wet. Could even feel them dripping off my chin onto my boobs.

I prised our lips apart – he was gasping for breath, but didn't seem to want to stop – and looked at the poor sod full in the face. He was really sob-sobbing, though he wasn't making any noise at all.

He sat back on the sofa, with his head leant on the wall, his eyes screwed shut, and I found myself holding his hand. Holding his hand, for fuck's sake. Never known anything like it. He was muttering something, over and over, so I tried to hear what it was. I think it was something like: "It's too late." At first, you know what I'm like, I thought he meant it was too late as in, y' know, too fucking late – as in . . . the horse had already bolted the stable. But now . . . now I'm not sure that is what he meant. People are so fucking obscure sometimes, don't you think?

He was the most obscure of the lot, was our Harry. Never known anyone like him. Because, you know what? We just sat there. We just fucking sat there, holding hands. We just sat there, for an hour, two hours, whatever. The newspaper bastards can say what they like about all-night romping sessions. I don't give a shit. Cos I know the reality – and the only other person who knows has buggered off, probably never to be laid eyes on again. Everyone else but him can go and fuck themselves for all I care. They don't know, and make shit up all the time. Fucking fuckers. Fucking fucking fuckers. God, it'd make me so fucking angry if I gave a fucking shit.

Right, deep breaths. Better take some deep fucking deep breaths and calm myself down. Don't want to piss off the twins upstairs, so they start howl-howling again. Deep breath. Deep fucking breath. I'm calm now, but I tell you, I still don't give a shit about what people say. It's okay. Deep breath.

I tell you, all I give a shit about is what's in my head, which is what really happened. I wouldn't have minded if we'd really had those 'lusty romps' all over the shop, that whole 'girlfriend experience' shit. God, I've done it enough times. I wouldn't have cared. Honest. But we didn't. We just sat there for an hour, maybe two hours, him fully dressed with my lippy on his mouth, me starkers apart from the stockings and stilettos, both of us holding hands, breathing in and out, in and out, like now, but more relaxed . . . And I kinda guessed he hadn't relaxed like that for a long while, him looking at his eyelids, me looking at him looking at his eyelids, wondering what he was seeing in there, glad, so glad I didn't know. And I was thinking too that he wasn't bad looking in profile, his nose maybe needed a bit of straightening, his nose hairs needed plucking, his cheekbones a bit hollow for a bloke – but, all things considered, he wasn't awful looking, and he wasn't a bad sort of bloke either, just fucked by the world, totally fucked, like so many of us are . . .

Finally, he opened his eyes, kinda squeezed my hand, kissed me on the cheek, and got up to leave. For a second, I thought he was going to offer me some notes – and, I tell you, the weird thing was that I didn't want him to. Fucking weird, cos I need all the money I can get with the twins. So I was actually kinda glad when he looked straight at me for a last time – actually fixed me in me eyes, like blokes hardly ever do – said something that sounded important that I didn't catch, then turned and left, letting himself out the front door.

Like I say, I was actually glad he didn't offer me any cash. How weird is that? I'll get struck off, laughed out of my own fucking profession if I carry that on. Not that I'm, like, in that profession any longer, understand. But no doubt if you let this shit out, I'll get loads of weirdos coming round, knocking on my door for a freebie. Soon sort those bastards out.

But I will tell you one other thing, for what it's worth. If it was Harry Comb who knocked on my front door again, if Harry Comb got himself un-lost and came round here, looking for a repeat performance, or something more – whatever the fucking neighbours think of me, or that Mrs. Bitch-Wife of his, or anyone else for that matter – I'd not turn him away. I'd not kick him out of bed.

VAR IV

Brahms and Liszt

"YOUR ENGLISH TEACHER – what's her name, Mrs. Kitsch or Kill or Kinky or something, the one who's deputy as well – she rang me up today, when I was busy," muttered Harry, not looking as if he could ever be busy, not turning his head away from the blank television screen, and not looking at Serena, to whom the muttering was addressed. Slowly, ever-so-slowly, he lifted a tiny piece of stilton and cracker from the plate on his arm-rest, and took a small bite.

"Oh?" asked Serena, dangling her school rucksack above the floor.

"Oh indeed," said Harry. "She said you absconded from her A-Level lesson earlier."

"Oh," said Serena, still dangling her school rucksack, not letting it touch the floor.

"Oh indeed," muttered Harry again. "Apparently, you walked out of her lesson during Dickens. You could at least have chosen Steinbeck – then I'd have understood." He took another corner-bite of his cracker, and shook the crumbs away from him. "Okay, to be honest, I haven't actually read much of either Dickens or Steinbeck; but given the number of invoices featuring them that I've processed over the years, I might as well have read the complete works. And Dickens's invoices were of a better quality than Steinbeck's, I can tell you. You'd only ever get a couple of orders with that American bastard, whereas Dickens'd go to entire university courses."

"Dad?"

"Yes, darling?"

"What're you going on about?"

"I'm going on about your woeful rudeness to Dickens, walking out on him like that. Show some respect to the old guy. Some appreciation. I don't care about Mrs. Kissy or whatever-her-name-is – you can be as rude to her as you like. But don't mess with Dickens."

Serena sighed and let her dangling rucksack fall to the floor. "I wasn't messing with Dickens. I . . . I just . . . I was . . ."

How could she tell her father what had happened? He wouldn't listen, and even if, for once, he did, it would never be for long enough to explain what had happened in English Lit that morning. It wouldn't be long enough for her to explain that she wasn't "messing with Dickens," or being "rude" to him. Whatever her father thought, she wasn't unappreciative of "the old guy." Quite the contrary: she had run out of the lesson because, in a sense, she appreciated the Dickens novel they were studying too much.

She hadn't flinched a week before when Mrs. King had asked them all to read a page of *Dombey and Son* each, round the class, from a chapter called 'What the Waves Were Always Saying' – and her turn had fallen, out of simple bad luck, on the page in which Paul Dombey Jnr. died in his sister's arms: 'The golden ripple on the wall came back again, and nothing else stirred in the room. The old, old fashion!'

Nothing had stirred in the classroom, whilst Serena had

read aloud this passage about a younger sibling dying. Nothing and no-one stirred in the classroom, whilst Serena had read slowly, steadily, giving each word its due weight, not looking up, not looking at Mrs. King – merely reciting the text, drained of emotion, as if it were one of her father's invoices to be processed. She reached the end, and still nothing and no-one stirred in the classroom – until Mrs. King had clapped her hands together and said: "Right. Okay, class. Moving on . . ."

After moving on, no-one had said anything to Serena about Paul Dombey Jnr., and she hadn't wanted anyone to say anything. It was fine, honestly, absolutely fine.

Then, a week later, the class had come to a passage in the novel which – to Serena's own surprise – wasn't absolutely fine, even though ostensibly it had little to do with the death of Paul Dombey Jnr., or anyone else's siblings for that matter:

> *Florence lived alone in the great dreary house, and day succeeded day, and still she lived alone; and the blank walls looked down upon her with a vacant stare, as if they had a Gorgon-like mind to stare her youth and beauty into stone.*
>
> *No magic dwelling-place in magic story, shut up in the heart of a thick wood, was ever more solitary and deserted to the fancy, than was her father's mansion in its grim reality, as it stood lowering on the street: always by night, when lights were shining from neighbouring windows, a blot upon its scanty brightness; always by day, a frown upon its never-smiling face . . .*
>
> *The spell upon it was more wasting than the spell that used to set enchanted houses sleeping once upon a time, but left their waking freshness unimpaired.*
>
> *The passive desolation of disuse was everywhere silently manifest about it. Within doors, curtains, droop-*

> *ing heavily, lost their old folds and shapes, and hung like cumbrous palls. Hecatombs of furniture, still piled and covered up, shrunk like imprisoned and forgotten men, and changed insensibly. Mirrors were dim as with the breath of years. Patterns of carpets faded and became perplexed and faint, like the memory of those years' trifling incidents. Boards, starting at unwonted footsteps, creaked and shook. Keys rusted in the locks of doors. Damp started on the walls, and as the stains came out, the pictures seemed to go in and secrete themselves. Mildew and mould began to lurk in closets. Fungus trees grew in corners of the cellars. Dust accumulated, nobody knew whence nor how; spiders, moths, and grubs were heard of every day. . .*
>
> *There was the great staircase, where the lord of the place so rarely set his foot, and by which his little child had gone up to Heaven. There were other staircases and passages where no-one went for weeks together; there were two closed rooms associated with dead members of the family, and with whispered recollections of them; and to all the house but Florence, there was a gentle figure moving through the solitude and gloom, that gave to every lifeless thing a touch of present human interest and wonder.*
>
> *For Florence lived alone in the deserted house, and day succeeded day, and still she lived alone, and the cold walls looked down upon her with a vacant stare, as if they had a Gorgon-like mind to stare her youth and beauty into stone . . .*

There was nothing in this description of Florence Dombey and her deserted house which should have upset Serena Comb. Nothing at all. No-one expected any reaction from her. She'd been determinedly poker-faced during the death of Paul Dombey Jr.; and this new passage was relatively benign – or so thought Mrs. King and the rest of the class. There were no death scenes, no 'old-fashioned' siblings, no illnesses here. Nothing at all.

Yet despite the apparent nothingness of the passage, when it came to Serena's turn to read from it in class, she stood up, pushed her chair under the desk, put her pencil case and folder into her rucksack, pulled the string to tighten the rucksack, slung it over her shoulder – and walked out of the room.

During her next free period, Mrs. King rang Serena's father: "I don't know why she walked out, Mr. Comb. Sometimes, Mr. Comb, I feel I don't understand your daughter. She has read out far more . . . disturbing passages before to the class, far more . . . shall we say, apposite passages. And yet, she deliberately walked out of my class today during something which should not have affected her at all. I can't help thinking, Mr. Comb, that there's a determined contrariness going on here, a conscious wilfulness, about your daughter's behaviour. I understand the grief that she . . . you must all be going through." She hesitated over the word "but," but could think of no other alternative: "But, Mr. Comb, I have to maintain discipline, grief or no grief, if only for the sake of all the students' grades."

"What do you want me to do about it?" asked Harry, yawning.

Mrs. King didn't know how to answer, and floundered for a few seconds. "Look, Mr. Comb, perhaps you could speak to your daughter? Find out how she feels? Find out her reasons for walking out of my lesson? I hear from the other students that she's become rather, shall we say, withdrawn of late. Again, understandable in the circumstances of . . . well, you know in what circumstances, Mr. Comb – circumstances which can only have been compounded by that ghastly incident with the poison-pen letter she received, only a couple of weeks after . . ."

"I don't want to talk about that," said Harry.

"I'm sure you don't, Mr. Comb, and there's no need. But about other things – about the more general circumstances, all I'm saying is that it might be a good idea to talk to your daughter. I'm a firm believer, Mr. Comb, in communication. It's what's enabled me to become deputy here – listening and talking, with students, staff and parents alike."

"I'm not asking you for your CV," said Harry.

Again, Mrs. King hesitated, unsure how to proceed. Finally, she decided to draw the conversation to a close: "Look, Mr. Comb. We all appreciate how difficult it must be for Serena, for you all, and how tough things must seem" – again she found the word "but" unavoidable, even though it seemed so inappropriate in the circumstances – "but . . ."

"But what? But what? But what?" barked Harry over and over, suddenly loud. Before, he had been muffled, distracted, but now Mrs. King had his full attention, and he was barking straight into the receiver: "But what? But what, Mrs. King?"

"But . . ."

"But what? But life carries on? But we need to get over it? But we need to think about Serena's future? Of her A-Levels and university and sodding career? Of what she's going to do with her life? Of what we're all going to do with our crappy lives? Of tomorrow and tomorrow and tomorrow? God, there's some English Literature for you, Mrs. Kint, Kit, Kunt, Kipper, whoever-you-are: tomorrow and tomorrow and tomorrow and tomorrow. There you are: that's English Literature for you. All of it. Tomorrow and tomorrow and tomorrow and on and on and on and tomorrow and on and on and tomorrow and tomorrow and . . ."

And, during this tirade, Mrs. King somehow felt sucked down into the receiver, into a whirlpool of tomorrows – a whirlpool which would spin her round and round forever, if she didn't extract herself from it right now. So she said: "Goodbye, Mr. Comb," and hung up. Disconcerted afterwards, she stared at the phone, wondering if she picked it up again, whether the tomorrows would still be whirling inside it. "God," she muttered to another teacher, who was frowning questioningly from across the room. "God help that family. God help Serena."

But no-one was even talking to Serena, let alone helping her. Behind a curtain of purply-black hair, she slouched into Sixth-Form College in the mornings, and stood alone in the corner of the Common Room, as if the blank walls had a Gorgon-like mind to stare her into stone.

Once the day's lessons started, Serena spoke only when spoken to, otherwise remaining stone-silent. Fellow students felt awkward round her and her silence. Most of them hadn't experienced anything resembling the death of a loved one, let alone a younger sister; so, after an initial "I was sorry to hear about your sister Melissa," they found it uncomfortable talking to her. And conversely, she seemed to find it uncomfortable talking to them. Old friends – even her best friend Sara Acker – found it increasingly difficult to get more than a few words out of her. They tried chatting to her about school work, boyfriends, alcohol, sex, but her moroseness either turned their conversations to stone, or, what was worse, made them feel like they were talking about Melissa, even when they (absolutely, definitely) weren't. The unspoken subject wove itself in inaudible counterpoint – like an enigma – around every other conversation topic:

"Ooh, look," Sara said, in their free period before the

English Lit lesson in question, "look over there," pointing out of the Common Room window, "it's that Jack – the bloke who's been picking up Terri every night in his 'Beemer,' as she keeps telling us, over and over a-bloody-gain."

"Oh," said Serena.

"He must be, like, fucking fifty-hundred years older than her. Look at him, Seri, opening the door for her. Suave bastard."

"Yeah, he does look a bit full of himself. Look at all that gold and shit on his hands."

Pleased she'd elicited a response from her taciturn friend, Sara pursued the topic: "And you know what they say about Terri's Mr. All-Gold, don't you? That he likes his A-Levels?"

"Y'what? He's a bit old to still be doing A-Levels, isn't he?"

"No, not A-Levels: *A-Levels* – y'know. Oh, for fuck's sake, Seri, get with it. A-Levels: *anal*. He likes it anal. Up the bum. Anal. Analanalanalanal."

Serena coughed into her drink, almost laughed: "Ugh, Sara, you're so gross. Stop it."

Despite Serena's protests, Sara carried on, because she was enjoying her friend's almost-laughter – an almost-laughter which she hadn't heard in a long while: "Anal, up Terri's bum, dirty bastard. Up the bum. Bet it hurts. Bet Terri'll be in tomorrow, all bow-legged, like."

"Gross. You're sick, Sara. You need a doctor."

"And that's why you love me. Up the bum! Up Terri's bum!" She mimicked a girl's and man's voice in turn: "'Oh no, Jack, please don't, not there,' 'It's got to be up there, Terri. I won't have it any other way. Not that I'm gay or anything, you understand,' 'Please please please,' 'It's going in, Terri, three-two-one-blast off,' 'Please, Jack, oh oh oh. Oh dear, Jack, I think . . . I think I'm going to . . . I think I'm going to do a poo.'"

"Ah, Sara, leave it out. Disgusting. You're as bad as them."

"I'm not. He should be arrested, the dirty git. He's, like,

almost a kiddy fiddler, a man that age messing round with us college-girlies. We're only just legal. You never know, p'raps he *is* a kiddy fiddler, but is, like, too scared to go younger – so snatches us just across the border. What a creep. Terri should know better."

"S'pose she should."

There was a pause, as Sara reached for something else to say, not wanting to lose the conversational momentum, not wanting Serena's almost-laughter to slip away: "She definitely should, dozy bitch. God, she should have her head unscrewed and then screwed on the right way again, hanging out with a wanker like that."

"Yeah."

Worried she was losing Serena and her almost-laughter, Sara kept trying harder: "Look at her – flouncing her hair extensions in his convertible. She thinks it's LA, and he's bloody-what's-his-name-Clooney. He's about as Clooney as my arse."

Now Serena was almost laughing again, the sound only muffled by a mouthful of crisps: "Clooney-arse. That's you, that is: Clooney-arse."

"Okay, that's me, Clooney-arse. But at least I'm not a stupid-sore-arse like her. God, Terri, take a look at him. He's got more wrinkles than a testicle. Mr. Testicle Head, that's what we should call him."

"Yeah."

On a roll, Sara seemed to be building up to a grand peroration: "Yeah, we'll call him that tomorrow when Terri swans up to us and tells us about his Beemer and his gold chains and frigid wife and backseat blow-jobs. We'll call him Mr. Testicle Head, and she won't know what's going on. She'll be as in the dark as she always is, stupid bitch. She's, like, so stupid, she wouldn't be able to tell a testicle from a face. She's so stupid, she shouldn't be allowed to live. There are some people, God, they're too thick to be allowed to grow up to be ad . . ."

Serena stared down into her empty crisp packet: "Yeah."

"Oh, I didn't mean . . ."

"No."

"I didn't mean, God, of course not. Of course I didn't mean . . . it was a joke . . . I didn't mean your sis . . . I mean, it goes, like, without saying, she wasn't stupid, anyone could see that – she was a genius, well, very clever, anyway, I mean, all that listening to your piano-ing, and the way she talked whenever I came round. You know I . . . I'm sorry, my Seri. I didn't mean . . ."

"It's fine. Nothing. It's fine."

. . . and Serena stood up, put the empty crisp packet in the bin, pulled her cardigan sleeves down, over her wrists – and then slouched off towards her English lesson, the curtain of purply-black hair falling back across her eyes.

In the English lesson, she read about Florence Dombey being turned to stone by an unvisited house, a house which seemed to recede from the rest of the street, hidden from everyone, its grief-stricken occupants isolated from the world around them and from one another . . .

. . . and suddenly, the classroom felt cold as stone, and she thought everyone else had frozen, their voices seeming unreal, echoey, their expressions blank, like carpet patterns which had faded, and she thought she could see her breath in front of her face, whilst no-one else was breathing . . .

. . . so she got out of the chair, packed her things in the rucksack, and left, to try and find a warmer place.

She didn't find that warmer place in her living room, a few hours later, as her father told her off for walking out on her English lesson: "Course you were messing Dickens about when you walked out on him. God, I feel sorry for Dickens, having to put up with ungrateful school girls all the time, chewing gum at him, saying how boring-yawn-yawn he is, slagging him off behind his dead back, flouncing out on him. I know how crappy all that feels from my own school days, poor sod. But he has to put up with it *ad infinitum*, now he's dead. An after-life of ungrateful school girls, how shit is that."

"Dad, you're talking rubbish," said Serena, knowing that she would never be able to find a slot in this conversation for her to explain what had happened – what had really happened – that morning. Instead, she stayed quiet and looked at the walls, the floor, her rucksack, anywhere but at him. With a fingernail, she scraped at an old sticker, which was peeling off the right shoulder strap of her rucksack – a sticker which read 'Brahms and Liszt forever,' with a cartoon of a German beer beneath. She'd managed to get her fingernail under one corner of the sticker, and was now scratching it off, bit by bit. "Rubbish," she said again.

"No, it's everyone else who's talking rubbish, and I've had enough of it for a whole bloody lifetime. You're talking rubbish, your teacher's talking rubbish, your stepmother's talking rubbish, your mother spouts rubbish down the phone, everyone on this shitty Close talks rubbish about hearing music they know sod all about – it's a huge landfill of rubbish, crap, nonsense. And all of it entirely unrecyclable. It'd be best for all of us to stay quiet, I think. Might save the planet from death-by-noise-landfill. Stay quiet. Stay quiet. Stay . . ."

"You're not doing that now," Serena pointed out, looking down at her fingernail. 'Brahms and Liszt forever' had come off the rucksack, in tiny, sticky rolls, which she was trying to flick off her fingernail onto the carpet; but they were clinging to her, stuck to this fingernail, then that, then back again.

"Stop making that nasty clicky noise with your fingers, whatever you're doing. You're giving me a headache."

"Don't be stupid, Dad. I'm not making any noise."

"You are – you're making too much noise in every way."

"So are you, Dad. That's what I said. You're making loads of noise too."

"No, I'm not. I'm telling you off, as a father should," he yawned, "I suppose. Anyway, I want to stop now. I'm busy, and I've had enough of noisy rubbish for one day. So let's wrap this up, shall we? To recap: don't walk out on Dickens again – stay and work like a good school girl should. Like a good daughter."

She finally ejected the remains of 'Brahms and Liszt forever' from her fingernails, and picked up the rucksack, slinging it over her shoulder: "Like a good daughter," she repeated, "like a good daughter? Doesn't a good daughter do what a good father does? Isn't that what good daughters do? They learn, like, by example. So I'm a good daughter, Dad. I've learnt by your example, walking out on shit like you walked out on your job. So actually, *Dad*, I am a good daughter, aren't I, following in your footsteps?"

She glared down at him, and he didn't say anything, didn't answer. Instead, he stared straight ahead, at a blank TV screen. For a few seconds, there was a silence between them – a silence which could have ended with his turning round, breaking down, sobbing with her; a silence which could have ended in his quietly taking her hand; a silence which could at least have ended with mutual rage.

But it turned out to be a silence which ended with his reaching – slowly, deliberately – for a cracker on the plate next to him, cutting off a little piece of stilton, and placing it in the centre of the cracker. By the time cracker and cheese reached his mouth – slowly, ever-so-slowly – the door of the living room had slammed shut, and Serena had gone, taking all other possible endings of that silence with her.

VAR V

Piano Sonata in B-Flat Major, D.960

VISITING HIS GRANDMOTHER and old neighbours, the Comb family, that Autumn, sitting with Serena in the living room of Number 4, Spark Close, flicking idly through a magazine or musical score, Simon Adler-Reeves gradually became aware of the regular appearance and disappearance of a figure at the other end of the room.

At first, Simon didn't see and certainly didn't hear this figure; at first, whenever the figure appeared, he only registered the change in the room's atmosphere with a shiver, or the hairs on the back of his neck prickling up.

Only gradually, over time, did this change come to disturb his consciousness.

Only gradually, over time, did his consciousness register the spectral presence, in the corner of his vision, five yards to his left . . . shuffling through the door from the hallway . . . footfalls muffled by carpet . . . four footfalls over to the piano . . . trying the piano fallboard . . . finding it secure . . . then quietly,

quietly lifting the ceramic lid of a little Jasperware pot on top of the piano . . . checking the piano key was still in there . . . replacing the Jasperware lid, slowly, slowly, as if sealing up a miniature tomb . . . then retreating, footfalls muffled, back to the doorway . . . creaking open the door . . . and out of sight again . . .

. . . And then, ten minutes later, the same apparition, the same ceremony of shuffles, muffled footfalls, piano fallboards, Jasperware pots, key-checkings, retreating footfalls, creaking doors, disappearances –

– as Serena's noiseless father checked the fallboard of the piano and the whereabouts of the piano key, for the hundredth, perhaps thousandth time.

As Simon started noticing Harry's obsessive checking of piano fallboard and key, he'd glance at Serena. She'd be sitting on the floor in front of the coffee table, her homework spread everywhere, or slumped in an armchair, a few inches from the television, its flickering colours seeming to reach out of the screen towards her, pulling her in. Her face would be blank, apart from the reflected colours, or, if she were engrossed in homework, set in a deep frown, as she concentrated on a complex Physics equation. She'd never say anything whilst her father was gliding in and out of the room. If she were watching the television, she'd lift the remote and turn the volume up on *Neighbours*, or whatever else she was watching; if she'd been talking beforehand, she'd stop even if she were mid-sentence, go still, and only continue when she heard the door creak (ever-so-quietly) behind her father, and he was gone.

Simon also found himself going quiet whenever Serena's father came into the room, leaving spaces for footfalls in the middle of his sentences. In those Limbo-moments, when the door swung open and they felt the draught of Harry's presence, Serena and Simon seemed turned to ice, and only the television carried on regardless, preaching at icicles.

And then Harry would leave, and the two of them would thaw, and Simon would look at Serena, and not dare to ask her about it, not dare to broach the subject. Serena and her occasional visitor never talked about anything except *Neighbours*, what they were going to do over Christmas or on New Year's Eve, the particular Physics equation she was trying to solve, the particular fugue she was trying to analyse, whether or not Simon was ever going to complete his Ph.D. As old neighbours and then family friends, they had their long-accustomed conversational topics, and didn't stray from them; and maybe Serena was happy with it that way. They never talked about her father's obsessive checking of the piano fallboard and the key; and they certainly never talked about how she'd hear Harry and his footfalls on the stairs even at night, at two, three, four in the dark, padding somnambulantly downwards. Perhaps Harry thought he could hear the piano murmuring from his bed, played by echoes, only to find – on creeping downstairs and opening the living-room door – the silhouetted monolith as silent as a tombstone.

Nor did Serena and her old friend talk about why – if Harry were now so determined that the piano should remain silent, that no-one should play it – he kept the key in a ceramic pot on top of the piano in full sight; why, that is, he didn't just pocket the key and keep it hidden. They didn't need to talk about this, because they both tacitly understood that what he was doing was tempting her, testing her, more or less saying to her: "You know I don't want you touching the piano, you know it is too painful for me to hear it, you know it reminds me of Melissa – so here, Serena, is the key, here is the piano, take it, play it, if you're insensitive enough, selfish enough, uncaring enough to disregard my wishes and trample on my terrible grief."

Similarly, in tiny, apparently insignificant ways, Serena's stepmother Lizzie was also continually testing Serena, trying to tempt her into anger – so she would have an excuse to bite back. Lizzie would use full-fat, instead of semi-skimmed milk, in Serena's tea, and then apologise: "Sorry, I wasn't thinking" – but nor had she been thinking the previous time, or the time before that. Nor had she been thinking, she claimed, when, for the fourth time in a month, she'd piled up all of Serena's magazines and music scores on her bedroom windowsill, blocking out the light. Nor had she been thinking when she repeatedly bought Serena the wrong nail varnish from Boots: ". . . but it's time you grew out of that grungey-gothy-purply rubbish. You need to learn to make more of yourself. You're hardly going to get a boyfriend worth having with nails that look like you've trapped them in a door, are you? And anyway, darling, it doesn't fit with the classical pianist image you like to put about – which, by the way, *is* a pretty good image for boyfriend-trapping. But it's an image let down, darling, by your nails – all black and jaggedy from biting. God, Seri, imagine your nails in close-up on one of those boring concert programmes your dad pretends to watch on BBC2. Your nails'd be as black as the – what-d'you-call-them? – 'ebony' piano keys."

"I don't want my nails or anything else on BBC 2."

"Why ever not?"

"Because I'm not that good at the piano. I'm not that standard."

"Don't put yourself down, darling," said Lizzie, brushing invisible dandruff from Serena's collar. "It's a bad habit, and won't make you any friends of the boy or girl variety." She turned her around, and put her fingers in the corners of Serena's mouth. "Smile, darling," she said, "smile and show off those nice ivory teeth – at least they counteract the black a bit."

guessing more. Rosa hadn't seen or spoken to Alexa in a long time, but Alexa had left her business number with her one-time neighbour, asking her to keep an eye on Serena whilst she was away.

Alexa had left Spark Close and Harry Comb in 1990, when Serena was eight years old. It was meant to be a temporary separation – Alexa had landed a job in a record company in Ottawa, Canada, for a year, which she had accepted to give Harry space to "sort himself out." But almost as soon as she'd got there, she'd been elevated to Chief Accountant, and, as if in celebration, had filed for divorce. A one-year job turned into a two-year contract, which turned into a permanent one. She sent money home for Serena and to pay for the mortgage – each year, more and more money – and she occasionally came back to the UK to visit. Never once did the suggestion of Serena leaving Stoke for Ottawa come up – or, at least, not within Serena's hearing.

Nor was it within Serena's hearing that, one day in November 1999, Rosa Adler phoned Alexa in Canada to talk to her about her daughter: "I know everyone like that Miss Kirsten next door thinks I'm, how d' you say, an old 'meddler,'" said Rosa, "but I wanted to tell you about Miss Serena, and all that has happened on the Close."

"God help her," said Serena's real mother, after Rosa had held forth for five minutes straight about the Spark Close Phenomenon, her ex-husband's obsessions, everyone's grief over Melissa. "I heard about the 'Phenomenon' over here," said Alexa, "and about the Melissa girl. Terrible shame." She paused for a moment, as if out of respect for the dead girl; then she added: "Oh, just a moment, I've got a call on the other line."

Please hold, an electronic woman said. There was some tinny-beeping Bach, electronic 'Sheep Safely Grazing,' whilst Rosa held for her.

Please hold.

"Hi there, sorry about that. What were we talking about?"

"Miss Serena, and other things."

"Ah yes, of course. Well, it all sounds terrible."

"It is not good. We should all be looking after the girl, I think."

"Poor Serena," Alexa said. "I mean, it can't make it any easier for her, stuck in that house with misery-guts Harry and that vacuous tart of a Stepford wife." She paused. "Sorry to talk like that to you, but you're an astute woman. You know what I mean."

Rosa didn't respond, so there was silence for a moment.

"Look," Alexa said, brusque and business-like again, "I tell you what I can do. I'll try and give Serena a call in the next couple of days, when I have a second. Or an email. And, if you don't mind relaying a message, you can tell her from me that I'll see her soon, probably very early 2000. I've got to come over to the UK then for a client, so I'll be able to spend some proper time with her. It's all in my diary. I'll get Serena down to London, and we can hit Oxford Street together. Yes, that's a plan . . . Oh, wait a minute, sorry, I've got a call on the other line."

Please hold. There was more beeping-bleeping Bach and electric sheep for three or four minutes.

Please hold.

Please hold.

Then the phone went dead.

That night, Rosa rang her grandson, Simon Adler-Reeves, to ask if he'd relay the message to Serena from her mother. She didn't want to do it – didn't want to be seen as a "meddling old woman" – and, anyway, Simon was closer to Serena, had better English, and so on. Simon grumbled about the errand ("I'm busy on my Ph.D"), but did what he was asked, and rang Serena. Awkwardly, he started telling her that his grandmother had spoken to her mother; that her mother would phone her soon from Canada for a chat; and that she was coming over to go shopping with Serena sometime in the New Year.

Halfway through the message, though, Simon realised he was talking to silence – and then the phone went dead. He called back, and the phone rang and rang and no-one answered. A few minutes later, he tried again, and eventually Harry Comb answered: "Hello."

"Hello, Harry. I was just talking to . . ."

"I thought it was you," said Harry. "Serena's flounced off upstairs. Since last night she doesn't seem to want to talk to you or me or anyone."

"Oh. What happened last n . . .?"

"Oh indeed. Goodbye." *Click*.

That was the last time Simon spoke to Harry or Serena for over a month; and it was seven months before Serena apologised, and explained why she'd been upset that night – why she'd hung up on him. For seven months, Simon wondered what he'd done. It turned out he hadn't done anything: it was the piano which was at fault.

For many months after Melissa's funeral, Serena hadn't gone against her father's unspoken wishes by playing the piano. Only in July, during the visit of a certain Prof. Sollertinsky – who had been investigating the Spark Close Phenomenon – had she dared, under the Professor's instructions, to do so. Otherwise, she hadn't dared take the key out of the Jasperware pot on top of the piano, hadn't dared unlock the piano fallboard, hadn't dared rest her fingers on the cold keys.

Sometimes, when her father was upstairs, or out at the shop, she'd sit on the piano stool, laying her fingers on the wooden fallboard, imagining the sounds locked underneath. She'd move her fingers, and make chords in her head. But whatever chord she chose – C major, C minor, E-flat minor 7 – she could never find anything but a dying away after it, never find any chord progression which sounded right. Musical lines seemed to disintegrate under her fingers, each imaginary chord drifting away from all the others. Worst of all was F minor, which had once been Melissa's favourite chord, for no reason she could adequately explain: "I like it the bestest," she used to say, "because it actually really sounds kind of like me, all tired and ill in a friendly-sad sort of way." Now, though, F minor merely sounded like some unresolvable discord, a cadence into nothingness. Serena's fingers found it impossible to imagine musical sense – whether in F minor, or any other key – emerging from that nothingness ever again . . .

. . . Until one November night, the night before Simon called her to relay her mother's message, when everyone else had gone to bed, and Serena had found herself sitting in front of the locked piano, holding a worn book of Schubert's Sonatas. It had fallen open on a movement she used to play – just about – to her younger sister: the 'Andante sostenuto' from Schubert's final not-in-F-minor-but-B-flat-major Sonata. The movement was in a key a reassuringly long way away from F minor; so Serena propped the book up on the music rack, smoothed the pages down, and remembered the music with her eyes. She knew she wasn't a particularly good pianist, she knew she wasn't her father, let alone a full-blown virtuoso, but this music had once made her feel like she was.

Her fingers too started remembering the music, sketching out the first C-sharp minor chord – low C-sharp in the left hand, E-natural and G-sharp in the right hand – on the closed fallboard. Of course, the chord sounded of nothing but dead wood, and so did the next and the next; so Serena stopped, frustrated, and reached to take the book off the rack, put Schubert away for another day, another lifetime.

But instead she found herself reaching higher, standing up, opening the lid of the Jasperware pot on top of the piano, taking out the key, sitting back down again, and unlocking the fallboard – quietly, ever-so-quietly, as if she were unlocking the lid of a coffin. *Click*.

And there were the keys, some chipped, some discoloured, on which she now perched her fingers: low C-sharp in the left, E-natural, and G-sharp, depressing the notes with the softest touch possible, first silent, then *pianississimo*. She played the next few chords at the same volume, ever-so-quietly, barely disturbing the sleeping strings, let alone anything or anyone outside the piano casing.

The piece didn't sound right at first: the strings had slipped slightly out of tune from disuse, and the left-hand rhythm – staccato quaver, dotted semi-quaver rest, demi-semi-quaver, quaver, crotchet rest – a rhythm which Serena had found difficult at the best of times – was *adagissimo*, limping, enervated, like a sick child.

Gradually, though, the sick child was revitalised under Serena's fingertips, and the rhythm coalesced into a steady beat. As no-one and nothing in the house seemed to stir, as no-one and nothing seemed to notice her playing, she grew in confidence, allowing her fingers a more definite pressure, moving from indecision to resonance, from *pianissimo* immobility to *mezzo piano* threnody . . .

. . . and from there to the A major middle section, which stretched her technique, her unpractised fingers, stiff knuckles, clicking wrists, with all those repeated pedal notes on A, all those semiquaver and triplet runs and arpeggios, which seemed to play her, rather than the other way round, forcing her fingers into a *mezzo forte* they had never intended . . .

... until that strange cadence from F major seventh, which fails to return to B-flat major, but instead moves onto a diminished chord, with F natural in the bass ...

... and then the *crescendo*, which always felt like the music had been inoculated with something horrible, building up to A minor, through long phrases, seemingly to *ff*, but in the end to nothing, to a dead end, a black hole, to ...

... the living-room door bursting open, and her father, stamping over to the piano, slamming the fallboard shut, missing her fingers, but only by a fraction of a second, a hemi-demi-semi-quaver, and the whole instrument underneath those fingers, from keyboard to soundboard to frame to hammers to treble strings to bass strings, booming with dissonance ...

... as Serena's father glared down at his daughter for another hemi-demi-semi-quaver, as if to say: "Why wasn't it *you* instead of *her*?" ...

... and then he turned and strode out, leaving the room to the dying echoes of a piano in pain.

VAR VI

Auld Lang Syne

SERENA FIRST RECEIVED the letter – what the journalists liked to call, in their old-fashioned way, her 'poison-pen letter' – on the 20th June 1999, less than a couple of weeks after Melissa's death. The police kept hold of it for a while, saying they wanted to run some forensic and graphological tests on it. The tests proved inconclusive, and they ever-so-kindly returned the letter a few months later, saying they'd finished with it, so Serena could have it back. "These sorts of things are often sent by someone close to home, someone you know well," said PC Fury, "but equally, it might be the work of someone you don't know at all, such as – and this is off the record, of course – some nut-freak from one of the spiritualist groups who keep haunting your Close."

Having covered all possible bases in his list of suspects, PC Fury handed the letter over to Serena.

"So you don't have a clue who sent it?" she asked.

"Sorry," PC Fury shook his head, "unless there's a repeat performance, I don't think we'll be able to find out who did send it. Do you have any idea, miss, who might do this sort of thing?"

No, she didn't have any idea. Or at least not then, not consciously. Only gradually, over the next few months, would it dawn on her, would the knowledge emerge into consciousness.

In the meantime, she folded the letter up, and placed it carefully in the left-hand pocket of her leather jacket – where it would remain for those next few months, often held tightly between her fingers, as if it were a concealed knife. And, indeed, when she'd first received the letter, Serena had cut her forearm once for every red-crayon word on it:

Seri, my dear older sis, I loved you.
Seri, my dear older sis, I am gone.
Seri, my dear older sis, it is your fault.

Notwithstanding the crayon handwriting, which was like Melissa's own, anyone who knew Melissa could tell the letter wasn't in her voice; but then, people's voices probably change when they're dead.

The psychics and spiritualists, of course, had a field day when they heard, via the local press, about Serena's letter from her dead half-sister. Every evening for two weeks afterwards, a huddle of them might be seen on the pavement outside the Combs' house, sitting around a makeshift table, holding hands. At the head of the table, a medium would be rocking backwards and forwards, mumbling and whimpering in a charlatan's child's voice – again, nothing like Melissa's.

While these séances continued on the pavement, the Comb household would be as silent as ever, the front door shut and curtains closed, no-one so much as peeking through to see what was happening outside. Visiting the Combs one night, Simon Adler-Reeves had a vision of Harry lying on the bathroom floor, in foetal position, groaning: "Please let it stop. Please let it stop stop stop." But no: when Simon stepped past the spiritualists, and rang the doorbell of Number 4, Harry answered as normal, nodded, and shuffled back to the sitting room, where he was watching the Proms on BBC 2. He slumped into his customary armchair, side-on to the television, his legs slung over the arm. He didn't seem upset or angered by the medium outside, who was audible from the living room, haplessly mimicking the voice of his dead daughter. His face was impassive, a hard surface reflecting, not absorbing, the medium's voice, the TV's sound and light waves. And it seemed to Simon that the other two residents of the house – Serena and Lizzie – copied Harry's attitude, reflected his reflection, and sulked around, not being angry too.

The problem was that Simon *was* angry about it, as if he had absorbed his old neighbours' displaced emotions. As the weeks and months went by, he found the situation in Spark Close, all the furore surrounding the Phenomenon, more and more intolerable. As an occasional visitor to the Close, he never got used to it, unlike some of the permanent residents – unlike his grandmother, Rosa, who told him to "calm down and concentrate on his studies, because his anger would end up doing no-one any good." He ignored her advice, and instead rang the police, sent letters to the local newspaper, complained to the Council about the disturbance, harassment, noise, even when he was fifty miles away from the scene. But the furore didn't go away – and the spiritualists, pseudo-spiritualists, crypto-spiritualists, New Ageists, Lay Line experts, alien abductionists, Neuro-Linguistic Programmers, Neo-Blakeans, American and Japanese tourists, Evangelical Christian tourists, Catholic tourists looking for a new Lourdes, medical tourists, musical tourists, spiritualist-Blakean tourists, New-Ageist-Blakean-Evangelical-spiritualist-Japanese tourists, all of them kept coming back to Spark Close. It never seemed to end.

And then, at ten o'clock on New Year's Eve, Simon arrived in Spark Close to spend the millennium eve with his grandmother and the Combs – only to find the street filled with a dozen stalls, fifty chanting spiritualists, a hundred New Ageists, a thousand scented candles, and Mr. Raymond Runtill from Number 2 yelling at them all, declaiming scripture at random: "'And my music has been turned to sorrow, and the sound of my pipe into the noise of weeping.'" After each random quotation, Runtill would nod to himself, and give the reference, as if he were being tested on his Biblical knowledge – as if anyone were really listening: "That's Job, that is, chapter 30, verse 31."

Simon parked his car on the kerb at the top of Spark Close, and got out. The moment he did so, someone accosted him, trying to sell what he called "millennium bugs": "They're, like, colourful lucky brooches in the shape of various minibeasts. Honestly, they'll make a great New Year's Day present for your girlfriend, or anyone, to ward off the airplanes that are going to fall from the sky, the nuclear power stations that are going to melt down, the economies that are going to, like, topple at the stroke of midnight. It's coming, man, it's coming. Only these little gold-plated insects can save you." The brooch-seller kept following Simon as he made his way through the crowds, shoving his "gold-plated insects" in his face: "It's coming, man, it's on its way. The end of computers. The end of airplanes. The end of all of us. I mean, just look at what happened to that little girl, Melodious Melinda . . ."

"Melissa," Simon said.

"Y'what?"

"*Melissa*. Her name was *Melissa*. Not Melinda, let alone 'Melodious Melinda,' for God's sake."

"Melissa, Melinda, Melanie, Mélisande, Mellifluous, Meringue, whatever. I tell you what, we've got brooches and badges with her picture on, if you want them instead." He reached forward with a brooch to pin on Simon's lapel, "There you go – you've been 'Melinda-ed,' as I like to say to my customers."

Simon shook him off, and then, glancing ahead, saw Number 4, Spark Close in front of him: the Comb household seemed blacked out, its untwitching curtains drawn, the whole place silent, shut up like a locked piano. That was when the rage finally came out of him. The house seemed so dark and dead to the outside world, and suddenly he was its anti-reflection, mirroring back fury to nothingness, noise to silence: "Fuck off, for fuck's sake, fuck off, you fucking parasite," he said, knocking Brooch Guy out of the way. The latter fell backwards, crashing over one of the stalls, which was manned by 'The Society of Musical Transmigrationists' ('In death, your soul is revealed as music'). The stall was covered with miniature paintings of Melissa's transfigured face looking up in wonder to a bright sky filled with trumpets and harps; on Brooch Guy's impact, the stall collapsed in two, and some of the paintings tumbled to the ground and smashed.

Hearing the commotion from the other side of the Close, Raymond Runtill looked up, and intoned in his most sonorous baritone:

> *And Jesus went into the temple of God, and cast out all them that sold and bought in the temple, and overthrew the tables of the moneychangers, and the seats of them that sold doves, and said unto them, it is written, my house shall be called the house of prayer; but ye have made it a den of thieves.*

But Simon's anger wasn't enough to cleanse Spark Close of all its thieves. Instead, he just stood there, seething, whilst Brooch

Guy looked up at him from the ground with something resembling fear – and thirty or so people around them stopped what they were doing, and stared, waiting for something to happen.

Nothing much did: Simon felt someone touch his elbow, and looked down at his grandmother, who'd come out of her house to meet him – guessing there might be trouble. "I know you really care about *her*," whispered Rosa to her grandson, nodding ambiguously in the direction of Number 4, "but this, it isn't the way to show it, dear." And with another touch on his elbow, Rosa guided Simon away – from the broken stall, from the crowds, and from Brooch Guy – towards the Comb household; and gradually, as they stepped towards it, as if they were passing over its event horizon, Simon felt all of his energy, all of his ability to express the fury he wanted to express, sucked out of him, into its blackness.

The last thing Simon heard, as though from an immense distance, before he knocked on the Combs' door, was Brooch Guy calling after him: "You're a bloody nut, mate. I'll sue your fucking arse off. They're all fucking nuts round here, the whole lot of them."

Simon and his grandmother spent the rest of that night – New Year's Eve of the millennium – shut up in the Comb household, away from Brooch Guy and all the other stallholders and spiritualists in the Close. With Harry, Lizzie and Serena, the five of them sat behind a dead-locked door and closed curtains, pretending the noises, shouts, music from outside weren't happening – doggedly un-hearing them all night.

As soon as the two visitors arrived, Lizzie Comb ushered them with oven gloves into the front room, where she'd laid the dining table in lavish style, as if it were Christmas day for a second time in seven days. Simon and Rosa sat opposite each other at the table – despite Rosa trying to offer to help in the kitchen ("No, please, no, everything's fine, honestly, please, sit down, sit down now, here, *now*"). Lizzie bustled out and then in again, with a bottle of rosé, which she poured for both her guests – again, despite Rosa trying to cover her glass with her hand ("I do not think I should, well, maybe a bit, no, that's too much, never mind, thank you"). Then Lizzie left again, saying, "Won't be too long, just enjoy the wine." So the two of them did, chatting away, blocking out the buying and selling, singing and chanting, laughing and crying in the Close outside.

Ten minutes of drinking and chatting went by before Simon noticed something in the room: in the corner of his eye, four yards to his right, was the back of a head, just visible above the back of an armchair. The back of the head had presumably been there since they arrived, but they hadn't noticed it, and, in return, it hadn't acknowledged their presence either. Simon frowned at his grandmother, and silently tilted his own head in its direction.

Rosa frowned back, and said, loudly: "What's the matter with you, dear? Crick of the neck? That is not a good way to start the millennium, is it, with a bad neck?"

"Grandma," Simon hissed, and nodded in the direction of the back-of-the-head once again.

Rosa's gaze followed her grandson's nod, and she saw the back-of-the-head herself: "Oh . . . I see," she murmured. She thought for a moment, then took an empty glass from the table, and tremblingly poured some of the remaining rosé into it. "This glass, take it to him," she whispered to her grandson.

Simon took the glass of wine, got up, and strode round to the front of the head. The head was Harry's, of course: he'd been sitting in the armchair in front of the TV all along, watching or not watching, listening or not listening, waiting or not waiting for the visitors to notice him. Simon offered him the glass, which he took, without even looking round.

Simon said: "Happy New Year and cheers, Harry."

Harry clinked glasses, and said: "Cheeeeers," elongating the word like a descending scale.

"Are you coming to sit at the table, Harry?" Simon asked.

"Not yet," Harry said. Outside, some druids had started chanting. "Not now."

There was a dead silence, during which Simon seemed unsure what to do or say, so just hovered around Harry, his mouth opening and shutting. A firework went whoosh outside. Simon suddenly felt an acute sense of frustration: outside, in the Close, he'd felt so angry for the Combs, so protective of them; and yet now, inside their house, confronted by Harry's silence, he felt like an unwanted add-on. Despite having been invited – perhaps because the three living Combs couldn't face spending New Year's Eve alone, as a 'family' – despite he and his grandmother being old family friends – perhaps the Combs' only family friends – Simon now felt like an unwelcome guest, in a place which, for many years, had seemed like another home.

For some years, Spark Close had actually been home for Simon: during early childhood, he and his parents had lived with Rosa at Number 12, whilst his parents tried to scrape enough money together for a deposit on a flat; and, ever since, he'd often been back, to visit his grandmother, to hide away during one of his parents' many split-ups, to babysit Serena whilst her father dated Lizzie, and later to visit Serena as a friend . . .

. . . and then . . . and then, one June some years later, to go spider-hunting with a five-year-old Melissa, who was distraught that her pet spiders had been ejected from her Planetarium by her mother – exploring together the overgrown alleyway between Spark Close and Forestside Grove, away from the rows between hysterical mother, sullen father and temperamental elder sister – working on the much quieter plane of the small of the world – collecting in their jam jars a dozen Garden Orb, Common House, and Snake's Back spiders, spiders of which Melissa seemed to have a near-encyclopaedic knowledge, as well as a good working knowledge of beetles, bees, ladybirds, and moths – even recognising a full-grown cockchafer which, when she'd disturbed some loose bricks, had flown in Simon's face and made him jump – but instead of jumping herself, she'd just watched it, as it circled their heads three times, singing a tune to it: "Cockchafer, cockchafer, where have you been?" to the melody of Elgar's 'Nimrod' – until, mesmerised, dizzied by its circling, she'd tripped over and bruised her knee, and she hadn't cried because she hadn't wanted her spider friends to see her upset – and, because she hadn't cried, no-one back at the house had noticed she'd hurt herself either, all of them too engrossed in their own selves and worlds – and so only Simon had wondered why, when he next visited Serena and the Combs a week later, the bruise was still there, dark as a cockchafer's shell . . .

Two and a half years later, Harry's tone was dark as a bruise when he repeated: "Not yet," to Simon's question. "Not now."

Eventually, after a bit more umming and ahhing, Simon retreated from Harry, back to the table. For a minute or two, he and Rosa sat in silence, staring down at the doilies.

Then Lizzie came back in, carrying a steaming turkey on a huge dish. She placed it ceremoniously on the table between Simon and Rosa, as if it were all for them. "We didn't have turkey for Christmas dinner," she said, glowering with narrowed eyes at the back of the head to her right, "because Harry forgot to defrost it. So here it is, just for you."

"It is lovely," said Rosa, "but I do hope it is not all for us. I do hope you are going to have some too. Is Miss Serena here, or is she out? If she is out, it is quite understandable on a night like tonight."

"No, Serena's around somewhere," said Lizzie. "In her bedroom, I think." Oven glove on one hand, carving knife in the other, Lizzie backed up and poked her head out of the door, directing a shout upstairs: "Serena! It's ready! Come down now, dear. *Now.*" She came back into the room and, in the same tone, said to the back of Harry's head: "Now, Harry, darling. *Now.*"

"Not yet," said Harry once again.

"Yet," Lizzie said, between clenched teeth. "*Yet.*" She swivelled on her heels, and left the room.

Slowly, as if he were twenty stone, not eight and a half, Harry prised himself out of his armchair, and shuffled over to the head of the table. Once there, he sat down without saying anything, or looking at anyone.

At the same time, the stairs rattled, as Serena took them two at a time, and burst into the living room. She sailed round the table and kissed Rosa on the cheek, genuinely pleased to see her. "Sorry, my Rosetta," she said, "I was upstairs in my room, talking with my . . . mum." She said the word "mum" with a slight hesitation, glancing at Harry for a micro-second. Harry didn't move.

"Oh," said Rosa, pretending to be unaware of micro-second glances and hesitations, "did your mother ring, then, my darling?"

"No, what I mean is – she sent me an email to say 'Happy New Year,' and I sent her one back."

"Emails, they are like the phone?" asked Rosa, who made a point of not keeping up with technology.

"Grandma, you know full well what emails are," Simon said to her.

Rosa laughed. "No I don't, not really. Come and sit by me, my dear," she said to Serena, patting the chair next to her, "and explain emails to me."

Serena sat down next to Rosa, and took a piece of folded-up paper out of her pocket. "This is an email," she said, unfolding the paper. "I printed it out, because my mum didn't . . . couldn't send me a card. You can look at it, Rosa, if you like." Rosa smoothed it out, and looked over it.

From:	Ms. Alexa Tarry (A.Tarry@beltonandjardincorp.com)
To:	Miss Serena Comb (serenadarkgirl@hurrymail.co.uk)
Re.	Happy New Year to you!
Date:	31.12.99

Hi Serena,

Am in a bit of a rush today – working right up to the end of millennium on Mr. Belton's new contract, and we've also got people in checking for this Millennium Bug thingymajig. Paying them astronomical amounts! So won't have time to phone you tonight. Never mind – will call you in the new millennium. How exciting. I'm sure you're off to lots of parties. Wish I was!

Everything here is busy busy busy as ever. I probably won't be coming to the UK after all for a few months. Just won't have the chance. Sorry about that. But I promise we'll meet up as soon as I can in the 2000s.

The good news is that I'll be able to increase your allowance, anyway, if we get this new contract sorted, so don't worry about your father losing his job. We'll manage!

Best wishes to everyone there, and love to you,

Mum xx

Rosa re-folded the print-out, and handed it back to Serena.

"Very nice, my dear," Rosa said, "and I can see how these emails might be quite useful. Perhaps I'll get some emails for myself. What do you think?" she asked, turning towards Harry. "Do you think these emails are a good thing? Are we being left behind, do you think, by progress, us older ones?"

Harry raised an eyebrow, as if it were the heaviest eyebrow in the world, and turned his gaze towards Serena, not Rosa, "I think I don't want to hear about my ex-wife on New Year's Eve."

Serena didn't react, just concentrated on putting the print-out back into her pocket. Everyone but Harry stared down at the tablecloth, which was embroidered with families of tweeting birds baked in pies.

Outside, fake bird song mingled with honking dolphins and whale song from one of the stall's tape recorders – and, for a moment, Simon imagined that the Close had been populated with Amazonian trees and flooded with an ocean, all at the same time. He wondered if he'd had a bit too much rosé, and pushed his glass away.

Lizzie returned, somehow balancing four huge dishes of vegetables, and caught him pushing the wine away: "Don't you like the wine?" she asked. "I've got red and white, or beer, or spirits if you'd prefer. Whatever you fancy, dear. Whatever you'd like, let me know."

Simon shook his head, but Lizzie had already left the room to open a bottle of red, which she brought in. "Here you are," she said, smiling, pouring some red into Serena's glass, and handing it to Simon.

Simon took the glass and glanced at Serena. "Hey," Serena said to Lizzie, "that's my glass."

"Don't be discourteous, dear, to our guests," said Lizzie, still smiling.

"Okay," said Serena, scraping her chair back and stepping over to the cabinet in the corner. She retrieved a tumbler, and came back to the table. She picked up the bottle of red, and was starting to pour, when Lizzie snatched the bottle from her.

"You can't have that, dear," said Lizzie. "Remember, you're only seventeen. The millennium doesn't change your age."

"Oh come on," said Serena, "it's New Year's Eve."

"You know the law, dear," said Lizzie, smiling at Rosa, as if for confirmation, "not till you're eighteen."

"Why did you put a wine glass out for me, then?"

"It was a . . . mistake, dear. I wanted the table to look nice, kind of symmetrical." She smiled again. "But one mistake mustn't lead to another. Let's not end the millennium by breaking the law, dear."

Unexpectedly, Harry stood up for a second, and took the bottle out of his wife's hands, speaking in a disinterested monotone: "I think you'll find the law slightly more ambiguous than that, *darling*, when it comes to under-age drinking. I do believe Serena can have some in our household, supervised by an adult." Despite saying this, Harry didn't offer Serena any of the wine. Having filled his own glass, he put the bottle down next to him, out of Serena's reach.

Serena sighed loudly. Lizzie handed her a serving spoon, and said: "Dear, rather than huffing and puffing, can you serve out vegetables for the guests? I'm sure they're starving hungry. I'll go and get the chestnut and garlic stuffing, if you can at least lend a hand with the serving."

Lizzie bustled out of the room, and Serena dipped the serving spoon into the broccoli dish. Wide eyed, observant as always, Rosa was looking from Harry to Serena to the open door through which Lizzie had left.

Then, with just a hint of a girlish grin playing on her lips, Rosa picked up the bottle of red from under Harry's nose, took Serena's tumbler in her right hand, and poured her a glass-full. She put the tumbler down, next to Serena, and returned the bottle to Harry, who said nothing, moved not a muscle. Patting Serena's hand, as she plopped a heap of broccoli on Rosa's plate, Rosa murmured: "There, my dear, you have a little. It's New Year's Eve, after all, and I used to get – how do you say? – 'sloshed' whenever I could when I was young. Getting sloshed, it is the only way to cope with being young." Still serving, Serena beamed at the table cloth.

At this moment, Lizzie strode back into the room, looked at Serena's full tumbler of wine, and then at Rosa, then at Harry, then back at Rosa, then back at the glass. She didn't look at Serena once, but had clearly sized up the situation: "Well, that's nice for you, to have such an . . . indulgent guest, isn't it, Seri?" Serena said nothing. "Say thank you to Miss Rosa, Seri."

Her short-lived smile gone, Serena muttered: "Thank you, Rosa," and continued spooning broccoli onto everyone's plates.

"Here, give me that spoon, young lady," said Lizzie, swiping the spoon from Serena, "you're being too mean with the portions." Lizzie continued with the serving, doling out more or less the same amount as Serena had done. Everyone watched the broccoli in silence, whilst outside the house someone was playing with wind chimes, running their hands through them like musical hair.

Back inside, Serena's hair sulked with her, a black curtain dangling over her eyes, over her plate. As if on cue, Lizzie pulled a long black hair, bit by bit, out of the broccoli dish.

"Yuckety yuck, Seri, what is this?" she asked, holding it above the table for everyone to see.

"A hair," muttered Serena.

"I can see that," said Lizzie, "but what's it doing in the broccoli?"

"It's not *in* the broccoli," said Serena.

"Yes it is."

"No it's not. It's between your fingers."

"I don't want to hear that kind of back-chat, *dear*, in front of guests." Lizzie didn't look at Rosa or Simon. She just continued dangling the black hair over the table, like some mini-sword of Damocles, which, however gossamer-thin, might cut off everyone's heads. "Tell her, Harry," Lizzie said, appealing to her husband, "tell your daughter I don't want any back-chat in front of guests."

Harry almost ground the words between his teeth: "Serena, dear, your stepmother doesn't want back-chat in front of guests."

Serena didn't flinch – she just focussed on the hair, which was silhouetted against the electric light from above. It was rippling slightly from side to side, caught in the micro-breezes moving between people, across the table. Gradually, the hair mesmerised everyone. Only the turkey seemed impervious to its hypnotic effect.

"Look at it," hissed Lizzie after a few seconds or so of hair-hypnosis. "Look at it. It's horrid."

"It's not horrid. It's part of me," said Serena, standing up, trying to grab it back from her stepmother. With super-fast reflexes, Lizzie evaded Serena's attempt to reclaim her hair by snatching at Serena's incoming wrist with her free left hand. For a moment, they stood there, facing each other over the broccoli dish: Lizzie holding the hair up high with her right hand, out of Serena's reach, whilst gripping her stepdaughter's wrist with her left hand. Lizzie stood upright, a good eight or nine inches taller than Serena, her face powerfully thin, sculpted bones outlining her like an exoskeleton, visible through her pink jacket and pencil skirt – an outfit which was still pristine, even though she'd cooked a turkey dinner in it. By contrast, her stepdaughter was dressed in dirty jeans and a black, baggy t-shirt with the faded motto '*Sic transit gloria mundi*' on it, above the image of a bombed-out skyline. Her face was pale, plump with the sulks; and she seemed to writhe and shrink in comparison to Lizzie. Indeed, her whole body seemed to twist downwards, as she tried to extract her wrist from her stepmother's grip: "Ow, that hurts, Lizzie."

Lizzie's fingers snapped away, and she turned and strode over to the bay window. She opened one of the side panels, and a hundred voices, wind chimes, chanters, sellers and potsmokers shared the room with those inside for a few seconds.

Lizzie parted her fingers, and ceremoniously dropped the hair outside, onto the pavement. Then she shut the window – and the outside voices were muffled again. Serena said nothing. She just sat down, head bowed, at her place. "You need your hair cutting, my dear," said Lizzie, as she strode back to the table. "That's the problem – that fringe of yours, it gets everywhere. I'll book you into my hairdresser's for a new-millennium hair-cut." She smiled at Rosa, as though she'd made a joke. Rosa nodded stiffly.

Standing back at the table, Lizzie picked up the carving knife and fork, and poised them above the turkey – which seemed to shrink into itself in her shadow, like Serena before it. "Right, carving time now," she said. "I'll do it this time, because I suspect Harry doesn't feel like it. And no doubt Serena would make a mess, wouldn't you, dear?"

Serena half-nodded underneath her hair.

"Exactly. So, what does everyone want?" She looked at

Simon. "Guests first. Simon: breast, leg, wing?"

Feeling strangely like he was being threatened with something, Simon asked: "Would anyone mind if I had one of the legs?"

Serena and Rosa shook their heads politely, and Lizzie moved the carving knife above the leg joint.

"I mind," said Harry.

Simon looked at him: "Pardon?"

"I mind."

"Harry, dear, there are two legs," Lizzie explained, slowly. "If Simon wants one, you can have the other one."

"That's not the point," said Harry.

"What's not the point?" asked Lizzie. Simon said nothing, because he'd been so thrown by Harry's unexpected response.

"I am the head of the house," said Harry, "and therefore I don't have to explain my reasons on matters pertaining to the house – and that includes turkey matters."

"I think you'll find the head of the house isn't here," hissed Lizzie. "I think you'll find the real head of the house is across the Atlantic, making the money that pays our mortgage. I think you'll find that you're head of nothing, not even yourself." After this outburst, she took a deep breath, and resumed her customary, controlled tone: "Harry, *dear*, there are guests here. One of the guests wants a leg. He has a leg, you have a leg – and we're all sorted."

"Actually," Simon tried to say, "I'm happy having some of the breast instead of . . ."

"No," said Lizzie, interrupting, "if a guest of mine wants a leg, a guest of mine gets a leg."

"Honestly . . ."

"You heard what he said," Harry interrupted Simon this time, "he doesn't want a leg after all."

"No, dear. *You* don't want him to have a leg. It's you, not him. Look, *darling*, our guest's just being polite. Why don't you want him to have a leg?"

Harry wasn't about to answer that question. Harry wasn't about to tell his wife, his daughter, the visitors that it was because he remembered past Christmas meals in this house – past Christmas meals in which the turkey was carved up, and Harry would have one leg, and a certain carnivorous toddler and, later, young girl would have the other . . . a toddler or young girl who, even when desperately ill, would chomp her teeth and kick her feet under the table with joy when presented with the huge leg on her tiny plate . . . a toddler or young girl who would teeth-prise the grey meat from the bone and gobble it as if it were her last meal . . . a toddler or young girl who would join with her father in making "bear-eating" noises, in a conspiracy of carnivorousness . . .

Nobody else in the room recalled those "bear-eating" noises, so nobody else understood Harry's reluctance to let anyone alive have that second turkey leg. Lizzie, for one, didn't want to understand, had no patience with him – and, ignoring his molten glare, sawed through the leg, and forked it onto Simon's plate. Simon had no idea what to do; so, when everyone else had been served, he just ate the leg, bit by bit, swallowing each tiny piece down like guilt. Only towards the end did he dare sneak a glance in Harry's direction. Harry was sitting silent as the turkey, not touching a thing, listening to the "bear-eating" noises inside his head – noises that none of the others could hear.

Outside Harry's head, there were no other noises round the table whilst the five of them ate. No-one spoke for a long time; they let the muffled sounds from outside fill up the silences between them. There was a group chanting, below which someone was droning Melissa's name – like some kind of incantation, some magic word, which would open the musical heavens. Perhaps it did outside, in the Close – those inside had no way of knowing. In this silent, static living room, nothing happened except time ticking on towards midnight and the new millennium. Just as this house had been the still centre during the Spark Close Phenomenon, now those inside seemed cocooned from the emotions all around. No matter how many times the people outside droned Melissa's name, or held her photo in the air, or cried for their tiny princess, nothing within the house seemed to stir – as though the house radiated all its grief, all its emotions outwards, and inside was merely a black hole.

As the black hole's singularity, Harry sat in front of his plate-full of food with his hands underneath him. When everyone else had finished, he pushed the still-full plate away from him, and said, very slowly, "Thank you, darling. That was *lovely*. Yum yum. You excelled yourself as ever." He dabbed the corner of his mouth with a napkin – despite having eaten nothing – and then scraped back his chair and declared: "After such a feast, I think the only thing a gentleman can do is retire to the salon, kick off his boots, and proceed to digest in front of that glorious marvel of modern technology, the television." He got up, and was soon ensconced in his favourite armchair, remote in hand, television glowering at him.

Rosa and Simon offered to wash up, but were shooed away to watch the TV as well. Serena hovered, and then decided that staying with the guests was less of a risk than trying to help her stepmother; so the four of them sat down, ranged on sofas, armchairs and dining-table chairs, in front of New Year's Eve TV. They were eventually joined by Lizzie, wiping her hands on a tea-towel. After the silence of dinner, the hair confrontation, the turkey-leg débâcle, only TV seemed safe. The party world on the TV was reassuringly distant, alien to the world of this living room. There seemed no points of contact between the two worlds, so no-one in this world could possibly be upset by what was happening in TV world. In TV world, there were streamers, lights, fireworks, music. In TV world, it was the end of a year, a century, a millennium. In TV world – when the time came – it was the beginning of a new one. Nothing in all of this seemed to apply to the Combs and their guests, in their dead living-room world.

Or at least, that seemed the case, until the twelfth and last bong of Big Ben – when TV world and living-room world unexpectedly converged. At that moment, Harry Comb suddenly leapt out of his chair, and, folding his arms across his chest, grabbed Rosa's and Serena's hands – and then, from the depths of his almost-tuneless voice, he sang, almost shouted, the words on everyone's lips:

Should auld acquaintance be forgot,
and never brought to mind?
Should auld acquaintance be forgot,
and auld lang syne?

For auld lang syne, my dear,
for auld lang syne,
we'll take a cup o' kindness yet,
for auld lang syne.

. . . And, carried away by the millennial moment, all five of them started swinging one another's arms – Simon linked to Lizzie, linked to Rosa, linked to Harry, linked to Serena, linked back to Simon – hands linked round and round in circles of grief, circles of friendship, circles of farewell . . .

. . . And some of those at Number 4, Spark Close that night wondered afterwards if, even as early as this, even in this first minute of the new millennium, it wasn't, or wasn't just,

Melissa to whom they were saying farewell, but, in joining in with that wild shouting-singing of his, which over-emphasised the first and third lines of the first stanza, they were also saying the beginning of a very long goodbye to Harry Comb.

Outside, the crowds were singing 'Auld Lang Syne' too; but, for the first time that night, the noise outside seemed a pale echo of inside, of Harry's over-the-top bass-baritone, and their over-enthusiastic linking of hands up and down, round and round. The energy seemed to have drained from the crowds' singing outside; and, even after 'Auld Lang Syne' had finished, the noises, the chanting, the buying and selling, though they returned, seemed more subdued than before.

Early next morning, the first morning of the new millennium, Simon Adler-Reeves left his grandmother's house, where he'd slept, and picked his way through the débris outside, the pot-saturated bodies, the burnt-down candles, the half-dismantled stalls, the vans picking up stalls, candles, bodies; and there seemed a certain malaise, a certain hungover disappointment in the moans and groans of the prostrate figures, and those clearing up around them. They'd expected apocalypse at midnight, or at least something important to happen, something major to change, some musical epiphany – and instead all they'd got was just another day.

VAR VII

Serena

"YES YOU FUCKING do."

"No I don't."

"Yes you fucking well do, you filthy-dirty bitch."

"Honestly, I don't. Honestly, Sara."

"Honestly, Seri, honestly, I can tell you do, you dirty slag. I know you too well. How long have I known you? Donkeys' years . . . no, donkeys' decades. God, we're, like, fucking ancient, you and me. Been around forever."

"Yeah. That's how it feels sometimes."

"Charming. But I bet it doesn't feel as ancient as him."

"Him who?"

"The him who you fancy – bet he's, like, even more fucking ancient than us."

"I told you, Sara. I don't fancy anybody or anything."

"You do. I can tell. I can see right through you, Seri. Is it a student? A teacher? A dog, a cat? Someone's great-great grandfather, you filthy-dirty slag? Tell me who it is."

"It's no-one and nothing."

"Go on, tell me. I'm not going to fucking rat on you by spreading it round, am I?"

"Yeah, right. I believe you. Millions wouldn't."

"Look, just answer some simple questions. First off, am I right in thinking this guy's old – ancient – pre-historic-al-ist – whatever?"

"I'm not answering," said Serena, sticking her fingers in her ears and singing: "Lah lah lah."

Sara knocked her friend's fingers out of her ears: "Stop lah-lah-ing your bloody Schubert or whatever it is, and tell me: is he fucking ancient or not?"

"Lah lah lah, lah lah lah. It's not Schubert, it's Brahms."

"Ah, you got down to *bras* already? Dirty old man. Dirty young Seri."

"We haven't got down to anything."

"Aha!" said Sara, as if solving a case, "I'm right then – there is someone, someone with whom you may or may not have 'got down' to something like *bras*. You dirty, dirty bitch, you."

"Sara?"

"What?"

"Shurrup."

"No, I'm not shutting up." She put on a deep, posh voice: "I'm going to pursue this case to its bitter end, I tell you, my good Dr. Watson. I'm going to find out who did what to whom with the bra in the –" she looked around "– Sixth-Form Common Room . . . or wherever."

"I didn't do anything in here with or without a bra."

"Where did you do it, then? Where? Go on, tell me. Is it like Terri in the back seat of Jack's Beemer? . . . or should I say, Jack in Terri's back seat?"

"Ah, Sara, you're soooo gross."

Sara sat forwards: "Come on, Seri, get on with it. Spill."

"It's nothing like that. There's nothing, nothing to spill. It's nothing like Terri and Jack."

"But I bet he is ancient like Jack, isn't he? Bet he is – and that's why you won't say anything about him."

"He's not 'ancient,' Sara, just older."

"Older's just, like, a polite word for ancient. I bet he's some teacher or parent or something, really ancient." Sara looked at Serena narrowly. "It's not that guy who's always round yours is it – what's he called – Simon Double-Barrelled-Name?"

"No it's not," said Serena, blushing slightly.

"Oh well, I thought it probably wasn't," said Sara, dismissing Simon Adler-Reeves as a possible candidate without a second thought. "He's not 'older' enough. The guy you wanna shag must be really ancient, for you to be so, like, embarrassed. Y'know what? I bet he's so ancient, his cock's got hieroglyphics tattooed on it instead of words."

Serena coughed back a laugh: "Gross. You nicked that from someone else."

"So what if I did?" said Sara, looking pleased. "Made you laugh anyway. Did his wrinkly-ancient cock make you laugh too?"

"I haven't seen it."

"God, Seri, you're slow. I thought it was 'luuurrrvvvve.'"

Sara started humming the tune to 'Love is in the air' by John Paul Young, whilst Serena talked over her: "I never said anything about 'love.' I just . . . well, y'know, like him."

"Ah, old-style romance is in the air. How sweet and old-fashioned of you, putting 'like' before 'love' before inspecting his ancient cock. From what I hear, Jack and Terri never bothered with things in that order."

"Well," said Serena, looking away, suddenly honest, "he's an ordered kind of bloke." She looked back down at the table. "That's how he seems, anyway."

"So, we've got an ancient bloke who's into ordering things. Sounds like a boring wanker, but at least it narrows it down.

Don't know many of them. I mean, I know a lot of wankers, but not ancient ones who're anally retentive OCD-ers."

Serena almost giggled into her Diet Coke can: "Don't talk about him like that."

But Sara was ready to talk about the subject forever, if it made her friend nearly giggle: "Oh, it's 'him' now, is it? 'Him'? Not Mr. A. Nall-Retention. Not Mr. N. Joy Wanking. No, it's 'him.' Soon, it'll be 'us,' and then . . . and then, like, you'll find yourself being banged by a fossil-cock."

Serena snorted through the Coke bubbles: "Ah, Sara, shurrup. You're sick."

"*I'm* sick?! *I'm* sick?! I'm not the one who wants to shag a fucking skeleton, a bony boner!"

"Shhhhh. For fuck's sake, don't let the whole college know. And anyway, he's not a skeleton. He's not ancient. He's just . . . he's just very . . . nice. Neat. Ordered."

Sara looked straight at Serena, a victorious grin, wide as a can of Diet Coke, spreading across her face: "Oh my God. Nice. Neat. Ordered. I, like, I know who it is."

"Who?"

"Not telling."

"What do you mean, 'not telling'? How fucking old are you? How can you not tell me what I'm not telling you?"

"Easy, but you can guess."

"I'm not going to fucking guess who you're fucking guessing I fancy. It's like going mad or something, round and round."

"Okay, I wouldn't want you to go mad . . . or at least no madder than you must be already to have fallen for him."

"Him who?"

"Him: the neat, ordered, ancient one. The one who actually talked about 'order' in our last fucking lesson with him. Just now. And you went scarletty red at something, and did your walking-out trick for the gazillionth time. God, Seri, you're so see-through, I can see your bra – no, worse than that, I can see outside through you, for fuck's sake."

Without thinking, Serena looked down at her body, to see if she really were transparent. Meanwhile, Sara continued crowing: "I knew it. I knew he was fucking ancient, and I knew he was probably a teacher or something, you dirty slag-of-slags. I knew it. But I didn't realise he was boring on top of it all. Boring boring boring. God, he's, like, *sooooo* boring, Seri."

Forgetting she was supposed to be denying her crush, Serena said: "No he's not. I think what he talks about is . . . dead interesting. And, well, I think he's just, like, a bit shy."

"How can he be shy at his age? At his fucking age – must be fifties, sixties, two-millions, as old as those black holes he goes on about."

"Sara, he's in his twenties. I mean, look at him."

"I don't wanna look at him, Seri, thank you very much. God, Seri, some girls go for squeaky Beckhams, some go for, like, suave and sophisticated olds like Clooney, some go for . . . I don't know . . . the Jacks of the world, giving it them up the bum. But Mr. Jenkins? Mr. fucking-death-by-Physics-Jenkins? I mean, come on. Come on, Seri." As usual, she was getting carried away: "I mean, he's, like, the most boringest, most straight-laced, most I'll-speak-in-a-monotone-for-the-whole-two-hour-lesson-in-case-anyone-starts-to-wake-up saddo in the whole fucking world. He doesn't have any discipline shit in his lessons cos everyone's either comatose or in physical pain, for fuck's sake, Seri. Even bloody Davy Lawson from up your street snoozes in Mr. Jenkins's lesson. Okay, so Davy stirred up a bit of shit in the last double Physics – but you got to admit that was pretty tame compared to his usual stuff, like throwing poos out of windows or setting fire to his hair . . ." For a moment, she got distracted: "Having said that, the hair thing's become a bit 'old hat' over the last year. If I see it again, I'll have to yawn in his face." Back on track, she carried on relentlessly: "But, fuck, not as much as I have to yawn during Mr. fucking Jenkins's endless lectures about order and disorder and particles and universes and shit upon shit. Talk about yawntastic. God, Seri, he'll turn us all to bones and dust with his lectures on en-trump-y . . ."

". . . entropy, it's entropy, Sara, and you fucking well know it is . . ."

". . . yeah, whatever. It's not even on the syllabus, for fuck's sake. He seems to think we're taking Physics cos we're interested in it. What an idiot." Serena giggled in spite of herself, and Sara continued: "I mean, for fuck's sake, Seri, doesn't he realise we're only bothered about his Physics shit as far as it'll get us enough marks to do something better instead? He can stick his en-trump-y-trumping up his arse – and then trump it out again."

"Sara!"

"Oh, sorry, I don't want to offend you, darling Seri, by taking the piss out of your beloved boyfriend. But fuck's sake, Seri. He goes on and on, showing us slide shows like there's no tomorrow of stuff he's nicked off NASA or the internet or somewhere, and even he'd be yawning if he wasn't taken up with droning on and on . . . God, that montone of his, it gets into your head and your bones and your dreams. All I, like, hear in my head now when I see pictures of stars and galaxies is that voice. I'll grow up thinking – that's the fucking sound of the universe, just an ancient guy droning on and on forever and ever. It's like that NASA shit he came out with the other day, something about the noise a black hole makes – that it gives off, like, a dead deep note for millions of years. That's him, that is: droning on and on . . ."

"I think it's interesting. And his voice is kinda . . . reassuring, lulling."

"Lulling like being lullabied to d . . . death . . ."

. . . and there was a short silence, during which time Sara struggled to keep hold of her malfunctioning smile. Suddenly, she felt terrible – not because she'd mentioned the unavoidable subject of 'death' in connection with a lullaby; but because she'd hesitated over the dreaded 'd' word, and because of the silence after it, which she struggled to fill.

Serena sighed, and got up to go to the next lesson: "Coming?" she asked – her hand hidden in the left-hand pocket of her leather jacket, touching the sharp creases of the letter she kept there: *Seri, my dear older sis . . .*

The next lesson was not Mr. Jenkins's Physics lesson – it was General Studies – but all the way through, Serena felt comforted, if only for a little while, by memories and daydreams of his lesson that morning – lullabied by his voice in her head, like a mental pedal point. Now and then, the pedal point was punctuated with a *Click* – the sound made when he pressed the button on the slide projector, to move on to the next slide.

Even the clicks were regular. Everything in Mr. Jenkins's lessons was stated methodically; everything in Mr. Jenkins's lessons was ordered – seeming a million miles from Serena's family's chaos of stasis and mania, a billion miles from her father's alternation of taciturny and hyper-nonsense, a trillion miles away from anything associated with a dead sister. Everything in Mr. Jenkins's Physics lessons was in its place, governed by equations and immutable laws . . .

Click: slide showing an image of the sun, with the words: 'Laws of Thermodynamics 2' superimposed in molten red on its surface.

"Now," Mr. Jenkins had started that morning, "the Second Law of Thermodynamics will not feature on your A-Level exam papers. Only the First Law of Thermodynamics is covered in the Cambridge GCE syllabus. Nonetheless, I believe that, to understand fully the implications of the First Law, one needs to study the Second Law as well. So that is what we are going to do for the two hours of this lesson."

Half-hearted groans rippled through the classroom, in concentric circles around Davy Lawson: "God, two sodding hours. Please can I hang myself now, sir?"

Mr. Jenkins ignored Davy and the groans, and carried on to the next slide.

Click: image of hot cup of coffee, with red arrows pointing outwards to indicate heat loss.

"The Second Law of Thermodynamics states that heat will transfer from a hotter to a colder body, and that process is not spontaneously reversible."

Sara hiss-whispered to Serena: "Yuck. I don't want him talking about hot bodies transferring their heat to colder ones. Sounds kinda creepy, coming from him."

"Shhhhh," said Serena.

Mr. Jenkins continued: "This law of heat transfer can be stated in various ways, and it suggests that the entropy of the universe, or any similar, closed system, always increases over time."

"The en-trumpety-trump of your lessons gradually increases over time," murmured Sara.

"Shhhhh," said Serena again.

Mr. Jenkins continued: "Let me explain. Entropy can be defined as the mathematical and theoretical expression of the order and disorder of a particular system."

Click: image of Big Bang, taken from Jodrell Bank's website.

"You might find it useful to envisage entropy this way: because of the Second Law, systems generally spread outwards, from a hot centre to a more diffuse and cooler state. Hence, the universe is expanding and cooling from the time of the Big Bang, approximately fourteen billion years ago, when it was (mathematically speaking) of infinite density and infinite temperature. The Second Law of Thermodynamics is one of the main ways we know that the universe can't always have been the size it is now. It must have expanded, and must still be expanding; and, therefore, the 'static state' model of the universe is not tenable."

There was no *Click*, but Serena shut her eyes and saw another slide-show image in her head: an image of her father ensconced in his armchair, watching snow on the TV, eating cracker after cracker; and she wondered – for a split second – if it were possible that Mr. Jenkins might be wrong, if what she was seeing so clearly behind her eyelids proved, in miniature, that a static state universe was possible.

"I'm sure you all know the case against static state universes already, so I won't elaborate further."

"Thank God," sighed Sara, her head an inch from the plastic veneer of the desk.

"However, I will elaborate on the ways in which the Big Bang and expanding model of the universe are fundamental to our notion of entropy."

Click: image of the universe as it is now, showing various overlaid galaxies.

"Evidently, entropy in its widest sense increases as the universe ages: the particles which make up the universe gradually spread outwards and cool. But that's only the general picture, and a crude one at that. Entropy as physicists understand it is a much more refined measurement than the generalised, crude and lazy versions put about by, say, philosophers or artistic types."

Mr. Jenkins frequently made unfavourable comparisons between, on the one hand, physicists and, on the other, philosophers, artists or musicians. Indeed, Serena felt he often singled her out at these moments; when talking about musicians or "English-Lit types," she could swear he usually looked straight at her – and it didn't matter to her whether or not the look was entirely complimentary. After all, at least he was noticing her, not just staring at his own diagrams and equations. Of course, logically she knew that he wasn't noticing her because he had feelings for her; it was because she was doing what he thought a bizarre concoction of A-Levels – Music, English, Physics, General Studies – and so he was making an example of her. Honestly, logically, that could be the only reason, she thought, doodling something or someone in her exercise book, and trying to focus on what he was saying:

". . . Physicists, you see, have found ways of encapsulating philosophical, literary, spiritual, even musical notions of the universe in elegant mathematical equations, rather than mere words. So philosophers or writers or artists might tell you that the universe is decaying and expanding, but physicists can tell you exactly how, at what rate and in what ways, using entropy as a model."

Click: image one of three equations for entropy:

$$\mathrm{d}S = \frac{\mathrm{d}Q}{T}$$

"Here, you should note, dS is the change in entropy and dQ is the heat added to the system."

Click: second of three equations for entropy:

$$S = k_B \ln \Omega$$

" . . . which is the expression of entropy according to statistical mechanics, which, as you know . . ."

"Do we?" asked Sara.

". . . treats the behaviour of particles *en masse* in probabilistic or statistical terms. You'll come across a few variants of this equation, but basically the entropy of a system (S) is defined to be Boltzmann constant (k) times the natural logarithm of the number of microstates (*omega*)."

Click: third of three equations for entropy:

$$S = k.\,log\,W$$

" . . . which is, of course, the most famous expression of entropy, whereby entropy (S) is Boltzmann constant (k) times the natural logarithm of microstates consistent with the macrostate (W)."

"What the fuck is he going on about?" whispered Sara.

As if in answer to Sara's question, Davy Lawson's hand shot up. "What is it, Davy?" asked Mr. Jenkins.

"Can I be excused, sir, for a few minutes?"

"Why do you need to be excused, Davy?"

"Because I need the toilet, sir. I desperately need to do a natural *log*-arithm, sir," said Davy. There were sniggers around Davy. Mr. Jenkins ignored them, and moved onto the next image.

Click: photo of Ludwig Boltzmann's gravestone, engraved with the same formula as before:

$$S = k.\, log\, W$$

"You see, the great physicist Ludwig Boltzmann (1844-1906) was so well-known for his formula for entropy, it was inscribed on his tombstone in the Vienna Zentralfriedhof cemetery. I visited the cemetery when I went to Vienna last year, to pay my respects, and took this photograph."

"God, what a saddo," hissed Sara, "most people go on hols to Ibiza and get laid – this guy goes to see the grave of some dead boffin."

"No doubt," continued Mr. Jenkins, "there is a kind of black humour in putting the entropy equation above his grave. After all, if entropy is, in general terms, the universal law that all systems seek a quiescent state, then death is the biological expression of entropy. Our bodies, like all physical systems, are gradually decaying, gradually dispersing heat-energy, inevitably moving towards an inert state. Therefore, to inscribe $S = k.$ log W on Boltzmann's grave is rather like declaring, well, that the famous equation applied even to the great man who formulated it. It was a little physicist's joke, I suppose." Mr. Jenkins half smiled, coughed and paused – though he didn't really expect anyone to laugh in the class: he'd long since given up expecting anyone to laugh at his scripted 'jokes.'

Much to his surprise, on this occasion, one of the students did. Davy Lawson slapped his thigh theatrically, and almost shouted with laughter: "Bloody hell, sir, that's so funny. That

Boltzmann guy, what a comedian. Hysterical. Call an ambulance, sir, I think I'm going to split my sides laughing."

"Yes, well," said Mr. Jenkins, adjusting his tie. "Let's not get carried away."

"But I can't help it, sir. It's so funny, sir, ha ha ha," Davy Lawson mock-laughed, enunciating each "ha" as if it were a separate word. At the same time, he looked round, prodding everyone else to join in with him. The classroom was speckled with laughter, but most of the students were too comatose to join in with much energy.

"Okay, Davy, let's move on, shall we?" said Mr. Jenkins. "Calm down, now. Everyone . . . calm . . . down." He stood there, trying to calm down the class by moving his hands up and down in front of him, like an awkward puppet. He waited until the laughter burned itself out, and then continued as if nothing had happened:

"Entropy, as I say, is a measure of the order and disorder of a particular system. What is interesting about entropy . . . "

"Is there anything interesting about anything anywhere any longer?" asked Sara. "Honestly, I think I'm, like, going to die, Seri."

"Shhhhh," said Serena

". . . is that, whilst entropy is often lazily understood as the increase of disorder over time, scientists have become intrigued in recent years by the ways in which spontaneous moments of order can occur within the context of a decaying system."

Click: image of the Solar System.

"To put this simply, the Second Law of Thermodynamics assumes that all systems, over time, are heading towards a quiescent state. Within this overall entropic process, however, there are also moments where spontaneous microstates of organisation, flourishes of energy, moments of 'beauty' (one might say, if one were being poetic) occur. In the long term, obviously, the universe is expanding, as heat disperses across space. In the long term, that is, the universe seems to be heading inexorably towards some form of heat death, whereby all the heat-energy in the universe has been spent. In the short term, by contrast, microstates, and microstates-within-microstates, such as galaxies, Solar Systems, stars, even human beings, form and then disperse, in spontaneous and transient moments of organisation. Even black holes, which apparently swallow everything within their event horizons, adhere to the Second Law of Thermodynamics, in complex ways which I won't go into here."

"Thank you, God, for micro-mercies," prayed Sara.

"These moments or microstates, like galaxies or suns or black holes, do not contradict the overall entropic process, but happen within it. The strength of Boltzmann's entropy equation is that it can comprehend these microstates, just as it can macrostates, in its beautifully simple way."

Click: image of Boltzmann's equation again.

"Fuck's sake, we're going backwards," hissed Sara, her head finally hitting the top of the desk with a thud. Mr. Jenkins didn't notice. "I could have died," whispered Sara, "and he still wouldn't notice."

Mr. Jenkins continued: "What Boltzmann's equation comprehends is that entropy is not merely an expression of increasing disorder, as it is popularly understood. Rather, it is simultaneously a measure of order. As heat-energy disperses, for example, what tends to happen is that a system levels out over time. Isolated microstates, where the temperature is concentrated, gradually disperse, until the macrostate becomes constant, and all microstates are uniform expressions of that macrostate. Similarly, if a gas is released into a closed box, the particles gradually spread out in a uniform manner. Hence, entropy is an expression not only of decay, but also of a levelling out over time, of – ultimately – an ordered and uniform, but diffuse universe."

At this point, Davy Lawson – whose earlier attempt at lesson-sabotage had fizzled out – decided he'd had enough, and raised his head, like a meerkat, above all those slumped around him: "So, sir, what you're trying to say is that things get more and more flattened out over time."

"In a sense . . ."

"No, sorry, sir, if I may interject," he put on a fake accent, mimicking his teacher's idioms, "if I may . . ."

Mr. Jenkins powerlessly opened his hands to indicate that Davy could continue.

"If I may proceed, like, I think what you're getting at, sir, is that things just drift apart over time, getting more and more the same, more and more boring, going on and on and never stopping."

"Well, that's one way of putting it. Nevertheless, as I say . . ."

"Yeah, sir, it's all about going on and on and on," Davy Lawson's audience began to perk up, smirk, snigger, "and never stopping, everything more and more boring and samey and boring and . . ."

"Thank you for that, Davy. Now I think, if you don't mind . . ."

". . . and on and on and Ariston and never stopping forever and ever and ever . . ."

The students round Davy were openly laughing now, egging him on . . . and on. Encouraged, he stood up, as if he were conducting them.

"Davy, please . . ."

"... and things just get further and further apart and drift and drift and go on and on and never stop like your lectures, sir, on and on and boringly on ..."

"Davy – please will you ..."

At that moment, Serena jumped up from her desk and stamped her foot: "Will you shut the fuck up, Davy?"

There was a chorus of "Ooohs" from around the room. Without much humour, Davy turned on her, and said: "Shut up yourself, you moody-fucking-goth-bitch." There were more "Ooohs," though this set of "Ooohs" was a restrained echo of the first.

Serena stamped her foot again, appeared to be about to say something, and then grabbed her bag and books, pulled her cardigan sleeves down over her wrists – and stormed out of the classroom.

A third set of "Ooohs," even quieter than the second, followed the swinging door. Davy watched her go, and sat down.

"Look what you've done now," said Sara.

"I don't give two fucking logarithms," said Davy.

Mr. Jenkins was quiet, watching the door Serena had left swinging, to and fro, mesmerised. Finally, he snapped out of it, and said: "Okay, class. Back to the subject we are discussing today. Entropy."

The class moaned in unison, all energy dissipated.

At the end of the school day, Sara asked Serena, as usual, if she would like to catch the bus back to Hanford and Trentham with her – and, as usual, Serena said, "No, not today, I think I'll walk home."

"It's like a million fucking miles," said Sara.

"It's not. It's two," said Serena.

Sara stuck out her bottom lip. "You always walk home these days. We used to catch the bus together and sit at the back and take the piss out of everyone. Now every night for weeks it's 'I think I'll walk home.'"

"I . . . just want the fresh air."

"Fresh air? In fucking Fenton?"

"You know what I mean."

"I know what you mean. You don't want to come with me."

"It's not that. I just want to be on my own for a bit."

Sara "humphed," slung her backpack over her right shoulder, and wandered off without another word.

When she'd got round the corner of the building, though, she stopped. She shifted her weight from foot to foot, and slung her bag over her other shoulder. Then she changed it back to the right one. Finally, she turned and peeked round the corner at Serena, who was heading off in the opposite direction, past the swimming pool.

Sara followed her.

Sara followed her past the swimming pool, across the football pitch, and past the Social Sciences block, which was gradually sinking into the quarry, a metre a year. She followed her friend down the track, past the quarry. She followed her over the road, under the railway bridge, past Bauble and Son's garage, and then through the subway underneath the A500 roundabout.

Sara kept hiding behind things – graffitied walls, ticking lampposts, rusting cars – expecting Serena to glance behind her at any moment. But she never did. Instead, she walked at a constant, moderate pace, in exact time with another figure, fifty yards in front of her – a figure wearing a brown mac, carrying a briefcase, who, like Serena, never once glanced back. When they went under bridges, or through subways, that second, more distant figure was often out of Sara's sight; but when the vista widened, he or she was still there, walking at exactly the same pace, whilst Serena remained equidistant between him or her and Sara.

The three of them – first the distant figure, then Serena, then Sara – emerged into Stoke town centre, passing boarded-up newsagents and cut-price card shops. They turned left onto London Road, and carried on, past the garage which marked the edge of the town centre, and then on towards Stoke's West End – an untheatrical West End of terraces and rundown off-licences.

Finally, after about half a mile, they turned left and left again into Tyke Street. By the time Sara was on Tyke Street, the more-distant figure had vanished, presumably into one of the terraced houses – and the whole symmetry of their walk, one following the other following the other at equal distances, was ruined, because Serena had stopped too. She was sat, perched on a garden wall, head in her hands.

Sara tiptoed up to her, and then wondered why she'd tiptoed. She touched Serena on the shoulder. Serena wiped her nose and eyes on her sleeve, and looked up at her friend. She didn't ask Sara why she was here, why she had followed her. She didn't say anything, just took Sara's hand, like she used to.

Sara nodded at the terrace opposite – Number 17, Tyke Street. "Mr. Jenkins?" she asked.

Serena nodded and breathed in deeply.

"Fancy a drink?" asked Sara.

Serena nodded again, slipped off the wall, and let Sara lead her away to a nearby off-licence. "Are you the right age?" asked the male shopkeeper. "Right age for what?" asked Sara, arching an eyebrow, licking her lips. "Well . . . you know . . . never mind," he said, letting them buy a cheap bottle of cider.

"God," said Serena taking a first swig of the cider outside, "you could twist anyone round your little finger."

"Yeah," said Sara, "especially desperate wankers like that. He'll, like, probably wank himself to death tonight – just over a seventeen-year-old licking her lips at him to get some cider. Can you imagine the headlines in *The Sentinel* tomorrow?" – she put on a deep voice, as if reading the news – "'Respected Local Shopkeeper Masturbates Himself to Death. Police in the West End are warning residents to take special care when drinking milk purchased from the man's shop in case . . .'"

"Ah, stop it," coughed Serena, spitting out some of the cider, "you're grossing me out."

"Yeah, right – you were laughing."

"Was not."

"Was too. Give me that cider."

Sara grabbed the cider from Serena, and knocked some back. Without even thinking about it, they wandered back to the wall on Tyke Street, where Sara had found Serena ten minutes before. This time, they both perched on it, taking turns with the cider.

Sara didn't need to ask if this was where Serena had been coming for weeks after school, following Mr. Jenkins on his long walk home from Sixth-Form College. Sara didn't need to ask if Serena often sat here at this time of night, perhaps for a few minutes, perhaps sometimes longer, staring at the man's house, running off if he opened the door to put the rubbish out. Sara didn't need to ask Serena if she knew what she was doing was stupid, what a besotted kid – say, a thirteen-year-old, as opposed to a 'mature' seventeen-year-old – might do.

"I'm fucking stupid, aren't I?" asked Serena, "like some loved-up kid."

"Yep," said Sara, "you're fucking stupid."

"Thought so," said Serena, swigging the cider again.

Then, all of a sudden, she was crying, like she hadn't done in weeks. "I really loved *her*, you know," she said.

"I know," said Sara, her arm draped loosely round her friend.

There was silence for a minute.

Serena wiped her eyes with her sleeve, and smiled up at her friend. "I am so fucking stupid," she said again.

There was a second, longer silence, which this time was broken by the roar of a boy racer on London Road, twenty or so yards behind them.

Sara nodded her head towards the road, "He's fucking stupid too. I s'pose we all are."

Serena nodded. "I s'pose we are." She felt like they were two *Daily Mail* duffers on a park bench, nodding at the stupidity all around them: "I s'pose I . . . we all do these things, like . . . like over-revving cars or like, just as an example, following someone we kinda fancy, even when we know it's fucking stupid. I . . . we'd like to stop, don't want to do it, really, but just can't stop . . . Do you know what I mean?"

"I know," said Sara, "and I also know the cure."

"The cure?"

"Yeah – the cure for someone who, for example, just a random example, follows someone they're in love with, even when they know it's fucking stupid. The cure for this example is fucking blindingly and deafeningly obvious."

"What is it?" asked Serena, leaning forwards.

Sara handed the bottle of cider to Serena. "The cure has three stages: first, you take a mighty heave of that cheap shit." Serena took a mighty heave of the cheap cider. "Secondly, you hop off that bird-crapped wall." Serena jumped off the wall, and smoothed down the back of her skirt. She guessed what was coming next. "Thirdly, you cross this road, go up to that door and knock on it – and see what happens."

Serena pretended to be shocked, and spoke in an uncharacteristically high-pitched voice: "You must be fucking kidding. How can I do that? How is that a fucking cure and not a fucking – I don't know – death sentence, for fuck's sake?"

"Isn't it obvious?" asked Sara. "Look, you knock on that door, and there are, I reckon, two possible outcomes. Either Mr. Jenkins screams, 'What the fuck are you here for? Get away from my house, you mad stalking bitch!' Or he says, in that seductive physicist's monotone of his: 'What are you doing here, Seri, dear? How lovely of you to drop by. Why don't you come inside for a moment and we'll make beautiful thermodynamics together?' Either way – get the brush off, or get laid – you'll have found the cure, and you'll never need to follow the fucker again. Just knock on the door, thinking of it like . . . – well, like some kind of science experiment, with two possible results."

"You must be kidding. I'm not knocking on that fucking door."

"Yes you are," said Sara. "Though let's have a look at you first." She forcibly twirled Serena round, and nodded. "A few little touches needed, madam," she said, hitching Serena's skirt up a little, undoing the top two buttons on her blouse, licking her finger to wipe off the mascara which had run when Serena had cried. Then Sara backed off, and nodded appreciatively: "Excellent, madam," she said, and grabbed Serena by the elbow, propelling her towards the door of Number 17, Tyke Street.

"I'm not going. I'm not fucking going. I'm not. I'm not" – but with each "I'm not," Serena was forced to take another step, across the pavement, across the road and onto the opposite pavement. Finally, still saying "I'mnotI'mnotI'mnot," she found herself a few inches away from Mr. Jenkins's door.

There, for a moment, she froze – reaching down into her left-hand jacket pocket, in which was a certain folded-up letter. She ran her index finger along one of its creases, as if feeling its sharpness, whilst mouthing its blade-like words to herself:

Seri, my dear older sis, I loved you.
Seri, my dear older sis, I am gone.
Seri, my dear older sis, it is your fault.

Immediately after mouthing these words to herself, her hand jerked out of her pocket, clenched itself into a fist, and raised itself to the door, as if she were no longer controlling it. Just before knocking, she glanced back at Sara – who nodded encouragingly, but who was also backing away, as from a ticking bomb.

Serena's hand knocked at the door – one, two, three times – loudly, slowly, resonantly.

Mr. Jenkins answered, still in his shirt and tie. He looked down at her, frowning, as though confronted by a particularly difficult equation on his doorstep.

"Mr. Jenkins . . . Hello."

"Hello?"

"Mr. Jenkins . . . I . . . I . . . I wanted to ask you something, Mr. Jenkins." She wondered how much cider she'd drunk, and whether she were slurring her words. "I wanted to ask you . . . a question, Mr. Jenkins."

"I don't understand. What question?"

"I . . . I wanted . . ." She looked around herself, as if a question might be lurking in the Welcome mat, the neat hanging basket, the rusting number plate next to the door. "I . . . wanted to ask you a question about . . . about . . . entropy and music, if you don't mind?"

"Pardon?"

"I wanted to ask you about entropy and music." Now

she'd hit upon a subject, she pursued it without looking back: "Entropy and music. Are they . . . like . . . related? Are there ways in which entropy might be sort of . . . kind of . . . applied, if you see what I mean, to music?"

"Are you serious?" asked Mr. Jenkins, now doubly bewildered, firstly by one of his female students knocking on the door, and secondly by that female student asking him about possible theoretical connections between thermodynamics and music. He'd answered the door expecting someone to ask him whether he wanted to swap gas companies, or buy some Tupperware. Instead, he seemed to have opened the door on some kind of alternate universe, to which the ordinary rules of logic and predictability didn't apply. "I'm sorry, but I don't understand anything you're saying," he said.

"You understand everything, Mr. Jenkins," gushed Serena, though somehow the flattery rang hollow coming from her. She wasn't very good at playing the awed and deferential teenage girl, fluttering her eyelashes at the older man. Unlike Sara, it wasn't a pose which came easily to her, and wouldn't have persuaded anyone – apart from Mr. Jenkins, who coughed and adjusted his tie.

"Well," he said a few times, shuffling his slippers on the mat. "Well . . . that's certainly not true. I certainly don't know everything. But I do know my laws of thermodynamics from my slippers, you might say." He paused, and she tried to laugh. He adjusted his tie again. "I would, of course, be more than happy to discuss thermodynamics with you at length. Perhaps, however, this isn't quite the right . . . context, shall we say? Perhaps we should leave the discussion till college tomorrow morning?"

That could have been the end of it. Serena could have turned and left. But now she'd got this far, she didn't want to retreat straight away; so she tried to prolong the conversation a little longer by saying the first thing that popped into her head: "It can't wait till tomorrow. It's . . . urgent."

"Urgent?" asked Mr. Jenkins. "I'm not sure I can quite see how a discussion about musical entropy can be classed as urgent."

"It *is* urgent," said Serena. "It's, like, been buzzing round my head all day, and I won't be able to go to sleep tonight if I don't ask you about it first."

Mr. Jenkins didn't know what to say, so he just nodded: "Okay."

"Thank you, Mr. Jenkins. It's very much appreciated. I know that you're busy at home, and I'm getting in your way . . ." She hesitated, and looked round him into the hallway, to see if there were a jealous partner lurking in the shadows – and also to give him a chance to contradict her: "Oh, no, of course you're not getting in my way. I'm never too busy for you, Serena, darling." He didn't contradict her, or say anything of the sort; so she carried on, improvising her speech just as her old music teacher had taught her to improvise on the piano: "You see, Mr. Jenkins, I know you're a busy man, but I thought you might be . . . interested in what I had to ask, and you might be able to help me. I hope you don't mind. I knew where you lived because . . . because . . . my . . . aunt lives on this street, and she told me. Honestly. Yes, that's how it happened."

"What's your aunt's name?" asked Mr. Jenkins, not quite realising what a pointed question it was until he'd actually asked it.

"Oh, that doesn't matter . . . I just call her 'auntie,' so I . . . don't know her actual name. Anyway, the point is that I was visiting my auntie, and I thought I'd, like, pop round, because I thought you – of all people in the world – would be able to help me with this question."

"What question?"

"The question I told you about – the one that's been buzzing round my head – the one about whether or not there's, like, any connection between entropy and music?" There was another pause, which Serena decided to fill. So withdrawn most of the time, here she was on an improvised conversational roll: "Please, Mr. Jenkins, what do you think?"

"What do I think?" asked Mr. Jenkins, genuinely unsure. "What do I think?" He looked at his slippers for a moment, and then looked up again. "What do I think? Well, Serena . . ."

He used my name, she thought.

". . . I think there must be some kind of connection. I think you've hit on something, and you must be right. I've never really considered it before, but I'm sure that the law of entropy must apply to music in some way or other. After all, the four laws of thermodynamics are beautiful and all-encompassing formulae which underlie all systems in the known universe. They determine everything, from cosmic history, to human brain function, to disease, to death. So I'm sure that musical systems must also be subject to a process akin to entropy. I'm generally averse to lazy metaphorical or analogical connections between scientific theories and the arts; but it's certainly the case that sound waves decay . . ."

"That's exactly what I've been thinking," interrupted Serena, who was now getting carried away by her own riff, almost to the point of forgetting why she was standing on Mr. Jenkins's doorstep in the first place. "I've been kinda thinking that musical phrases are like miniature versions of entropy, if you see what I mean: they reach a sort of climax in the middle, and then that energy dies away in the second half of the phrase, until the music, well, kind of comes to a rest in the cadence at the end. That's what I've been thinking."

"I'm not sure . . ."

"That's like entropy on a tiny scale, isn't it?"

"As I say, I don't like . . ."

"On a much bigger scale, you might say that music doesn't work like entropy, because things by people like Beethoven often get louder and more energetic at the end. Not less. Y' know, like Beethoven's Fifth Symphony – it's all noise and trumpets and drums at the end. So perhaps I'm wrong – perhaps we're wrong – and entropy and music aren't connected, y'know, on a big scale.

"But then I'm also thinking about some other pieces of music, and I'm wondering: p'raps there are some which are kind of . . . shaped like entropy. Do you get me?"

Mr. Jenkins, who was still caught up thinking and mumbling about lazy analogies, and the physics of sound waves, didn't "get" her, and shook his head.

"Okay, I'll try and explain what I mean," said Serena. Mr. Jenkins started to wonder who was the teacher, who the student. Serena continued: "There are lots of examples I can think of to explain. I mean, there're all those musical collapses in Mahler's Ninth Symphony . . ."

"Musical what?"

"Collapses. Like, the music builds up to these huge great climaxes, then it kind of falls to pieces – and the tunes and the instruments all sound like they're drifting away from each other, and the energy's draining away to nothing, and it feels really . . . cold. Do you know what I mean?"

Mr. Jenkins shook his head again.

"Okay, think of . . . think of another example . . . Look, do you know Shostakovich?"

"Not personally," answered Mr. Jenkins. It was often difficult to know whether or not Mr. Jenkins was being funny, and Serena didn't laugh. She just carried on:

"Okay, what I mean is: do you know Shostakovich's music?"

"Not very well," said Mr. Jenkins.

"I don't either. But I do like some of my dad's LPs of his symphonies. That's where I got to know the Mahler symphony too – though I don't reckon my dad ever listened to it in his life. Just likes having it there to show off. Anyway, there's this other symphony by Shostakovich – the last one, the Fifteenth – which we've been studying in Music A-Level. This one, I reckon, is kind of a musical picture of entropy, if you see what I mean. It's like the Mahler piece: the orchestra keeps building up, and then disintegrating into . . . into tiny bits and pieces of tunes, or instruments playing solo, or two instruments playing totally different tunes against each other. In the second movement, the music ends up really, like, I don't know the word, 'sparse,' I s'pose, and kinda broken. And in the last movement, the music *crescendos* to this huge climax, and then collapses – I s'pose a physicist might say, 'diffuses' – and gradually, everything seems to drift away, till all you've got left is this long-held string chord, going on and on . . . kind of chilling, like everything, all emotions, even the music itself, have diffused and become this one, uniform sound. It's amazing, and it's dead like what you said about heat death and entropy in the lesson."

"Oh," said Mr. Jenkins, wondering what else there was to say in response to Serena's enthusiasm – feeling like "Oh" was the only word left in the universe.

"Oh," said Serena, looking down at her shuffling feet.

"Oh," said Mr. Jenkins again.

And then.

And then there was a silence.

And then there was a silence of just a few seconds.

And then there was a silence of a few seconds, during which Serena peeled off a tiny strip of rusty paint from the door number on the wall next to her.

And then there was a silence of a few seconds, in which Serena peeled off a strip of rusty paint from the door number on the wall next to her, and let it fall.

And then there was a silence of a few seconds, in which Serena peeled off a strip of rusty paint from the door number on the wall next to her, and let it fall – along with all her energy and enthusiasm and illusions and dreams – into an invisible black hole, which seemed to have opened up on the Welcome mat, between her and Mr. Jenkins's slippers.

And then.

And then she suddenly pulled herself upright, and said: "Thank you for that," as if it had been Mr. Jenkins who had been talking – as if it were he who had enlightened her, not the other way round. He nodded, taking the credit without thinking: so used to teacherly authority, so used to others deferring to his superior knowledge, it never occurred to him that this time it was the student who had widened his vistas – that this time it was the student who had imparted more than information to him.

The student in front of him scratched one last piece of rust off the door number, and then stared up at him – or, rather, at his tie. She said: "Yes, thank you very much for this talk, Mr. Jenkins" – and turned . . . and closed her eyes . . . and breathed in . . . and shoved her hand into her jacket pocket, to feel the folded-up letter in there . . . and opened her eyes . . . and took a step away from the house . . . followed by another step . . . followed by another step . . . each one slightly quicker than the last.

Behind her, Mr. Jenkins's mouth opened and shut with every step she made, but he couldn't assemble the words or mathematical formula which might express everything he felt about the retreating student. So, eventually, he sighed, turned and shut the door.

And Serena would not have known that Mr. Jenkins subsequently paced into the living room, sat down on the edge of the sofa, flicked off the TV, and stared at a cup of tea on the coffee table – a cup of tea which he'd poured for himself before the knock on the door, but which was now too cool to drink. Serena would not have known that he dipped his finger into the tea to test its temperature, the dispersal of its heat-energy. And nor would Serena have known that, the next time he was in Hanley, he visited HMV and bought himself a copy of Shostakovich's Fifteenth Symphony in A Major, Op.141 . . . and took it home, put it on the stereo in his cold and empty terrace . . . and breathed in-out-in-out in time to its desolate cadences . . . *calando*, *calando*, *morendo*, *morendo*, like the slowing breathing of a dying child. Serena had no way of knowing any of this.

No, all Serena knew was that, the night after knocking on Mr. Jenkins's door, she came down with a cold, and dreamt a chaotic, feverish dream of an equation in statistical mechanics . . .

$$S = k_B \ln \Omega$$

. . . where entropy (*S*) equalled Boltzmann constant (*k*), times the natural logarithm of the number of microstates (*omega*) . . . or entropy (*S*) equalled her father's constant waiting, watching in the sitting room (*k*), times the natural logarithm of the number of micro-emotions for Mr. Jenkins, her father, her mother, her stepmother, Sara, Simon (*omega*) . . . or entropy (*S*) equalled her father's never-ending piano ban (*k*), times the natural logarithm of tears she hadn't cried (*omega*) . . . or entropy (*S*), which might also have been *S* for Serena, equalled everything in the world (*k*) times an *omega* which, in her dreams, looked more and more like a dead sister's face, a face she loved . . .

. . . until she woke up with a start and a scream into a lonely house *sans omegas*.

VAR VIII

Lizzie

LEAVING HARRY IN his customary armchair one cold February morning, Lizzie slammed the front door shut behind her, and almost collided into Davy Lawson, from Number 3, Spark Close. She tried to say "Sorry" and "Good morning," but he looked uncharacteristically embarrassed, lowered his head, and hurried past, crumpling a newspaper in his hands.

That was the first strange thing she noticed that day.

The second strange thing she noticed was at school, where the kids pointed at her car as she pulled into the driveway, and sniggered behind their hands – even more than usual.

The third strange thing she noticed was in the staff room at break, when no-one had used her Little Miss Neat mug for their coffee. For once, she didn't have to rinse out her mug before using it herself, and she almost felt offended on its behalf, as though it had been quarantined: "Why doesn't anyone like my mug today?" she wondered.

She was sipping coffee from her mug, when the fourth and final strange thing happened: the Head of Year asked her into her cubby-hole office, and offered her a sports biscuit – engraved with a heroic javelin-thrower – along with "whatever kind of help might be required in these trying circumstances."

Lizzie had assumed that the "trying circumstances" were now such ancient pre-history to everyone outside herself that they'd been all but forgotten, except as a passing whispered comment: "Ah, there goes that poor woman. Always smartly turned out, her. Would die for her steepled nails. Talking of which, her daughter died, you know. Terrible story. Cancer or suicide or something. Can't quite remember which. Poor girl. Poor woman. Still, it was a long time ago in a universe far, far away, and she seems to be handling it quite well, considering the nails. Time mends all. Anyway, as I was saying . . ."

Or, at least, Lizzie thought that was what everyone had been saying behind her back; but perhaps not. Perhaps she was wrong, and other people didn't think it was a long time ago. She was no longer sure what a long time was in the outside world; in the inside world, a long time was no different to a short time which was no different to no time at all. Often, time felt as still as a man sinking into an armchair.

Sinking into the Head of Year's armchair, she took the sports biscuit, and nodded at the offer of help. "Thank you," she said, "it's very kind of you." She'd come out with such responses so many times, they'd become automatic, mechanical. "I think we're managing okay."

"That's very commendable," said the Head of Year, "in the circumstances."

"We do the best we can." Lizzie dipped the javelin-thrower into her coffee.

"I can see that, Elizabeth. But it's important to know, *in the circumstances*" – she kept repeating the three words, with heavier emphasis each time – "that you're not alone."

"Thank you," said Lizzie. "It's nice to know." She bit the head off the javelin-thrower. Usually, she only nibbled biscuits round the edges, but today already felt different.

"It's not only nice," said the Head of Year, "it's vital for you to know that the school recognises that you have been a punctual and attentive teaching assistant. It's been a successful experiment, employing you, Elizabeth – so much so that the LEA as a whole is thinking that they might, in the future, pilot more assistants in other schools. Indeed, the scheme might go national. It is neither the school's nor the LEA's policy to overlook such success."

"I'm glad to hear it," said Lizzie.

"You'll also be glad to hear that the school will stick by you. Myself, the deputies and the Head, we held a breakfast meeting this morning, and we all decided to back you, Elizabeth, whatever the . . . repercussions."

"Back me?"

"Of course. You can count on our support in these trying circumstances. We will do whatever it takes to help you get over this . . . difficulty. We feel you have been an asset to the school, and we do not want to punish you for something that is no fault of your own."

"Punish me? No fault of my own?"

"Absolutely. The circumstances are clearly not of your own making, and anyway, we feel it would do the school's reputation more damage than otherwise to discipline you or ask for your resignation now. As I say, you will be pleased to know that we have decided to stand by you, despite the seriousness of the circumstances which confront all of us."

"Stand by me?" Lizzie felt like a questioning echo, but a sudden rage broke her out of it, and she jerked forwards, spilling coffee down her blouse. She took out a handkerchief, and started dabbing at it, speaking down at her own chest: "What do you mean? I don't understand. You can't be serious."

"Of course we are serious, Elizabeth. These are serious circumstances. We need to have a concerted policy in the school to deal with them."

Lizzie was trying not to cry, her voice increasingly high-pitched: "You're damned right they're serious circumstances. You're damned right. But what kind of 'concerted policy' are you talking about?A policy of what? A Leukaemia policy? A dead-daughter policy? A grief policy? A grief . . ." She couldn't finish the sentence, because she knew at the end of the sentence were tears, and she didn't want to reach that full-stop, not here, not now. So she stood up, smoothed down her skirt and started saying: "I'm going now. I'm going and I'm not sure I'll be . . ."

The Head of Year held up her hand, and interrupted: "Look, I'm beginning to think there's been some kind of confusion here. We don't seem to be on the same . . . wavelength. I'm not talking about your . . . about Melissa, Elizabeth. Did you think that?"

"I don't know what to think," said Lizzie, hovering between standing up and sitting down.

"Please don't think that of us. It's got nothing to do with Melissa or her Leu . . . illness, Elizabeth. I think we've been supportive about that, over the last few months. Haven't we?"

Lizzie nodded automatically, wondering what the definition of "supportive" was. They had all expressed the usual condolences. There'd been cards and flowers and school representatives at the funeral. She'd been given compassionate leave by the school for a week, which was then extended for a second week to cover the funeral. Coming back to school, people had been slightly more touchy-feely than usual, holding her elbow or knee when they were saying good morning, or pouring her a mug of coffee. She'd tried not to flinch at these incursions into her physical space, tried to welcome them, but had failed: the touches and near-touches served only to jerk her awake and reconnect her with a world of feeling – a world of which she was now terrified. Those who sensed her reaction didn't try touching her again, feeling they were intruding on someone's personal horror; and those who verbally expressed their condolences soon stopped, feeling there was nothing much more to say than "I'm so sorry," and "Let me know if there's anything I can do," and "I'm so very very sorry, please please please do let me know if there's anything whatsoever I can possibly do." Repetition or silence seemed the only two options when faced with her loss, and, within a few days, most colleagues had chosen the latter. So Lizzie came to feel that, for everyone else, her loss was all but forgotten, and she was alone – except for the odd sympathetic glance, or awkward pause when someone else was talking about a daughter, or family illness, or hospital visit, or even just a happy day out. This was the kind of "support" she had received from colleagues, which was neither more nor less than could have been expected. If Lizzie did expect more, she couldn't possibly have said what that more might have consisted of, and probably wouldn't have welcomed it if it had materialised, for that matter. She didn't want people to ask her how she felt. She didn't want people to give her reassuring hugs. She didn't want to share tears with someone else who'd suffered a similar bereavement. She didn't want any of this "support" . . . or perhaps deep down she did . . . but no, she certainly, definitely didn't . . . or perhaps she did, but . . .

. . . but the Head of Year wasn't referring to this kind of support anyway. She was talking about what she called an "invisible form of support, whereby we've tried to lighten your load behind the scenes, preserve your timetabled slots, ring-fence your free periods and lunchtimes, remove children with behavioural issues from your sphere, and not . . . not worrying too much when you've departed from normal school protocols. In these ways, behind the scenes, we've tried to be supportive, Elizabeth."

"I do appreciate all this," said Lizzie quietly, sitting down again. "Honestly I do." She sighed the anger out. "But I don't understand why you're talking about disciplinary action, or standing by me, or not standing by me 'in the circumstances.'"

"We're not talking about your . . . loss, Elizabeth. We're talking about the . . . *newer*, more recent circumstances."

"There are no other circumstances," whispered Lizzie, staring at the floor, which was a tiled brown and black carpet; the black patch into which her right heel dug was surrounded by eight brown tiles. "There are no other circumstances, that I know of."

"I see." The Head of Year puffed up her cheeks, and then opened her mouth with a slight pop, like a teenager blowing imaginary gum. "I see." She was still for a moment, and then reached down into her desk drawer. Taking something folded and red and grey out, she got up, stepped round the desk – and handed Lizzie what turned out to be a newspaper. Then she backed away, and perched on the desk in front of Lizzie.

Lizzie unfolded the paper, and laid it on her lap. She didn't open the paper, merely stared at the front page, which might as well have been red, white and black hieroglyphics. All she could make out was the date: 'Friday 18th February 2000.'

"Turn to page 12," said the Head of Year.

Lizzie shook her head, and tried to hand the paper back. "I don't need to. I've seen the sorts of things they say about our Close – well, even about us – before. It's rubbish."

"I know, but this is . . . different rubbish, shall we say? God knows, Elizabeth, I didn't think it'd be down to me to show you this. I assumed you'd already have seen it. In fact, we all assumed you wouldn't come in today. So please, Elizabeth, just turn to page 12."

Elizabeth turned, page by page, to page 12. There was a tiny article in one column about a man who'd lived for the last year by eating flies, and there was an advert for the National Lottery in the bottom right-hand corner.

In the middle of the page, though, was a photo of two stockinged feet, meeting two stockinged legs, spreading over to page 13, where the two stockinged legs became bare thighs, and then a black negligée, pulled down at the breasts to expose the nipples, then a neck adorned with pearl-imitation necklace – and finally the heavily-lipsticked face of someone she gradually recognised as Ms. Kirsten Machin of Number 10, Spark Close.

Lizzie's eyes travelled to the top of the right hand of the article, where the main headline was in white on black:

Sparks Fly in the Close:
Machin Love with the Neighbours.
World Exclusive.

Lizzie skim read the article and interview, eyes flitting between paragraphs, from sub-titles back to the beginning, from inset black and white mugshot of her husband, to Kirsten Machin's vital statistics, from one sentence about the Spark Close Phenomenon, to a sentence three paragraphs before about Harry's amazing love-making skills – as if Lizzie's ability to read in a linear way, the way she taught children to read, was falling to pieces before her eyes.

Finally, her eyes blinking with weariness, she folded the paper up, and handed it back to the Head of Year. She stood up – straight this time – nodded a couple of times, and said, "Thank you for showing me that. If you don't mind, I might take up the offer of having the rest of the day off."

"That's fine. I'll arrange cover for today and next week."

"No need for that. I'll be in again on Monday as usual. I just want today to sort a few things out. In the meantime, please could you convey my thanks to the other members of the Senior Management Team for being so understanding?"

The Head of Year nodded. Lizzie stood still for a moment, staring at a poster about the life-cycle of spiders, which was pinned on the wall above the Head of Year's desk. Then she breathed in, and left the office.

"God," said the Head of Year to herself, "I'm glad that's over. That was ghastly."

The day's ghastliness, though, had only just begun for Lizzie. Driving home, she wound the tinted windows up, and put on the radio. She didn't want to see anyone, didn't want anyone to see her. She now understood the peculiar behaviour of some people this morning – crappy *Sun* readers, she thought. She herself had never read a newspaper cover to cover in her life.

She pulled into Spark Close, and parked outside her front door. She checked no-one was around, and let herself out of the car. Right at that moment, out of nowhere, came a hard, bony hand on her elbow, and a whisper in her ear: "I told her," crackled the voice, like an old LP, "I told her not to do it."

"Told who what?" Lizzie looked down at the bony hand, which was connected to a bony arm, which was connected to Miss Rosa Adler. She was dressed all in black with an embroidered collar, held together with a blue brooch in the middle. She looked like she was in mourning for something. In her free hand, she was brandishing a copy of *The Sun*.

"I told her not to talk to the people who came from here," she whispered, more out of hoarseness than anything else, waving the newspaper. "She shouldn't have done it. She shouldn't have done it. She shouldn't have . . ." She kept repeating herself, and Lizzie wondered for a moment if her mind was going. Or perhaps both their minds were going.

"It was a horrid thing to do," Rosa continued. "We are old friends, myself and your family, and I know you are going through a terrible time at the moment. I can see it clearly. And then this, on top of everything, the – how do you say? – icing on the cake. It is not right. Loud so-called 'music' is one thing. Too many gentleman callers is another thing. Too many gentleman callers whilst your babies are crying is still another. But to do this. It is not forgivable. I told her so. I watched from behind my curtains, and I knew who the photographers were, who the reporter was. I guessed what was happening. So I knocked on her door afterwards, and told her what I thought. I told her: it is wicked, this thing you are doing. Please, take it back. But that Miss Machin, she wouldn't listen. She told me she needed the money for the mortgage, the twins, their milks, anything and everything, all these excuses. She told me to take my nose and stick it somewhere else. Where, I won't tell you. She thinks I am some kind of 'nosy old bat' with lots of those f-words thrown in too. Maybe everyone around here thinks the same, Elizabeth. I am just trying to help."

Lizzie didn't have time to deny or confirm Rosa's anxieties about people's opinion of her. She shook off the bony hand and muttered: "Thank you, anyway, for trying to stop her. Shame it didn't work." She thought for a moment, and then added: "And a shame you didn't warn us . . . me beforehand."

Rosa looked at the ground. "I am truly sorry about that, Elizabeth. I wasn't sure how to tell you, and by the time I'd summoned up courage, I was too late. I am sorry."

Lizzie said: "I'm sorry too," unlocked her front door, stepped into the house, and slammed the door shut on her neighbour. She put her bag down on the hallway mat, smoothed her skirt down – and then a pre-verbal growl welled up in her, gradually coalescing into words: ". . . Harry? . . . *Harry*! I want a word with you, Harry. Where are you, *darling*?"

"In here, *dearest*," came a reply from the sitting room.

She walked into the sitting room, and there he was – or there the back of his head was – in his armchair, in front of the television. Next to him, on a wooden stool, was an untouched cup of coffee from the morning, and next to that was a newspaper – today's *Sun*.

Harry muted the television, but didn't turn away from it, and the flickering images remained a silent yet colourful ghost between them for the rest of their 'conversation.'

"From your early return home, I would guess that you have heard about our renewed fame?" asked Harry, and Lizzie knew instantly that he had been preparing this all morning – rehearsing in his mind the archness, the detachment, the coldness of his tone.

"Harry," she said, and then stopped, feeling like she was strangely losing her balance, despite many years on high heels. She put her hand on the back of his chair, and steadied herself. Harry didn't turn round, didn't ask if she was okay. He just continued staring at the television, like an infant fascinated by lights.

"Harry, please," she said.

"Harry please what?" he asked.

"Harry, please, look at me."

His head turned with reptilian slowness: "Why?" he asked.

"Why?"

"Yes, why? I'll get a crick in my neck."

That was it. All of a sudden, the stasis between them was broken, and she cried, "You'll get much more than that, by the time I've finished with you," as she shoved him in the shoulder, once, twice, three times, each shove harder than the last. Finally, he caught her wrist, with unexpected force, and pushed her backwards into the armchair next to him.

"That hurt," he said.

"Good," she said, nursing her wrist, wriggling it around. "Good." She was almost choking as she spoke, "Harry, please." She'd so wanted to unleash all her rage, despair, fury on him – but her voice was letting her down. It sounded weak, almost pleading: "Please."

"Please what?"

"Just please. Just please. Just pleasepleaseplease." She took a deep breath. "Please make it stop."

"What?"

"Everything. Anything. Make it stop. You used to be able to make things stop."

"No I didn't. I couldn't make anything stop. Nothing ever stops. It just goes on and on and down and down. What happened proved that once and for all."

"But, Harry, you've got to understand . . ." she was saying.

"There's nothing to understand. It all happened, and I couldn't stop any of it."

"You could have stopped . . . you could have stopped yourself."

"I couldn't. I don't think I could. It wasn't my fault."

"Are you saying it was *her* fault, then?"

"Which *her*? Which *her* is to blame? Or is it all three of them, all three *hers*?"

"I don't know who or what you're going on about," she said, though deep down she did. "I'm talking about *her*," she said. "*Her. Her.*" She grabbed the newspaper from the stool next to him, and rifled through the pages till she found the article. She spread it out on the coffee table in front of them both and pointed: "*Her*. Are you saying it was all *her* fault?"

"No," said Harry, his tone hard, "I'm not saying that. Her fault was just . . . being there."

"Well, I'm there . . . I mean, here, aren't I?" Lizzie asked. "I'm here all the time. Why didn't you come to me? Why do you sit there . . . here, wherever, and never come to me? I wear high heels, don't I? I can wear stockings, can't I? I can . . . We can . . . We could . . ."

"We could what?" he asked. "Fuck? Is that what you want? All right, let's go and do it now." Again, with unexpected agility, given his usual torpor, he sprang out of the armchair, and grabbed her wrist for the second time. "Come on then. Let's go and fuck, like man and wife. You can dress up if you want, in stockings, heels and shit. But the important thing is the fucking, which we haven't done in quite a while. Not since last millennium, in fact. It's like learning how to ride a bike, though, isn't it? You never forget, especially when it comes to bikes – bikes like you were when I first met you. But that's all forgotten now. We can forget everything, wipe everything clean away, with a good, hearty fuck. Come on," he wrenched her by the wrist out of the armchair. Her legs wouldn't carry her, and she found herself on the floor. "If that's what you want, let's do it. Let's go. We could even make another M . . . baby. Yes, that's what we'll do. We'll replace the old one. We'll fuck for a new one. That's what we'll do. Come on. Chop-chop, fuck-fuck."

On her knees, on the rug, Lizzie was sobbing.

"Don't cry," Harry said. "We're going to fuck. It's a cause for celebration, not crying. Like Christmas – we only come once a year. And we don't cry at Christmas, do we? No-one'd ever cry at Christmas, it'd be fucking ridiculous, what with all that tinsel and presents and family fun. So let's not cry now either. Let's just go upstairs and have an uncrying fuck. Now."

He pulled at her wrist, trying to drag her along on her knees – but she wrenched it away and breathed in, out, in, out, levelling out the sobs, and whispered: "You're horrid, Harry, and I'm going to leave you."

"Nope," he said, grabbing his coat, which was slung across the dining table. "I think you'll find I'm leaving you. I'm going for a wank, sorry, I mean walk." And with that, he strode out of the room, and out of the house, slamming the door behind him.

Meanwhile, Lizzie picked herself off the floor, smoothed herself down, and went to look in the hallway mirror. She grimaced, and climbed the stairs to the bathroom, where, with trembling hands, she washed her face in cold water. After that, she dipped a cotton-wool pad in cleansing cream, and, with neat, circular motions, scraped off all her make-up.

For a minute or two, she glared, hard and straight, at the unfamiliar, ageing woman glaring back at her.

She shook her head, as though dispelling a hallucination, and started to re-apply the same make-up as the morning. Gradually, her face travelled backwards in time, wiping out the last few hours. If only it were more. She put on lipstick, and stepped into the bedroom to pick out some earrings; and then she almost skipped down the stairs, not out of delight, but because she wanted to get out of the house before anyone returned.

Too late: as she reached the front door, a key clicked, and in walked not Harry, but Serena, early home from college – probably skiving, thought Lizzie, though it was understandable in the circumstances.

Lizzie didn't look at Serena and Serena didn't look at Lizzie. Neither knew what to say to each other. So they didn't say anything, and Lizzie brushed past her stepdaughter into the street, pulling the door closed behind her.

In the street, Lizzie breathed in-out-in, and turned right. Walking – even striding – towards Number 10, Spark Close, she tried to keep her head up high, her back straight, her posture correct. But she kept glancing down at the cracks in the pavement; and in every crack, she seemed to glimpse something she didn't want to remember, further and further back in time . . .

. . . In the first crack, she remembered today, the getting-on-with-it morning, the meeting with Head of Year, the newspaper full of bare thighs, the argument with Harry.

In the second crack, she remembered yesterday, and the day before that, and the day before that, before she knew any of this was going to happen – although maybe she'd sensed that the armchair-bound *status quo* wouldn't last forever, that something might be round the corner.

In the third crack, she remembered Harry giving up work, Harry giving up everything apart from his armchair and cheese and crackers.

In the fourth crack, she glimpsed an eight-month-old darkness, and closed her eyes.

In the fifth crack, she saw long strands of Melissa's auburn hair on a pillow, on the back of the sofa, blocking the plughole in the bathroom.

In the sixth crack, she saw Melissa catching spiders in jars with Simon and Serena.

From the seventh crack came Serena's piano music, as she played to Melissa to calm down her baby-screams.

From the eighth crack, rising up like steam, came a prehistory, a rush of pre-Melissa memories; and she felt acutely Melissa's absence from those memories, as if she were losing Melissa even before she was born.

In the ninth crack, Lizzie saw a moment a year and a half before Melissa had been born – the moment in which her younger self had first met Harry's younger-and-nearly-divorced-from-first-wife self. She had been living at home, working part-time as a support assistant in a Burslem primary school. One lunchtime, Harry had come to visit the school from Alma Mater Bookshops. He'd set up a display in the school hall, and given a presentation on new resources to a small group of teaching staff who were interested. Not particularly interested herself, Lizzie had been in the hall at the time, lining up chairs for a Year 3 music lesson after lunch.

At first, she hadn't taken much notice of Harry's droning presentation – and most of what she had heard didn't mean much to her anyway: " . . . and for Key Stage 2 Science, we have this new and revised edition of *Black Holes Are Fun* . . . and for Key Stage 1 Numeracy, we have this, *Number Days* . . . and for primary English teachers, we have this new series, which includes an updated version of *Midsummer Night's Dream*, where the language is tailored for inner-city schoolchildren from the Midlands . . . and this, a comic pop-up version of Aeschylus's classic, *The Sacrifice of Iphigenia*, suitable for . . ."

At this point, one of the teachers had interrupted him: "Oh, come off it, mate. Do y'know what you're saying?"

"I beg your pardon?" Harry had asked.

"No, I beg *your* pardon," the teacher had said – a teacher who'd happened to be someone Lizzie disliked, who'd never deigned to give her the time of day. She'd looked up, and started following what was happening more closely. "Look, mate," the teacher had said, "you can't be serious: a pop-up book of Aeschylus. You must be kidding." He'd looked round at his colleagues: "He must be kidding, right?" His colleagues had nodded.

"I'm not kidding, it's . . ."

"Well, if you're not kidding, and the publishers aren't kidding, then you've all got no fucking clue. Sorry, mate, and sorry about the language, but *really*, you people . . ."

Harry had suddenly stood up straight and glared at the teacher: "What do you mean, 'you people'?"

The teacher, a little taken aback by Harry's tone and stance, had opened his hands, and shrugged his shoulders: "Mate, look . . ." He'd looked round at the other colleagues for support, but they'd stopped nodding.

"Don't you 'mate' me," Harry had said. "And don't call me 'you people.' I'm not 'you people.' You think I'm so inferior to you. It's always the same. You bloody teachers think I don't have any idea what I'm selling. You think I'm some flunky who you can sneer at. Well, get this –" and Harry had strode over to the small upright piano in the corner of the hall. He'd sat down, opened the lid, and hammered out the opening of Grieg's Piano Concerto from memory. As soon as it was over, he'd stood up, slammed the fallboard shut, and glared at the group of teachers. "Do you know Grieg?" he'd asked.

The teachers hadn't answered. There'd been a pause, and then they'd all got up and left, shoulders slightly hunched, muttering to one another.

Only Lizzie had remained. It'd suddenly felt warm in the hall, and she'd found herself sitting down, trembling slightly. As Harry had started packing up his books in boxes, she'd tried to put her thoughts in order, tried to decide how she might make him notice her. In the end, half-remembering the title of one of the books he'd mentioned, she'd got up, touched her hair, and walked over to him: "Hi there. I just wondered, before you put everything away, could I possibly buy a copy of . . . Ease-key-loosses's . . . *Sacrifice of Fridges*?"

Harry's anger had instantly dissipated, and he'd laughed so hard that he'd ended up asking her out.

Back in February 2000, the ninth crack in the pavement reminded Lizzie that Harry had laughed once . . .

By the tenth crack, Lizzie was there, in front of the door of Number 10, Spark Close: Kirsten Machin's house. She tried the bell. It didn't work. So she knocked. She glanced to her left and saw the net curtains of Miss Rosa Adler's bay window waft in and out. She knocked again.

There was no answer, but when she pushed at the door, it gave. Maybe Kirsten had been expecting her; maybe she had got distracted by the twins and hadn't shut it properly.

Whatever the case, Lizzie opened the door, peered inside, and murmured: "Hello? Is anyone there?" – and then she realised that a tentative tone was by no means appropriate, given the nature of her visit, so she spoke loudly, harshly: "Look, I'm coming in. I want to speak to you."

A voice from a distance responded: "I'm in the back garden."

Lizzie stepped through the door, shutting it behind her. The front door of Number 10 led directly into the sitting room, which was littered with nappies, baby wipes, used baby wipes, washing, old underwear, old magazines and newspapers, old takeaway boxes, baby bottles, very adult bottles, and second-hand baby toys, which started playing out-of-tune nursery rhymes when Lizzie stepped over them. She wondered how this room could have been conducive to any kind of erotic liaison.

The kitchen, behind the living room, was no better, and the smell of damp rose up the walls around her. She pushed at the back door, which was ajar, and stepped into the back garden.

The back garden was full of bubbles. Refracted through them was Kirsten Machin, who, despite the February cold, was wearing sunglasses, vest top and jeans, and reclining on an old cloth deckchair. Now and then she took a sip from a long straw, which looped into a drink perched on the edge of a plastic table next to her. In between sips, she was blowing bubbles over a faded play mat, where misshapen giraffes and tigers leered over her twins. The bubbles swirled over them, then dispersed, eddied, spiralled and popped around the garden.

Kirsten didn't even glance at Lizzie as she stepped into the garden – she just carried on blowing bubbles. At times like these, Lizzie felt she was only half-visible: Harry, Serena, Kirsten, teachers at work never seemed to look at her, never so much as turned in their chairs when she approached – as if, without Melissa by her side, she were gradually fading away, not worth anyone's attention.

Kirsten's attention was limited to half-offering Lizzie a drink: "Would you like to join me in a little 'Ginny and Tony'? If so, you can help yourself – the bottles are all in the kitchen, somewhere or other." She blew some more bubbles.

Lizzie shook her head, and then realised that Kirsten wouldn't be able to see her, so she said. "No thanks."

Now she was here, in this woman's presence, she didn't know what to say, and she found herself staring at the twins, wriggling on the play mat. Kirsten sensed her gaze.

"Lovely, aren't they?" she said in a monotone, bored with the topic even before it was begun. "It was all for them, if y'know what I mean."

"What was?"

"*It*. That's, like, what I'm guessing you came here to talk to me about. *It*."

"Oh, *it*," said Lizzie, absentmindedly. Here she was, a yard or two away from the woman who appeared to have had sex with her husband, who may have destroyed her marriage, and yet, unexpectedly, she found she couldn't focus on anything – with the exception of the twins on the mat.

"That one – the one on the left," Lizzie said, pointing, "he's been a tiny bit sick. Possetting, probably."

Kirsten leaned forwards for a moment, yawned, "Oh, yeah," and slumped back in her deckchair. She blew a few more bubbles, then picked up the drink from the table, and stirred the ice with the straw.

"Shall I get a wipe and clean it off?" asked Lizzie.

"Yeah, if you want," said Kirsten. "Knock yerself out."

Lizzie went back in the house, through the kitchen into the living room, and found a packet of wipes on the floor. Standing up, she looked around, and remembered the article. "God, what am I doing?" she wondered out loud. Still, she didn't throw down the wipes, rush out of the back door, and scream at Kirsten. There was something about the atmosphere here, something so gin-soporific, that she felt she was moving, thinking, even raging in a dream.

She dreamed out of the house and back into the garden again. Kneeling down by the play mat, she dabbed the first twin's cheek clean. She pinched his toes, and was surprised how cold they were. "Do you think they're cold?" she asked.

"Might be," shrugged Kirsten, engrossed in blowing – slowly, slowly – a huge wobbling bubble out of the plastic dipper.

So Lizzie went back into the house, and rooted round for a blanket. Finding one screwed up in the corner of the living room, she came back into the garden, shook it out, and tucked it round the twins' feet and legs – just as she'd done with another baby, many millions of years before. "There, you poor things. There."

Suddenly, the huge bubble Kirsten was blowing burst, and she sat forwards, snapping, "Why d'you say 'poor things'?"

"Because . . . because they were cold."

"Because you thought I'd, like, made them cold? Is that it?"

"Pardon?"

"Because you think I'm not fucking looking after them? Is

that why they're 'poor things'? Is that what you think? That you can look after them better than me?"

"Hey, wait a min . . ."

"No I won't wait a minute. I fucking won't. I get all this shit from that miserable old bitch next door. Then I've got all this shit from the paper, who swan in here like they're my mates, and go ahead and print lies about me, and rip me off for my fee. And now you swan in here too and accuse me of being some kind of shit mother. Well, I'm fucking not."

"I never said you were. But honestly, you shouldn't be using language like that in front of them," said Lizzie, patting them. "Shhhhh," she said to them. "It's all right."

"Don't you 'shhhhh' my babies," said Kirsten, as if Lizzie were invoking a curse, not a comfort. "They're my fucking babies. Get away from them." Lizzie jerked backwards, and stared up at Kirsten, who only moments before had seemed so calm, and who was now slamming down her drink on the garden table. For months, Lizzie had felt self-conscious around other people's babies, when teachers brought their newborns into the staff room; for months, she'd worried that parents were keeping an eye on her, in case she got too close, in case she somehow infected their new families with what had happened to hers – and now Kirsten's behaviour seemed to confirm those fears.

"I was only 'shhhhh-ing' them," said Lizzie.

"'Shhhhh' yourself," said Kirsten. "You lot come round here, shhhhh-ing my twins, judging me, when you've got no idea. You don't know how I am with them. You and that bitch next door, you don't fucking know how I get up at six every morning, change them both, then they shit everywhere, and I have to change them again, and then I have to get their milk, and then they throw up all over me, and then the phone goes, and it's some bloke who wants a quick wank-off at eight in the morning, eight in the fucking morning I tell you, and I'm covered in baby sick, but I need the money, so I stay on the line making the right noises, whilst the twins are shrieking and crawling and breaking stuff in the next room, and then I hang up, and find one of them has shat on the other one, and he won't stop screaming and screaming, and it's like the beginning of that bloody noise we all heard in the Close, except we never get to the nice music bit – there's just the shrieking going on and on forever and fucking-ever till I'm half-dead in the fucking head, and it's only ten a.-fucking-m.

"And then, just when we've finally got to a bit of chillaxing in the p.m., you swan in here and tell me I'm a shit parent. Perhaps I am, but no more nor less than any of the other shit parents around here."

"I never said you were a . . . bad parent, Ms. Machin. Kirsten. I never said that. I didn't come here for a discussion about parenting. I came here to discuss you and my husband. You and my husband and nothing else. For God's sake, I should be the one shouting and banging gin and tonics around – not you."

"Bollocks," shouted Kirsten, now on her feet, and waving around her arms and the bubble mixture, which spurted everywhere. "You came round here to spout exactly the same fucking lies that are being pedalled by her next door, by those wankers at the newspapers – that I'm a slapper, that I'm a crap parent, that I'm some kind of fucking alchy. It's all lies. They promised me, the lying bastards, a certain, like, sum, and they promised me they'd print the truth. Instead, they print fucking bullshit. I am not a slapper. I am not an alchy. And finally, finally, fucking-final-final-finally, I didn't have any fucking romps with your fucking husband."

Kirsten had ranted the last "finallys" in Lizzie's face, who leant backwards, away from her. There was a silence, as

Kirsten caught her breath. Then she picked up her drink from the table, and slumped back down in her deckchair. Twitching slightly, taking a sip from her straw, she spoke calmly once again: "And that is my last and final word on the subject. Like what they say in TV costume shit: I bid you good day, *madam*."

Lizzie opened her mouth and closed it again. In the end, she almost squeaked when she spoke: "So what you're saying is that . . ."

". . . that I did not, and never have, in any way, shape or form, romped, made love to, slept with, shagged, fucked your fucking husband. Though I might do it now you've pissed me off so much."

"Oh," said Lizzie.

After that, she said nothing more to Kirsten. She just bent down, kissed her fingertips, and pressed the fingertip kisses onto the twins' foreheads. Then she swivelled round on her heels and, with her back straight and gaze forwards, strode away from the bubbles, away from the twins – one of whom had rolled over and was trying to crawl after her – out of the back garden, through the house, out of the door, and down the Close. Halfway back, on the fourth or so pavement crack from home, she hesitated slightly, her footfall more tentative for a millisecond, not noticeable to anyone who might be passing. In that millisecond, on that crack, she thought of all the things she'd meant to shout at Kirsten, and considered retracing her steps. But by the time her heel clacked on the ground again, she'd decided to leave everything else unsaid, and propelled herself forwards.

She let herself in to the house, wondering if Harry had returned from the newsagent's, or Bargain Booze, or wherever – perhaps already wondering if there'd come a time when he didn't come back at all. His trips to the shops – at least, that's where she presumed he went – were getting longer, as if the distance between the house and outside world were lengthening, imperceptibly, over time.

She peeped round the corner of the living-room door, and found it empty: Harry hadn't yet returned from the outside world. She took off her shoes, massaged her heels, and stepped into the room. Padding over to Harry's chair, she looked down at it, half expecting him to be there – or, at least, a smaller version of him, shrinking into the leather.

But no. The chair was empty, the imprint of his bottom hollowed out on the seat. Lizzie pulled the cushion up, brushed the cracker crumbs off it, shook it around, hit it twice to plump it out, and replaced it, spick and span.

Then she sat down on it, on Harry's chair, and looked around – to see what was so special about the chair, and about the view from the chair, that he wanted to spend all of his time there. There was nothing startling: a good face-on view of the TV, the coffee table and footstool easily to hand, the other armchair, sofa and bay window all ranged round him in a semi-circle. Here, Harry was at the centre of a small and usually empty amphitheatre, a miniature concert hall.

Something in the middle of this concert hall caught Lizzie's attention, something on the coffee table. She bent down, and pulled the coffee table closer so she could see it properly. There, wide open for all to see, was *the* article, spread across pages 12 and 13 of the newspaper. There was the small, grainy photo of her husband – who, at this moment, seemed small and grainy to her in real life. There was the 'exclusive interview' with Kirsten Machin. There, in front of her, and no doubt in front of a million other people, were the lies, or not-lies, or mixture of the two, about her husband's adultery, or *faux*-adultery, or mixture of the two. And there, in the middle of it all, was the photo of Kirsten Machin reclining, smug and victorious in lingerie.

Or not.

As Lizzie's eyes once again travelled up her stockinged legs, skimmed over those bare thighs, saw through that transparent negligee, and then alighted on the bare breasts, she realised with a start that they were no longer breasts, but eyes, with spectacles drawn round them, a pointy nose between them, and a big moustachy grin underneath. Above this Magritte-ish breast-face, everything, including the original face, was scribbled out with a black-biro hair-do. The moustachioed, bespectacled, cross-dressing, stocking-wearing, shrunken and misshapen man, with his huge Afro and out-of-proportion legs, was signed with a flourish underneath: *Serena Comb*.

Lizzie closed her eyes, opened them again, found the cartoon still there in front of her . . . and started giggling, and then laughing and then crying and then laughing again and then laughing-crying-snorting-giggling – all things she hadn't done in a very long time. Serena, who was buttering herself some toast in the kitchen, heard the animalish snorts, snuffles and giggles, and crept up to the living-room door, to see what was happening. At the door, she saw the back of her stepmother's head rocking back and forth, and wondered if she was having some kind of fit, if she were ill, if she'd finally gone mad.

But if Lizzie had gone mad, Serena thought, it was a nice kind of mad, infinitely preferable to the silent sanity, which had turned the house to stone over the last few months; and Serena smiled at her toast, and carried it back into the kitchen.

Because she was back in the kitchen, she didn't hear her stepmother – after wiping her eyes and trying to catch her breath – whispering, "Thank you. Thank you, Serena. Thank you."

Those "thank yous" were the last words Lizzie spoke in

the house for a long while, because, a few minutes later, she leapt upstairs, threw a suitcase on the bed, threw as much as she could into the suitcase – clothes, shoes, make-up, jewellery, a small music box containing a strand of Melissa's auburn hair – dragged the suitcase down the stairs, stepped into her heels, breathed in-out-in, stepped out of the front door, put the suitcase on the backseat of her car, sat in the front seat, waved absentmindedly at her soon-not-to-be-neighbours, Mr. Rajesh Parmar, who was outside his house watering a hanging basket, and Mr. Paul Higgins, who was shuffling past the car, munching a packet of beef and mustard crisps, turned the key in the ignition, raised the clutch, released the handbrake, did a quick three-point turn, and let the car roll down the hill towards Clermont Avenue, then Diarmid Road, then New Inn Lane, then Stone Road, then the A500 – and finally, forty minutes later, her mother's home in the northwest of the city.

VAR IX

Email

From: Mrs. Elizabeth Comb (lizzieharrymelandseri@hurrymail.co.uk)
To: Miss Serena Comb (serenadarkgirl@hurrymail.co.uk)
Re. Leaving
Date: 19.2.2000

Dear Seri,

I can write to you from this email address, because I know that Harry won't check it.

I didn't want to leave you without any explanation. But I couldn't face talking about it yesterday evening, after everything that had happened. I hope you understand.

I had to leave, just for now, because of the stuff with the newspaper and all that. Your father and I had an argument about it, we said some things we'll probably regret, and I decided we both needed some time out, if only to calm down. I think your father needs some time to think about where he's going, and perhaps find another job.

Try and look after him, if you can, whilst I'm away. Both of us know he's difficult to live with, and I get frustrated because it often seems impossible to know how he's feeling or what he's thinking. Trying to see into his feelings is like, well, I don't know how to put it – like staring into one of those black holes you have on the space posters in your bedroom – staring and staring till you get kind of dizzy and have to turn away. But you never know, perhaps Harry thinks that way too: I don't think he really understands how he feels himself. Or perhaps I'm just talking nonsense, I don't know any more.

Everything's been a bit of a black hole lately, and I wanted to say I'm sorry if we've not got on so well. I am very sorry if I've behaved badly. No, I HAVE behaved badly. It's been a difficult time since, well, you know.

You probably also know where I am. I'm staying with my mother in Talke Pits. You are welcome to come and visit or stay any time.

With apologies and love,

Lizzie xx

VAR X

Happy Birthday

After her stepmother left, Serena half-wondered if, mathematically speaking, the change would mean she was less lonely than before: now there was only one, not two people ignoring her at home. Surely, mathematically speaking – surely, in terms of the kinds of equations she studied with Mr. Jenkins – that would mean that home life was less, not more, desolate than it had been. Loneliness should obey an inverse-square law, she thought, whereby the further away people like her stepmother and mother were, the less ignored, and therefore the less lonely, she felt.

But no, it seemed that the loneliness equation didn't obey an inverse-square law; instead, without Lizzie there to ignore her, Serena felt as if home itself were drifting and collapsing outwards, away from her – the walls retreating from her touch, even the smallest rooms full of echoes, unwatered house plants shrivelling, blown light bulbs unreplaced, reflections in mirrors strangely small, as if seen down a tunnel.

It all seemed to happen so quickly: the central heating stuttered and moaned and gave up the ghost; the fridge emptied, apart from one mouldy patch at the back, shaped like a child's face; the living-room carpet was patterned with cracker crumbs; dust settled everywhere, like sleep; the cooker was cold and unused; the window frames rusted up and wouldn't open; the front door wouldn't open or shut properly; cupboards contained only damp; and even the cobwebs seemed tatty and neglected, as though the spiders – including those once caught and serenaded by Melissa – had abandoned the house to ruin . . .

. . . and Serena *lived alone in the deserted house, and day succeeded day, and still she lived alone, and the cold walls looked down upon her with a vacant stare, as if they had a Gorgon-like mind to stare her youth and beauty into stone* . . .

Finally, one and a half months later, on the morning of Tuesday 4th April 2000, Serena woke up as cold as stone, and decided to call an emergency plumber from the Yellow Pages to try and revive the boiler. She paid him an interim fee with her mother's allowance – or, rather, with the money she took from her father's wallet, which was ultimately from her mother's allowance.

After the plumber had gone, she went to the shop and bought some light bulbs. She came home, and balanced on a stool at the top of the stairs to try and change the bulb there. The light fitting crumbled at her touch, and she fell and hurt her ankle; but immediately she got up again, and went to replace some of the other lights which had blown in the bedrooms – even the one in Melissa's room. Then she put on her stepmother's marigolds, and scrubbed the worktops in the kitchen with an old scourer; she wiped the toilet seat down, and rinsed the bath out; she found a duster under the sink, forced open some of the windows, and tried to exile dust, dead skin, cracker crumbs from the house; and finally, she hoovered the carpets, including the living room, around her father's unmoving feet. Under the sofa, the Hoover knocked against one of Melissa's old spider jars, which Serena quietly picked up and took upstairs. Back in her sister's bedroom, she shut the door behind her, switched on Melissa's Planetarium, and lay on the bed, holding the jar like a teddy whilst she dozed.

She awoke next morning into renewed grief, and crept out of the room, not wanting her father to know where she'd slept and cried. In the harsh morning light, the house seemed almost as much of a mess as before. The boiler had started clanking and stammering again, one of the light bulbs she'd replaced had fallen out and smashed, some of the dust had resettled, and her father had dropped more cracker crumbs in the living room. Later that day, whilst he was in the bathroom, she picked up the crumbs one by one. She thought of Hansel and Gretel following breadcrumbs out of a forest; but her father's crumbs led nowhere, just round and round the armchair.

At that moment, her father wandered back into the living room, following the trail to his own personal nowhere. Still holding a couple of the crumbs between her thumb and forefinger, Serena sprang up from the floor, red in the face.

"What are you doing?" he grunted. It was the first thing he'd said to her for two days . . . or maybe three . . . no, surely it couldn't have been three. "Why are you looking guilty?"

"I'm not looking guilty," she said. "I'm trying to keep the place a bit tidier."

Harry pointedly glanced around himself, "You're not doing a good job then."

"At least I'm trying."

"Very trying," said her father, yawning at his own non-joke. He pushed past her and plumped himself back down in his armchair. He picked up the remote control, and peered round her at the blank TV screen. "Can't you at least go and do this so-called 'tidying' stuff elsewhere? You're in the way here – in the way of my silence."

Serena stamped her foot. "I could say the same about you," she said. "I could say you are in the way of my tidying."

Harry looked at her with a dead stare. "Okay then, why don't you tidy *me* away?" It was not said as a joke, Serena thought, nor even as a challenge, but almost as a request. He said it so plainly, without any kind of inflection, yet it caused something to rise into her eyes, something unwanted.

Blinking the unwanted something away, she looked down and realised she was still squeezing forefinger and thumb together. By now, the cracker crumbs she'd been holding had all but disintegrated, and she let the remains fall back into the carpet.

"God, Dad," she whispered.

"What's God got to do with it?" asked Harry, sharply again. "What's God got to do with anything, let alone tidying up? He's pretty crap at tidying up. If it weren't for humans and their obsessive tidying, the world'd be covered in dust and cobwebs and crap. Bloody environmentalists on my TV all the time going on about pollution – they don't seem to understand that, if it wasn't for humans, this crappy world would be a fucking mess. Without us, God'd just let it all go to shit. That's the so-called 'natural order' he set up."

"Dad, I wasn't talking about God or natural orders or anything." She knelt down in front of him and his armchair. "Dad, listen to me. Dad, look at me. Are you all right, Dad?"

Harry narrowed his eyes, "What do you mean 'Am I all right?'"

"I mean, are you . . . all right?"

"Of course not," he snorted, as if she were being a silly girl, and that was the end of the conversation. "Of course I'm not all right." He looked away.

"Dad, honestly. Look at me, Dad." Reluctantly, he looked down at his daughter's face again. "Look, I don't mean 'all right' as in, like, 'all right.' I know you're not 'all right' like that. I mean . . ."

"What?"

"I mean . . . 'all right' as in '*all right*.'"

"Well, that clears that one up then," he said, turning up his nose.

"But, Dad, I don't know how to ask you what I mean. I don't know how to ask you without you going m . . . getting angry. What I mean is: are you 'all right,' in like . . . perhaps you need . . . I mean, you go off on such tangents, talking about – I don't know – environmentalists and God and stuff, when I've just said one thing about tidying. Then other times you're totally, like, silent for days on end and I feel sort of like I don't exist, or that no-one exists apart from you in this chair. I don't think that's 'all right,' but I don't know if it's me or you who's not all right. Perhaps it's both of us. So what I mean, Dad . . . what I mean is: are you 'all right' as in, like, do you need to see, perhaps, I don't know, perhaps, maybe, you need to see a doctor or something." She gabbled the last few words so quickly, to get them out before she thought better of it, that she wasn't sure he'd heard them the first time. So, when he said nothing in response, she repeated them, more slowly, more clearly: "What I mean, Dad, is perhaps you're not 'all right,' and you need to see, like, a . . . doctor."

There was a pause, during which Serena held her breath and jerked backwards, falling on her bottom – imagining he was about to burst into a rage, leap up at her, push her away, throw his crackers onto the floor and stamp them into the carpet around her, shouting all the while: "How dare you? Who do you think you are, you jumped-up shit of an adolescent, telling me I'm going round the twist? Do you want me committed or something? Do you want me on fucking pills, drugging me up so I forget my daughter fucking died? God, I tell you what: if pills can do that, please give me fucking millions of them."

But Harry didn't do or shout these things. Instead, he merely picked up the remote control in his right hand, and pointed it at the television, directly behind her. He pressed a button, and pressed it again. He looked down at the remote, shook it, then held it at arm's length, and pressed the button again. "Will you move?" he asked.

"What?" asked Serena, who was still on her bottom, looking up at him.

"I said: will you move out of the way?" He spoke slowly, as though to someone who didn't speak English: "You're in front of the television. Will you move, so I can use the remote? I'm trying to change channel." His voice hardened as he growled: "You're in the way. At present, I'm shooting laser beams into you. If you don't move, you'll get cancer."

He said the last word in the same tone as everything else, but, for Serena, it worked like a remote control, and she shuffled quickly to one side.

"Thank you," said her father, again pointing the remote at the TV, and then putting it back down on the arm rest next to him. The TV had been blank to start with, and was still blank when he finished. Serena looked between it and him, him and it.

"Dad," she whispered.

"What?" he said, staring ahead at the blank screen.

"Dad, that's . . . what I mean."

"What's what you mean?"

"What you're doing now."

"What am I doing now, *dearest*?"

"You're watching a . . . blank screen." She hesitated over

the words, wondering if she were destroying some kind of comforting delusion – and, at the same time, wondering if it might be her, not him, who was deluded. Perhaps there *was* something on the screen, and it was she who couldn't see it.

Still, neither of these possibilities stopped her pursuing the subject she'd finally broached – the subject, that is, of doctors and some kind of "help." Having got this far, she felt she might as well pursue the subject to the bitter end. "Dad, I don't want to argue with you . . ."

"Who's arguing?"

". . . but you *are* watching a blank screen." She pointed behind her at the television. "There's nothing there. Can't you see it – it's totally blank, grey, empty?"

Harry picked up the remote, and waved it at the TV. "That's exactly what I'm talking about. There's nothing on. There's never anything on." He pressed a button on the remote. The TV remained blank. "See," he said, "nothing here." He pressed the remote again. The TV remained blank. "And nothing here. All the same nothingness. God, what do I – or should I say, your mother? – pay all that fucking licence money for?"

Serena got up, stepped over to the TV, and pressed the 'On' button. The TV flickered, and some blurry images of models in colourful lingerie appeared on the screen. A newscaster was reporting something about one big lingerie retailer taking over another. The lingerie flickered, rolled, stabilised.

Harry pressed standby on the remote. The lingerie collapsed into a line in the centre of the screen, and disappeared. "I preferred the original nothing to the nothing you just put on – or, for that matter, the nothing that those women had put on." He pressed the remote a few more times, as if flicking through nothing-channels. Finally, he nodded his approval, waving the remote at the TV: "This nothing'll do," he said. "I think I like this nothing the best. The nothing-silence is so reassuring, don't you find? Much better than the noise that comes from the TV when it's actually on – or, for that matter, the noise that comes from your piano playing, or Lizzie's nagging, or that God-Botherer-Runtill's stereo down the road, or . . ."

Serena looked from remote to TV and back again. "Dad, please, put the remote down and listen to me instead of – well, instead of the silence. Please."

Harry put down the remote on the arm rest.

"Thank you," she whispered. Although she was the one standing, there was no doubt he was controlling everything – like a captain on the bridge. He was unmoveable, unsinkable: armchair confrontation after armchair confrontation, with his wife, his daughter, anyone, it was always the other person who argued, cajoled, gnashed their teeth, but who ultimately backed away, out of the room. He was always victorious here, if nowhere else. Here, in his living-room command centre, he could control the TV, the cheese and crackers, the arguments. Elsewhere – well, elsewhere was elsewhere, and he didn't really want to concern himself with elsewhere any longer. And certainly not today.

"Do you know what today is?" asked Serena, trying a different tack, shifting her weight from one leg to the other.

"Thankfully, I have no idea."

"Yes you do. You know it's the 5th of April. And you know what yesterday was too."

"Well, dear, I'm taking a wild guess that it was the 4th of April."

"You know what the 4th of April is . . . was . . . is."

"No I don't."

"Yes you do. You know it was . . . you know full well it's *her* birthday."

"Whose birthday?"

"You know, Dad. Course you know. Don't make me say it."

Silence.

"Melissa's."

"Oh *her*," he said, almost grinding the words out between his teeth. "*Her*. I'd almost forgotten about *her*."

"Shut up, Dad. Shurrup."

"Why?" Now he was shouting, finally: "Why should I shut up when you say whatever you want to me? You can say: Dad, you're a fucking nut-job. Dad, you need a nut-doctor. Dad, you need nut-pills. There's something nut-ologically wrong with you, Dad. Of course, daughter dear, how stupid of me not to notice." He theatrically hit his head with the palm of his hand. "How fucking stupid of me. Of course, I hadn't noticed there was something wrong with me. I hadn't noticed that my daughter had died. Thanks for pointing that one out."

"Dad . . ." Serena was crying now, holding her hands over her ears, but he didn't notice.

"Don't fucking 'D-a-a-a-a-a-ad' me," he elongated the word 'Dad' as if it were a multi-syllabic insult. "Don't fucking stand there, pretending to be the victim, when it's you who's just told me I'm a nut-job, and that I need to see a doctor. Well, yes, that's a good idea. The doctor can tell me there's something wrong with me too. The doctor can say: you're a nut, and you need some nut-pills to calm down the jumping-bean-nuts in your head. The doctor can say: take these Pro-nut-zac pills once a day, and soon everything will be hunky-fucking-dory. You'll be nut-less, no longer feeling stupidly sad. You'll no longer notice every time you trip over one of your dead daughter's dusty toys, which you're sure wasn't there yesterday. You'll forget you even had a dead fucking daughter."

Harry took a breath, and stared coldly at Serena. "Why the fuck are you crying, Serena, dear? Perhaps there's something wrong with you too. Perhaps you need some nut-zac pills as well. After all, crying after your daughter or your sister has died, it can't be fucking natural, can it? A bit of misery, bloody hell, it must be treated. It's been, what, nine months now. For God's sake, aren't you over it yet?" Harry's tone changed almost every sentence, as the different voices he mimicked – some posh-BBC, some high-pitched-female, some patronising-medical-professional – mingled with his own: "Grief is a process, don't you know. We agony aunties call it, in technical terms, the 'mourning process.' You have to take your time, let grief flow through you, and soon you'll feel better about the world.

"But then, you know, there are some people who take it too seriously. Their grieving processes are a bit unhealthy. A bit un-English. A bit OTT. There are some people who seem to think that grief might be more, well, more *passacaglia* than sonata form. Poor fellows: the grief just repeats itself over and over, never getting anywhere.

"These poor fellows are a bit lacking on the old Serotonin front. They need to pull up their Serotonin socks, as it were. After all, the only real problem is that someone died. Come on, people die all the fucking time. Get over it, son. And if you can't, well, at least there are pills and self-help books and waiting lists and psychiatrists and counsellors and a million other optimistic fuckers in the world. Their sort don't die, can't die, and even if they do, they come back, and you have to chop their heads off, and then their bodies and heads come back separately and get you all the same and . . ."

"Dad, shurrup, you're talking crap, shut up, SHUT UP!" Serena yelled, stamping her foot and staring down at him. There was no more patience left in her: all of a sudden, she felt furious at him – furious that he seemed to feel he was the only person hurting for Melissa, the only person who had loved her, the only person who now felt that loss. He sat in his chair like some armchair Lord of Grief, surveying and dismissing minions who wouldn't, couldn't match his despair.

That's how she felt at that moment, but she didn't say it to him. She just made some unintelligible, animalish noise, stamped her foot again, and ran out of the room.

Instead of running upstairs, she grabbed her jacket, and stormed out of the front door. Taking a deep breath on the doorstep, she turned left, walked down Spark Close, and then turned right onto Clermont Avenue. She walked down Diarmid Road, following the end of New Inn Lane onto the A34. She turned left on the A34, and walked the half mile or so to Trentham Cemetery. She paused just outside, as cars roared behind her – and then took the three steps up to the cemetery. She strode past the decaying war memorial, past gravestones which had been reclaimed by nature, past gravestones which had been effaced by nature, and past gravestones which had been knocked over by the Council, to pre-empt them toppling of their own accord.

Finally, she found herself standing in front of *the* gravestone. The engraving on it was stark and simple, because no-one had been able to think of a suitable epitaph at the time:

MELISSA COMB
(1992–1999)

. . . which inscription seemed to Serena as obscure, as abstract, as incomprehensible as an equation on a dead physicist's grave.

Serena knew she should have been at her sister's graveside yesterday. She'd waited all day for her father to say to her: "Look, it's Melissa's birthday, p'raps leave the cleaning for now, and we'll go and visit her." But he'd never said it, time had ticked by, and, by the evening, she'd realised he wasn't going to – wasn't even going to mention the fact of the birthday.

At least someone – presumably Lizzie, and perhaps her mother too – had replaced the flowers on the grave. Serena went to fetch a watering can and some water. She watered the flowers, and stood for a while in the cold and creeping darkness, shifting her weight from one foot to the other, crying and not crying, running her index finger up and down the sharp fold of the letter she kept in her left-hand pocket.

Eventually, she sighed and turned away from the graveside, in much the same way that she'd left her father in his armchair a couple of hours before; both were immovable objects, and ultimately the only option was retreat.

On her way back through the cemetery, she walked under the dusk-shadow of the Sutherland Mausoleum, all Piranesian gothic, all angles and haunches, its Ashlar blocks blackening against the sky, its four grilled faces facing outwards with gorgon-like stares. She'd wondered what was inside for seventeen years, and now, for the first time, the oak door was unlocked; so she heaved the door open, and stepped over the threshold.

Here, inside, had once been laid out the corpses of the Sutherland dynasty. Here, in a moment of Poeian fantasy, the family had kept a bell, in case of premature burial. Here should have been coffins, crucifixes, catacombs, ever-burning candles, echoing darkness, maybe even ghostly choirs. The gothic-pyramidical exterior demanded such things.

But such things weren't here. Instead, all Serena found inside was emptiness – and a magnolia emptiness at that, more like some vast abandoned living room than a tomb: the inside walls had been painted a few years before, and the paint peeled off when her hands brushed against it. On the floor were the remains of a spliff, and a couple of empty cans of cider.

Someone had scratched a half-hearted upside-down cross on the opposite wall, along with a picture of a cock and balls.

Otherwise, there was nothing, nothing at all – apart from a second sigh, a turning away, a weary trudge back home.

VAR XI

God Loves You

LATE IN THE afternoon of the 8th June 2000, on the eve of the Spark Close Phenomenon's first anniversary, Mr. Raymond Runtill and his stereo seemed to be conspiring to reconstruct the Phenomenon with Evangelical Worship Music. Belting out of the open window of Number 2 was an ecstatic refrain:

God loves you, He does and you know it,
Even when you're at the end of your tether,
God loves you, He does and you know it,
God loves you, forever and ever and ever . . .

After about two and a half hours of 'forever and ever and ever,' Harry Comb was seen striding out of Number 4, slamming the door behind him, and marching up to the door of Number 2. He banged on the door, but no-one answered – presumably because no-one inside could actually hear the door-banging over the music:

... Everyone, you should hold up your hands,
Cos your Father, He loves you and understands ...

Harry banged on the door again, but still no-one answered, and his fury seemed, for a moment, to be going nowhere. Just as he was backing away, the refrain came round again, and he glimpsed a chubby forefinger pointing out of the window to his left – as though finger-preaching to everyone in the Close that:

God loves you, He does and you know it ...

A moment later, Harry Comb was gripping hold of the finger, pulling its owner forcibly to the open window – until he and Runtill were face to face on either side.

Mr. Runtill was taken aback: "What the ...?"

Harry yelled over the praise music: "God loves me, does he? God loves me, does he?" He kept repeating the same words, just as the music itself kept repeating its refrain. Mr. Runtill, caught between these two ever-repeating refrains, seemed mesmerised, letting his forefinger be crushed by Harry's grip.

Finally, Mr. Runtill pulled his finger away and shook it slightly. He reached forwards and placed a hand on Harry's shoulder: "Yes, Mr. Comb, He truly does love you and blesses you, Harold Comb."

Harry screwed up his nose, then his whole face, and glared down at the hand on his shoulder, as if the physical contact were more wasp-sting than Christian blessing. "Get your fucking blessing off me!" he shouted, and pushed the hand away so hard that Mr. Runtill toppled backwards, and disappeared from view. When he reappeared, brushing himself down, his face was blank, his eyes wide. He didn't seem to realise what had happened. No doubt, in his night-job as a bouncer, he was used to sudden violence – but today he'd been in his other role, as lay-preacher to the Close, a role which didn't usually involve physical assault. So he wasn't prepared for Harry's behaviour, and didn't respond in kind – which was lucky for Harry, given their relative strengths, heights and weights.

"Harold, Mr. Comb, I don't under . . ."

"No, you don't," said Harry. "You bloody Christians never do. God loves you, he does and you know it, you know it, knowitknowitknowitknowit . . ." He seemed to get stuck on the song lyrics, like a stammer that wouldn't go away. He took a deep breath and carried on: "I keep hearing that God fucking loves me and I should knowitknowitknowit . . . I keep hearing this shite coming out of your front window. We all keep hearing it. It's so fucking loud it's making the blood in my veins vibrate. Will you please fucking turn it down and don't subject us all to your 'God is so fab' crap. I tell you what: God is a total wanker as far as I can see – getting sadistic kicks out of killing . . . killing . . . little girls like . . . well, like some kind of evil Maurice Chevalier: 'Thank heavens for little girls, so I can fucking kill them in lots of horrible and painful ways.' Ooh, God says, wasn't that fun. Must do that again and again for the next umpteen millennia, never stopping even for a fucking Sabbath break. Doesn't the wanker ever get bored of the same cruelty? Can't He invent something new? Oh, yes, I forgot – how disrespectful of me to underestimate Him. He has invented something new – in fact, every single minute, there's some new form of cruel shite to put little girls through, and everyone else for that matter. 'I believe in a cruel God' – wasn't that Verdi? Wasn't it? Wasn't it?"

With every insistent question, Harry leant further in through the open window, until he was only an inch from Mr. Runtill's face. At the same time, Runtill shook his head over and over. Whether he was indicating that he didn't know if the quotation came from Verdi, or, more generally, that he didn't understand a word Harry was saying, was unclear.

Meanwhile, a few people in the Close were peering round net curtains, tentatively opening doors, even stepping out, to see what the commotion was about. Further up the Close, to Harry's left, Rosa Adler was hovering on the doorstep of Number 12, clutching a half-empty Tesco's bag, which she'd been unpacking when she'd heard the noise outside. She was readying herself to intervene in the row, if it proved necessary.

Back at the window of Number 2, Mr. Runtill hardly seemed involved in the row himself: "I don't under . . ." he whimpered.

"Just try for once. Try to understand." Harry was almost spitting his words at the round pale face in front of him. "Make an effort. Stop sticking your big head in the fucking happy-clappy sand, and look around you. Listen to what's around you. It's all a cruel fucking trick. This God, He's a fucking sadist. So, once and for all, I don't want all this God loves you, he does and you know it, know it, knowitknowitknowit . . ." Again, he breathed in to stop the loop, and then continued: ". . . and more than anything, I don't want his cancerous fucking blessings anywhere near me, thank you very much."

As he said this, Harry was visibly shaking with rage, leaning into Mr. Runtill as if he might kill him with proximity. Anyone else would have backed away, perhaps to the phone to call the police. But Mr. Runtill suddenly looked straight at Harry, his face transfigured into an expression which seemed a hybrid of the bouncer's and lay-preacher's, mingling controlled aggression with benevolence. And he spoke in a voice which seemed to still the whole street: "'We made music for you and you did not take part in the dance; we gave cries of sorrow and you made no signs of grief.'"

There was silence for a moment – even the music on the stereo had stopped – and then Runtill nodded to himself, and rather ruined the effect: "That's Matthew, that is. Matthew 11, verse 17."

In response, Harry stood still, quivering for a few seconds. Then he turned on his heels, to glare at all the people in the Close who – on doorsteps, in cars, round net curtains – were staring at him. He seemed to have nothing to say in response to anything or anyone, apart from: "Bollocks."

After that, he might have returned to his house, slammed the door, sat back in his armchair, eaten some crackers; but, just as everyone thought the fuss was over, somebody who'd been scampering down the Close quietly fell over – like Brueghel's Icarus falling into the sea, in the corner of everyone's eyes.

It was the largest gathering of Spark Close residents since the 9th June 1999: Lelly and Davy Lawson from Number 3, Kirsten Machin from Number 10, Mrs. Hayley and Mr. Frank Hutchinson from Number 8, Mr. Paul Higgins from Number 6, Mr. Rajesh and Mrs. Sejal Parmar from Numbers 9-11, one of the Shelley sisters from Number 5, Ralph the Cat from Number 1, as well as various hangers-on – all of them were crowding round Rosa Adler of Number 12, who'd fallen over in a cascade of oranges. On her way to intervene in the row between Harry and Raymond Runtill, her Tesco's carrier bag had broken, and the oranges inside had started rolling away. Rosa had bent down and tried to catch them. Then she'd bent down some more. Then some more – until her body formed a kind of archway with the tarmac. Then the archway had collapsed in the middle, and she was nose-down on the road.

A number of people had run over to her. As they approached, the first person they saw bending over her, rolling her onto her back, and whispering to her was, of all people, Harry Comb.

"What's he fucking saying to her? What's he fucking doing to her?" asked Lelly Lawson, jogging up to the scene.

"Probably perving," said her brother, Davy. "He's dirty Harry, the one what shagged the slag at Number 10, and was in the papers for it. Now he's having a go at Number 12 too."

"Yuck, but she's like a million years old."

Kirsten was now bending over Rosa too. Only she thought she caught Harry's words – though admittedly she'd had a few cans of cider in the garden earlier. It was two days before her birthday, so she felt she deserved it, and, anyway, the twins were at her mother's that morning, to free her up to look for work.

Instead of looking for work, she'd found herself running down the Close to help her neighbour. She got to Rosa second, just after Harry. He was almost shaking Rosa, clutching onto her arms and whimpering something which resembled: "Please tell me, pleasepleasepleasetellme it's worth it. You of all people must know. Please tell me."

Rosa didn't respond. Kirsten told him to "Shut the fuck up," and shoved him away.

People huddled round them, murmuring: "Is she okay?" "Shall I ring the ambulance?" "Is she alive?" "What shall we do with her if she's not?" "Do you ring the ambulance anyway?"

Ralph the Cat squeezed through the small crowd, and purred up to Rosa, rubbing himself against her ankles. Rosa's eyes quivered and opened.

Seeing her regain consciousness, Kirsten took one arm, and Harry took her other. Half-lifting her, they guided her to the pavement, where she sat down on the kerb, Kirsten and Harry ranged on either side. Ralph the Cat weaved between their six legs, whilst everyone else milled around, mumbling, some of them already drifting away.

"Are you okay?" asked Kirsten.

Rosa looked from Kirsten to Harry and back again. "I am not sure," she said, croaking slightly. "Tell me, is this heaven?" She looked around, grinned and shook her head. "Obviously not. It must be the other place. To be honest, I thought I'd already seen that. Perhaps it is neither."

"You're right," said Kirsten, "it's neither. You're not dead, just a bit sick." She got her mobile phone out of her pocket, and started punching in 999. Rosa's hand shot out like a claw, and stopped her. Given that she'd just collapsed, her grip was surprisingly powerful.

"Ow, that hurts," said Kirsten. Rosa didn't let go.

"Don't call," she said.

"You need an ambulance, medics."

"I don't want them."

Kirsten said slowly: "Okay then," and Rosa withdrew her hand. "You might need to go see a doctor, though. What about that guy at the top of the Close, what's-his-name, Williams or something. I could go and get him. He wouldn't hurt – he seems dead gentle, like."

"Who says he wouldn't hurt?" asked Rosa. "These doctors, they're all the same. They've always hurt, right from . . . right from, well, a long time ago. For many years after that long time ago, I didn't want to see any more doctors. Even when I had my baby, all I saw was the midwife and one doctor who – how d'you say – turned his nose up at me and walked off, because I wasn't married. Because I didn't want to get married. I didn't care what the doctors thought, not after that . . . long-ago time. I didn't care. I didn't care. I didn't . . ."

"Okay, okay," said Kirsten, "I get the f . . ." – she stopped herself swearing in front of the old woman – "picture."

Kirsten rolled her eyes at Frank Hutchinson over the smaller woman's head, as if to say: "God, the old biddy's frigging nuts." It was the first time she'd really returned his gaze or even acknowledged his existence – a momentary thing, but when it passed, Frank beamed, and nudged his grandmother: "She's amazing, don't you think?"

"Who're you muttering about?" asked his grandmother.

"No-one," said Frank, looking down at his shoes.

By the time he looked up again, the "amazing" Kirsten was already moving away, leading Rosa back to Number 12. Harry tagged behind, carrying the remaining oranges, followed by the Hutchinsons and Paul Higgins. All the others, including the Lawsons, the Parmars, the Shelley sister, and Ralph the Cat, had got bored and drifted away. Ralph had retreated to the windowsill of Number 1, where he was scratching fleas and singing a tuneless cat-song.

Meanwhile, Kirsten half-carried Rosa into her house and up the stairs. "She's so capable, isn't she?" Frank mumbled to anyone who would listen.

"Who, Rosa?" Paul Higgins asked.

"No, Kirsten – Ms. Machin. Look at her."

Paul looked at her, dragging Rosa up the narrow staircase. "She's not just capable," he said, "she's bloody strong."

"What're you two are muttering about?" asked Mrs. Hayley Hutchinson.

"Nothing, grandma," said Frank.

"Good," said Mrs. Hutchinson. "This poor woman is ill, and we mustn't disturb her."

Despite not wishing to disturb Rosa, Mrs. Hutchinson followed the rest of the small group into Rosa's house, up the stairs, and into her bedroom.

Kirsten lay Rosa down on the bed, put a blanket over her, and propped her head up on some pillows. Then Kirsten sat on the bed next to her, and Rosa took her hand and patted it: "Young lady, you are not as bad as you want people to think."

Kirsten withdrew her hand, "Shut up."

For a minute or two, Rosa did shut up, and her eyes closed. Everyone stood and waited, uncertain whether or not to leave, uncertain whether to ring Rosa's grandson, Simon, uncertain whether to ring for a doctor in spite of Rosa's own wishes.

Just as everyone but Kirsten was on the verge of going, Rosa's eyes opened. "Don't go," she hissed.

"But you need your rest," said Kirsten.

"I don't. Or perhaps I do. But the point is I like having people here." She grinned. "It is a long time since I had anyone in my bedroom." She patted Kirsten's hand again. "You know, Miss Kirsten, that was what the doctor didn't like when I was pregnant: that I wasn't sorry. That I'd enjoyed myself." She was suddenly animated, and pulled herself up a bit on the pillows: "I mean, wasn't I – how d'you say – entitled to a bit of enjoyment, after . . . after what had happened? But then, I suppose the doctor, he didn't know about that. I never told people, and people didn't seem to want to know, anyway."

"Told them what?" asked Kirsten.

Rosa looked at the faces around the room, and shook her head.

"It is too late to tell you about it all now." She shut her eyes, holding her hand over the tattooed number on her forearm, seeming to drift off: "It is too late . . . I am too tired, too old, too sick to tell you . . . to tell you about . . . to tell you about that . . . that long-ago time . . . that long-ago place . . . that . . ."

(*. . . that long-ago place where music had gone up in smoke, rained down as ash, sunk into grey clay-mud, been sucked down with still-twitching corpses, risen again ("Aufstehen!") before frozen sunrises from the three-tiered cojas, pulled on* *the blue skirts, woollen stockings, striped jackets and white head scarves, swallowed metallic soup, marched in rows of five from Block 12, past the electrocuted Stoffpuppen hanging off the fences, three hundred or so yards to the Mädchenorchester's platform, stands, stools, and then shivered out of their instruments, Arbeitsmarsch after Arbeitsmarsch, for the hundreds, thousands, shuffle-marching past them to work, and then back again, to a place where major keys sounded like terrible dissonances, where common chords shocked the ear as much as the Leichenwagen's rattle, the gunfire, the boom of five belching chimneys, the dogs, the unheard screams from the Experimenteller Block, the rasps from the Revier, the barked orders of the Selektionen, the hiss of Zyklon-B, so that, afterwards – and for her at least there was an afterwards – the violin she had played there seemed permanently detuned, and the music she had once loved no longer anything but rattles, gunfire, booms, dogs, screams, rasps, orders, hisses . . .)*

. . . but no, Rosa wouldn't, couldn't tell them about all of this, because long ago her memory had locked itself up in a terminal *Blocksperre.*

Instead, when she opened her eyes again, all she would say, very quietly, was directed at Harry – who stared at the floor like a piano pupil being told off for a fudged note: "Some people, you know, their musical selves must be very strong, so they can overcome the most terrible things. But for others, for the weaker ones, for the ones who aren't quite talented enough, for the human beings like *us*, the musical selves are . . . well, turned to stone when faced with what is terrible. Afterwards, all we can hear is noise, dissonance, hell."

VAR XII

Fantasia for Four Hands in F Minor, D. 940, Op. Posth. 103

COMING BACK FROM Rosa's that evening, hoping, wishing she wasn't right,

finding his daughter Serena in the sitting room, looking up at him slouching in, his shoulders drooping, mouth sagging,

putting her magazine down, getting up to help him, as one might help an elderly man on a bus, trying to guide him to his customary armchair,

but he just shakes her off,

instead shuffling over to confront the piano, as though it is an enemy,

taking down the Jasperware pot on top, lifting the lid, taking out the piano key, replacing the lid with a scraping sound, tossing the Jasperware pot away, so it smashes behind him, unlocking and opening the fallboard with a creak, sitting down on the stool, and placing his hands on the keys, which aren't cold as he'd expected, but the same temperature as his fingers,

resting there, right thumb on middle-C up to small right finger on G, left thumb on middle-C down to small left finger on F, doing nothing, merely touching, ever-so-lightly, keys hardly touched since the funeral, and then, casually, as if nothing extraordinary is happening, the fingers starting to flutter by themselves, playing silent scales of an octave of C Major in contrary motion, flowing like tears, up and down the face of the piano –

flowing outwards, and then sucked back into the eye of middle-C, flowing outwards again, only to be sucked back down again –

and then two-octave arpeggios, wrists loosening, and the finger motion taking over from any conscious resistance in the brain, C Major in contrary and parallel motion, D Major, E major, C Minor, D Minor, E minor, and finally F minor, a certain little girl's favourite key, over and over again as if stuck in a vortex . . .

until abruptly, the soundless arpeggios stop, and Serena, who's been watching from a few feet away, thinks it might all be over, everything shut up again, her father's F minor arpeggios locked under the lid, trying to get out . . .

. . . but no, rooting beneath himself in the piano stool, for a tatty, yellowing score of a Schubert piece he'd once played – the only piece he'd regularly played in F minor, but which unfortunately needs four, not two hands – pulling it out, flicking through it, then unfolding the music in front of him, like a concertina on the stand, fingers poised on the keys, ready to play the opening F minor chords of the lower, *Secondo* part,

without thinking, shuffling over to the left half of the piano stool, making space for an invisible partner from his younger days – probably his piano teacher, whose thigh once touched his during this piece, but who might now be dead, a ghost, for all he knows

– a ghost who doesn't turn up to play with him, so there is no-one sitting beside him on the stool, no-one ready for the delicate entry of the *Primo* part in the second bar, and he might be sitting here forever, his fingers poised, waiting for nothing and no-one . . .

. . . and certainly not waiting for Serena to fill the ghost's place next to him on the stool, which she does nonetheless, expecting every second that his trance will dissipate, that he'll push her away, smashing the lid of the piano shut with a terrible discord,

deporting the piano once and for all to an endless, musicless limbo, in which the tuning slips, the wrest pins loosen, moths devour the piano felt, the overstrung frame rusts, the whole internal mechanism crumbles, fails, collapses in on itself . . .

. . . but her father's trance isn't dissipating,

is instead intensifying, leading him to play actual notes, bringing forth actual sounds from the piano, F-minor sounds,

Allegro molto moderato,

leading to her entry, the Hungarianesque first theme, that reminiscence of Schubert's beloved pupil Carolina Esterházy, stammering its syncopated sadness in crushed notes, meandering through major and minor keys, recurring throughout the piece like a dream of someone lost, always in the background, never going away, whispering like grief through everything that follows,

whispering through the more assertive second theme, with its angry exchanges between *Primo* and *Secondo*, the former *sfozando* at first, shouting repeatedly in the soprano register, the latter carrying on as if nothing is happening, and then echoing anger in the bass, and finally the dying echoes of both first and second themes weaving together,

then *crescendo*-ing to the recitative frame of the *Largo* movement, through grand trills to the miniature *Largo* itself, a love song for soprano and baritone, which can't stay still, can't stop drifting from key to key, haunted by outbursts of *fortissimo* rage and murmured echoes of the recitative trills,

giving into the *Allegro vivace scherzo*, where *Primo* and *Secondo* are always ready to erupt into *forte*, always ready to change back to *piano*, never settled, often working in contrary motion, trying to escape from each other – and sometimes, when their hands are farthest away from each other, at opposite ends of the keyboard, Serena wonders if his will ever gravitate back to the middle, back to hers,

but they do, with the recapitulation of what's been there all the time, whispering in the background, the original F-minor theme,

and in that terrible F-minor sadness, in his rocking accompaniment, in their crossings of hands, in this moment of musical closeness, Serena understands,

she understands that her father loved and loves both of his daughters,

and that this music is more or less the only language he's got left to express that love,

and she understands this language, understands all of this, even though it was he – she knows, in a way always has known – who wrote the red-crayon letter from a dead Melissa,

it was he who wrote the letter, now folded away in the left-hand pocket of her leather jacket, accusing her of being responsible for her little sister's death,

accusing her of this because it was her transplanted bone marrow which had failed to cure her sister's Leukaemia – which instead had triggered Graft Versus Host Disease, and she has to live with, sleep with, play with this knowledge, like bone-ache, every second of every day, forever and ever,

she has to live with, sleep with, play with this knowledge, as the two of them launch into the second, more assertive theme, now used as the basis for a final fugue, a desperate flight, in which Serena is always chasing her father, trying to catch up with his wildness, sometimes managing only one line at a time, sometimes a whole bar behind, sometimes losing him round musical corners, sometimes drowned out by his *fortissimo* virtuosity, sometimes sounding like she is begging him not to leave her behind, as he seems to be building up to something world-shattering,

something he never quite reaches,

and, in the end, the whole fugue disintegrates beneath them both, its crashing climaxes coming apart at the seams,

their lives crashing round their ears,

and out of the rubble, wandering, lost, dazed, staggers the first theme, unseeing, like the ghost of a girl who once was . . .

. . . And also like Harry the next morning, when, after fitful sleep, he got up at 7.05 a.m., showered, dressed in trousers, cardigan, shirt and tie, breakfasted on black toast with marmalade, muttered something through Serena's door about going to the shop for the morning paper "to look for jobs," left the house, shut the front door behind him – just as Serena was coming down the stairs – walked down Spark Close, turned right onto Clermont Avenue, right again onto Church Lane, walked past the bus stop, the newsagent and the Staffordshire Knot pub, right onto Stone Road, after which he was spotted by a couple of motorists walking up the hard shoulder of the A500 towards Stoke, where he caught a train to London Euston and then . . . and then . . .

. . . and then, apart from a few rumours and dubious sightings, nothing.

Harry Comb vanished into nothingness, silence.

And, however distraught they were, neither Serena nor Lizzie were really surprised by this vanishing act. Serena for one knew that their last piano duet, their final *Schubertiade*, hadn't been a true reconciliation, because a reconciliation necessarily implies a future, something afterwards; and that was precisely what Harry could never cope with – an afterwards. As he himself had once said to Lizzie: "Why can't things just finish like they do in music, instead of growling on forever?"

Coda

2003

Oft denk'ich, sie sind nur ausgegangen,
Bald werden sie wieder nach Hause gelangen.
(I often think they have just gone out,
And will come back home soon).
– Friedrich Rückert and Gustav Mahler, *Kindertotenlieder*

HARRY COMB MIGHT not have been able to cope with an 'afterwards' to the events on Spark Close, but others had no choice. What follows are some of the other residents' 'afterwards' – up to the time of writing, nearly four years after the Spark Close Phenomenon.

One of residents who has attained a certain public notoriety since the Phenomenon is KIRSTEN MACHIN, formerly of Number 10, Spark Close. Having 'retired' from her short-lived career in glamour modelling, Kirsten founded *Sex Yap!* Ltd., an internet and phone sex-chat service. She set up the business with the compensation she received from an out-of-court settlement with a major newspaper. At first, she managed the business from her own living room. It was an overnight success, and she subsequently moved away from Spark Close, Stoke-on-Trent, to London. She no longer operates the phones and chatrooms herself, but oversees a team of women from her office in Docklands, whom she reportedly rules with "a rod of iron." This is what SARA ACKER, Serena's best friend, claimed in a tribunal, after having worked for *Sex Yap!* for a few months. After winning her case for constructive dismissal, Sara has since gone on to concentrate on her career as an 'in-yer-face' stand-up comedienne.

Despite a high staff turnover, and numerous tribunals, the *Sex Yap!* team has continued to expand over the years, and the company share price has risen steadily; the company has more or less cornered the 'sex and sympathy' market, focussing as it does on the reassuring-motherly-"aren't-you-a-poor-thing" end of the sex-chat spectrum. *Sex Yap!* is now seeking to broaden out from this market into unchartered territory: the company is currently funding world-class research into the effect of music on erections, with a view to opening up an entirely new, niche market in 'musical sex.' Meanwhile, *Sex Yap!*'s founder is also about to release her first book, a work of self-help psychology, financial advice and autobiography entitled *Call Me*, one of the chapters of which discusses the Spark Close Phenomenon as a major turning-point in her life.

If it was a turning-point for her, it was too for MR. FRANK HUTCHINSON of Number 8, Spark Close, who is rumoured to be one of the most frequent callers to *Sex Yap!* phone lines. Apparently, Kirsten Machin makes an exception for him, by always accepting his desperate calls herself. They never meet – he's still living with his grandmother in Stoke – and she has no photo of him on her desk. In fact, the only photo she owns of anyone on Spark Close, hidden away in a locked desk drawer, is an old, grainy one of Harry Comb, which she takes out now and then when no-one is looking.

Still, in Harry's continued absence, Kirsten and Frank seem a happy telephone couple. MRS. HAYLEY HUTCHINSON is far less happy when her phone bills arrive, but she puts up with them because at least her grandson remains with her at home.

When asked about the phone calls, she shrugs her shoulders and says: "Well, he was in the Territorials, you know. Soldiers will be boys will be soldiers."

DAVY LAWSON from Number 3, Spark Close, seemed to be heading for a life as a soldier, but he dropped out of basic training to move in with a pregnant girl in Biddulph. She promptly left him, taking his bank cards with her, and emptying his account. He is now in prison for armed robbery. By contrast, his sister, Elizabeth 'Lelly' Lawson, surprised everyone with her A-Level results, and is now on her way to university to study Medicine, inspired by her experience of the Spark Close Phenomenon, and her meeting with various doctors, consultants and neurologists, including Prof. Christopher Sollertinsky and Dr. Terence Williams.

While Lelly Lawson is looking forward to her chosen vocation, PROF. CHRISTOPHER SOLLERTINSKY – well-known neurologist and author of various articles on the Spark Close Phenomenon* – has recently announced early retirement from his post as Consultant Neurologist at St. B***'s University Hospital, following a number of unsubstantiated allegations concerning a relationship between himself and a younger, female patient. He is looking forward to spending more time on his work with the FIN ('Fat is Neurology') campaign, and is also said to be planning his first major work of fiction, a novel inspired by the events and people on Spark Close.

MR. RAYMOND RUNTILL of Number 2, Spark Close, is similarly going to have more spare time on his hands. He has taken (very) early retirement, from both his position as doorman to a local nightclub, and as lay-preacher in his church; he is currently being treated for chronic depression. Likewise, MR. PAUL HIGGINS of Number 6, Spark Close, recently resigned from his position in the BNP to "spend more time with

* See 'Variations: Pavane pour une infante défunte,' above.

his family." No-one has ever seen his family, or anyone else visiting his house on Spark Close for that matter – with the occasional exception of his new-found friends, MR. RAJESH PARMAR and MRS. SEJAL PARMAR of Numbers 9-11, Spark Close, with whom he sometimes shares his evenings, watching war documentaries and ballroom dancing programmes. In his resignation letter to the BNP, Paul admitted that what happened on Spark Close in 1999-2000 had compelled him to revise his opinions somewhat. He found it hard to tow the BNP line after playing football with Mr. Parmar on the 9th June 1999, and even more so after finding out about Rosa Adler's background, during her funeral in September 2001.

MISS ROSA ADLER of Number 12, Spark Close, died on 10th September 2001, following a series of strokes. Both her son and grandson, SIMON ADLER-REEVES, were amazed by the number of mourners at the funeral. Over 175 people attended, most of whom Simon had never met or heard of – but with whom Rosa had kept in contact through phone calls and prolific letter-writing. There were residents from the Close, nurses, doctors (including Prof. Christopher Sollertinsky who first met her during his investigations on the Close), people she'd known at work, people she'd known through various voluntary organisations, people she'd known through synagogue, old friends, relatives, charming ex-lovers – and two elderly women who recalled, in their eulogy, that long-ago time when Rosa's music had been turned to ash.

Immediately after this, Simon Adler-Reeves decided it was time to act on Rosa's last instruction to him, before she died: "For goodness sake, dear, you really need to – how d'you say? – pull your finger out, and ask that young lady you care for out on a date." At the wake, he asked the young lady in question this, and she said, "Okay."

The young lady no longer lived permanently on Spark

Close, but her stepmother now did. After HARRY COMB disappeared on the morning of the 9th June 2000, apparently for good, LIZZIE COMB decided to return to Spark Close to look after her stepdaughter. At first this was a temporary arrangement; but, to their surprise, both Lizzie and her stepdaughter found that the arrangement suited them, and Lizzie stayed. In fact, she's stayed there ever since, looking after the house whilst her stepdaughter is away at university. The upshot of this is that, oddly enough, Harry's ex-wife, ALEXA TARRY, has ended up subsidising the residence of Harry's second wife, Lizzie. In a sense, Lizzie is a kept woman – kept by her husband's first wife.

Meanwhile, in October 2000, Lizzie's stepdaughter, SERENA COMB, went to L*** university, to study for a degree in Music History and Appreciation. Away from home, she found she had to start mourning for her sister from scratch – and her missing father too. She used to ring up Simon Adler-Reeves in tears, and ask him to visit her at weekends. So he did, at first as friends, then, after Rosa's funeral, as more-than-friends.

Over two and a half years later, they are still together. Serena is in her third year at university, and is completing her final-year dissertation, which will probably be publishable, on 'The Musical Structures of Entropy.' Uniquely, her dissertation draws on her knowledge of Physics from A-Level, and particularly the laws of thermodynamics. At the same time, Simon is trying to complete his Ph.D thesis – some years late – whilst undertaking part-time university teaching, and working in a call centre. Unlike Serena's dissertation, he doesn't feel his thesis is unique, and doesn't really believe he'll ever finish it.

In fact, Simon doesn't really feel clever enough for Serena in general. He is not convinced they'll last as a couple. He can't help thinking she's too good for him, and everyone else for that matter. He can't help thinking of her in thirty years, on her own, surrounded by nothing but music, thinking in music, speaking in music, understood by no-one – except perhaps the birds in the trees, and the descendants of Melissa's spiders.

Acknowledgements

MANY THANKS TO the residents of 'Spark Close' for their kind cooperation, help and advice in making this book possible.

Many thanks to Will Buckingham, Rowland Cotterill, Nico Lehmann, Francis Bowdery, Eric Leveridge, Kathleen Bell, Simon Perril, John Schad, Lorna Piatti, Simon King, for their advice, assistance and expertise. Thanks to Leicester University, De Montfort University, LOROS and Rainbows Hospice for their help and support with the book.

Many thanks to Jen and Chris Hamilton-Emery for their invaluable advice and support.

My thanks and love to Maria, Miranda, Rosalind, Robin, Anna, Sam, Naomi, Erin, Karen, Bruce, Finola, Tancred, Conal, Helen, Ben, Dylan, and, of course, my mother.

Obviously, many articles and books form the basis of a work such as this one; below are a selection of some of the sources to which I am most indebted:

Adair, Katherine, *Adam: The Story of a Child with Leukaemi* (London: Hodder and Stoughton, 1987).

Atkins, Peter, *The Laws of Thermodynamics: A Very Sho Introduction* (Oxford: Oxford University Press, 201

Ball, Philip, *The Music Instinct: How Music Works and W We Can't Do Without It* (London: Vintage, 2011)

Bishop, John and Graham Barker, *Piano Manual* (Sparkford: Haynes, 2009).

Brecht, Bertolt, *The Threepenny Opera*, ed. and trans. John Willett and Ralph Manheim (London: Methuen, 1979). The quotation in the chapter 'Mack the Knife' is from 'Notes and Variants,' p.84.

Buckingham, Will, *Happiness: A Practical Guide* (London: Icon, 2012).

CancerBACUP, *Understanding Acute Lymphoblastic Leukaemia* (London: CancerBACUP, 1999).

CancerBACUP, *Understanding Stem Cell and Bone Marrow Transplants* (London: CancerBACUP, 2001).

Combs, Allan and Stanley Krippner, 'Collective Consciousness and the Social Brain,' *Journal of Consciousness Studies*, 15:10–11 (2008), 264–76.

Critchley, Macdonald and R. A. Henson (ed.), *Music and the Brain: Studies in the Neurology of Music* (London: William Heinemann, 1977).

Fénelon, Fania, *Playing For Time*, trans. Judith Landry (London: Sphere, 1980).

Greaves, Mel, (ed.), *White Blood: Personal Journeys With Childhood Leukaemia* (London: World Scientific, 2008).

Jourdain, Robert, *Music the Brain and Ecstasy: How Music Captures Our Imagination* (London: Avon, 1998).

Lasker-Wallfisch, Anita, *Inherit the Truth, 1939–1945: The Documented Experiences of a Survivor of Auschwitz and Belsen* (London: Giles de la Mere, 1996).

Levitin, Daniel, *This Is Your Brain On Music: Understanding a Human Obsession* (London: Atlantic Books, 2008).

Mahendran, R., 'The Psychopathology of Musical Hallucinations,' *Singapore Medical Journal*, 48:2 (2007), e68–70.

Miller, Arthur, *Playing For Time* (London: Nick Hern, 1990).
Newman, Richard, and Karen Kirtley, *Alma Rosé: Vienna to Auschwitz* (London: Amadeus, 2000).
Rangell, Leo, *Music in the Head: Living at the Brain-Mind Border* (London: Karnac, 2009).
Rushton, Julian, *Elgar: Enigma Variations* (Cambridge: Cambridge University Press, 1999).
Sacks, Oliver, *Hallucinations* (London: Picador, 2013).
Sacks, Oliver, *The Man Who Mistook His Wife For A Hat* (London: Picador, 1986).
Sacks, Oliver, *Musicophilia: Tales of Music and the Brain* (London: Picador, 2008).
Storr, Anthony, *Music and the Mind* (London: Harpercollins, 1997).